THE CALYX

Donald Neil McIlhone

TRAFFORD

• Canada • UK • Ireland • USA •

© Copyright 2004 Donald Neil Mcllhone.
All rights reserved. No part of this publication may be reproduced, stored in a retrieval system, or transmitted, in any form or by any means, electronic, mechanical, photocopying, recording, or otherwise, without the written prior permission of the author.

Note for Librarians: a cataloguing record for this book that includes Dewey Decimal Classification and US Library of Congress numbers is available from the Library and Archives of Canada. The complete cataloguing record can be obtained from their online database at:
www.collectionscanada.ca/amicus/index-e.html
ISBN 1-4120-4772-2
Printed in Victoria, BC, Canada

TRAFFORD

Offices in Canada, USA, Ireland, UK and Spain
This book was published *on-demand* in cooperation with Trafford Publishing. On-demand publishing is a unique process and service of making a book available for retail sale to the public taking advantage of on-demand manufacturing and Internet marketing. On-demand publishing includes promotions, retail sales, manufacturing, order fulfilment, accounting and collecting royalties on behalf of the author.
Book sales for North America and international:
Trafford Publishing, 6E–2333 Government St.,
Victoria, BC V8T 4P4 CANADA
phone 250 383 6864 (toll-free 1 888 232 4444)
fax 250 383 6804; email to orders@trafford.com
Book sales in Europe:
Trafford Publishing (UK) Ltd., Enterprise House,
Wistaston Road Business Centre, Wistaston Road, Crewe,
Cheshire CW2 7RP UNITED KINGDOM
phone 01270 251 396 (local rate 0845 230 9601)
facsimile 01270 254 983; orders.uk@trafford.com
Order online at:
www.trafford.com/robots/04-2580.html

10 9 8 7 6 5

I would like to thank my family and friends for their patience and encouragement.

Thank you, Wendy, for your creative touch. A special thank you, Sue, for your keen editorial eye, for your genuine credence and for your relentless support.

Thanks for travelling with 'The Canadian Lynx'

Yours,

Donnie Mc.

PROLOGUE

"Evidently, nobody wants to experience a disaster.
However, a twisted and uncontrollable urge to encounter the alien can sometimes overtake the rational mind and trigger a reckless adrenaline."

I write these words, based on my experiences, working on an oilrig, in the late 1970s, in Alberta, Canada.

I learned that when a crew is put together to work a rig, it is run through a disciplined drill to calmly and collectively flee from a blowout.

But like a fire drill in an elementary school, the drill is one thing and the fire, from which the children flee, is another. It is that thing, out there, that some fear and others use to instill fear.

It reveals a unique side of the human condition.

Paranoia can make us do and think things that, under normal circumstances, we wouldn't... well, that is, some of us wouldn't!

Donald Neil McIlhone
August 2004

PART ONE

SLEEPING WITH EYES WIDE OPENED

- CHAPTER 1 -

COLD HANDS, WARM HEART

He kissed her.

The cold drive, to Lana's, was still tingling the ends of his toes.

He could taste champagne on her lips.

She said, "I have had a busy day. I have had only two small glasses."

Her mouth, nevertheless, tasted deceptively strong.

There was a time, when he was aloof to the demands of her job.

He never really understood why, after work, she would need a drink.

Now he knew.

She needed to talk about her job. That was normal.

He didn't mind listening. That was convenient.

He loved her.

She loved him.

Her career had taken her down many paths. Fifteen years had been busy—successful and busy. She was the assistant principal of a large high school in Edmonton, Alberta.

The name of the school was: *Edmonton Central High*.

Her name was Lana Lois.

At the school, the students called her Ms. Lois.

Most of the staff did the same.

Her fellow administrators called her Lana.

Her *super* man was a driller named Jed.

There was a time when he would tease Lana about her name.

"When reversed," he proudly proclaimed, "It sounds like the name of Clarke Kent's favorite reporter: Lois Laine."

At that, Lana would roll her eyes and tell Jed that only he would think of something like that.

He tried to convince her that her parents probably thought the same.

She disagreed. "They weren't that creative."

He has since stopped teasing her.

Jed was working on an oilrig, which was situated seventy miles northeast of Edmonton, Alberta, Canada.

The rig site was near a rural community called Cold Lake. It was appropriately named.

The rig, on which he was working, was on *short change*. This enabled Jed to drive to Lana's, for the night and not be due back at the Lake, until 8:00 p.m. the following night.

His feet were beginning to warm as he poured her another glass of *Summer Hill*.

They laughed; they loved; they slept.

- CHAPTER 2 -

THE SWAN

The early morning sun brightened Alberta's *Big Sky*.
Jed dragged himself to the living room and sat in the chair facing the alcove.
He looked out at the skyline.
He followed the sparkling crystals as they danced in Edmonton's frosty air.
They reminded him of butterflies, he had seen, years ago, fluttering by a bush, in a Cuban garden.
His sleepy eyes were beginning to come alive.
He got up. He made his way into the kitchen.
He prepared a pot of coffee.
While he waited for the drip, he returned to the living room and picked up the T.V. remote control.
He pressed the numbers for channel four.
With only a semi-concentrated eye, he read the words of the *information network*.
He thought about how much the technology had improved, in his thirty-six years.
As the coffee dripped and the news unfolded before him, Lana appeared in the doorway.

She looked tired, but apparent fatigue hadn't darkened her bright eyes. They still radiated the warmth they had emitted, hours before, amidst the candlelight and champagne.
Jed asked how she had slept and she responded, "Fine, I think, and you?"

"Not long enough, I never do." He yawned.
"I know what you mean." She yawned.
Jed smiled. "It's catchy, eh?"
"What?" Lana frowned.
"Yawning."
"Oh ya." She nodded and then yawned, again.

They made small talk, as they sipped their coffees.
They both felt weighted, however, by the same, overhanging, cloud.

Jed read the news.
"Look! Air Canada and Canadian are talking about a merger."
"That'll be the day," Lana smirked.

Jed thought about his return to the Lake.
He would have to head back, in a few hours.
Lana would then begin another long, lonely week of working and waiting.
She was already beginning to feel the heartache.

On the screen, the temperature indicated that Edmonton was sitting at a balmy -19°. "Another hot one," Jed chuckled, as he got up to replenish their two mugs.

"Yes," agreed Lana. "Typical."
Jed sat down beside her. He filled their mugs.
"Thanks."
He placed the pot on one of the magazines that was, conveniently, angled on the coffee table.
Lana took a sip. "Ooh, that's good!"
She looked at Jed. " What do you feel like doing today?"
Jed paused. "Well." He tilted his head. "I don't have to be back at the rig for a few hours. Do you want to go for

a little hike along the riverbank? We could bundle up and stop at that little café, by Parkway Close."

He stood up.

"What's that place called?"
He looked out the window.
"You mean the *Grabba Java*?"
"Ya, that's it!" He leaned against the alcove. He looked up at the sky and then up and down the street below.
"It looks cold out there. We had better dress in layers. I have an extra pullover in the truck, if you need one."
"Okay. Give me a few minutes to get ready."
Lana headed for her bedroom.
Jed returned to the *information network*.
He took a sip of his coffee.
It warmed his throat.

The walk along the river was romantic.
As they inched their way closer to the café, Lana commented on how smoothly and steadily the waters of the North Saskatchewan were flowing. Jed compared the scattered ice to sculptured bergs.
"Look Lana," he pointed, "those two look like swans—glacial Arctic swans! Frozen lovers—sailin' down the river!"
He studied their flow. "You know, Lana, they actually look warm. With the sun on them like that, they're probably quite toasty."
"Wo Jed! You should write poetry. Only you could see warmth in ice." Lana tugged at Jed's arm and pulled him closer to her side.
"You're gifted." She touched his cheek—then she kissed it.
Jed laughed. "No, Lana. You're the one who's gifted."
She touched his chin. She gently turned his face to-

wards hers. "Are you blushing, Jed, or is that red on your cheeks, from this frosty wind?"

He shook his head. He stopped walking. Lana stood beside him. Jed looked into her eyes.

"Maybe it's from your lipstick." He smiled, then, he kissed her lips.

"Ooh!" Lana sighed. "Thanks. That feels nice."

The *Grabba Java* was crowded.

Jed said that everybody looked like hippies. Lana corrected him and told him that they weren't called that any more.

"Now they're called yuppies."

Jed frowned.

He looked around the restaurant.

Hats and scarves were vicariously draped on and over heads and shoulders.

He liked the artistic atmosphere. He found it entertaining – even uplifting. It was so unlike the world of the oil patch.

As his eyes panned the room, he remarked on how therapeutic the whole thing was:

"The walk along the river; this crowded restaurant." He looked around.

"And your kisses, Lana."

He touched her hand.

"It's good to see you."

Lana smiled. "You too!"

The sandwiches were filling but tasty.

"Generous portions." Jed licked his upper lip.

"This should keep me going until I'm back on tower."

"How has Marty's cooking been?"

"He does his best, considering the crew he has to serve. Rig food doesn't taste like this though." He pointed to his crumb-filled plate. "Nothing at the rig is like this."

"How much longer will you be there?" Lana scooped some whipped cream from the top of her latte.

Jed shook his head. "I know you think I'm crazy driving back and forth like this but I love the rigs, Lana. I love the fresh air. You know that."

His reply sounded apologetic.

Lana sipped her drink.

She placed her hand on top of Jed's and then moved her chair in closer, beside his. She looked deeply into his analytical blue eyes.

"You didn't answer my question." Jed thought that she looked angry.

"I know you love the fresh air. I know you love the drilling and that damn oil patch. But I asked you how much longer you will be, at the site, in Cold Lake. You know, the one that you'll be going to in a few hours." She looked away from Jed. She removed her hand from his. She tucked her hair in, tightly, behind her ears. "The place that is so unlike this place." She waved an arm. She sounded sarcastic.

Jed understood her frustration.

He looked down at his plate and then raised his head to look at her.

She leaned back.

She sighed.

Jed struggled to say something encouraging.

He looked at his watch.

"It's a slow hole, Lana. I don't know. Maybe another month or two."

Lana shook her head. "Sometimes I wonder why I wait for you, Jed." She made a growling sound. Jed thought that it sounded like a cat or something.

Lana leaned forward. She pinched Jed's elbow.

It was an affectionate pinch.

Jed was, momentarily, relieved.

"I'm sorry I'm like this, Jed. But," Lana paused, "It's just that at one time, I thought your drilling life was adventurous and romantic. Now, I see it as something that just takes you away from me."

Jed's eyes, once again, panned the room.
He studied the eclectic, loquacious crowd.
Then, he looked at Lana.
He smiled.
She smiled.
He leaned over.
He kissed her.
Her lips tasted like coffee.
"I think I know how you're feeling."
He paused.
She frowned.
He squinted.
She returned his squint.
He started to repeat his thoughts.

"I think …"
She placed her hand, over his lips.

- CHAPTER 3 -

NO WOMAN, NO CRY

The drive to Cold Lake was slow.

The fog and icy conditions compelled Jed to travel at a moderate speed.

The drone from the blasting defrost, though, was rhythmically soothing. The forced air warmed his face and hands.

Ordinarily, Jed would listen to the local radio station, but for this trip, he thought that the sounds of reggae king, Bob Marley, were a more suitable accompaniment, to the droning defrost.

He slid the tape into the cassette player.

He adjusted the seat and tilted the steering wheel.

He glanced at the dash and noted his speed: 85 k.p.h.

He angled the mirror for night vision and pressed the switch for cruise control.

The truck felt safe.

He felt safe.

He sang along with Bob and the Wailers:

"No woman, no cry."

As Lana prepared herself for the ensuing week, she, too, was establishing her own 'sense of control'.

The condominium felt empty.

She felt empty.

She could hear the ticking of the kitchen clock.

She tried to fill her mind with things, other than thoughts of Jed.

She couldn't.

She fought to hold back tears.

She lost that battle, too.

Beads trickled down her cheeks forming tiny streams upon her chin and neck.

Her emotions swung like a pendulum: from sadness to anger; from love to hate; from emptiness to overflow.

Lana felt torn.

For a moment, she viewed her relationship with Jed as something like yesterday's news: once alive and hopeful but, now, distant and fading.

Their personalities were skewed, she thought.

He was the strong quiet man of the outdoors, with a tender but independent heart. She was the determined devoted leader, with an emptiness that pained and a longing that chilled.

"Why are we still together?" She asked herself, out loud, as she turned on the tap.

Lana added her favorite bubble bath to the cascading water.

She lit a candle.

She adjusted the volume of her trusty ghetto blaster.

Like the drone in Jed's truck, the soft music, moving with the rising steam would hopefully sooth and comfort.

She reclined, into the tub.

Meanwhile, for Jed, miles away and deep in the Alberta woods, the lights of Mustang Two, illuminated the trees and dark skies, of Cold Lake.

Lana thought of him and he thought of the drilling.

Her bathroom mirror was smoked with steam.

His rearview mirror was clearing.

Lana began to relax.
Jed began to unpack.

The solitude of the condo made time stand still.

At the rig, the 8:00 p.m. shift-change was only minutes away.

- CHAPTER 4 -

THE MONSTER

Based on its size and drilling capacity, Mustang Two was a model rig.

It was what the oil patch called a *triple derrick*. It was standing on ground that was filled with rocks, the size of elephants and chunks of coal, the size of grapefruits.

The ground, through which the Canadian Diamond Drill Bit (the CDDB) relentlessly crushed, was described as slow ground or 'slow hole'.

Due to the stress placed on the CDDB, as it chipped its way through the rock and mud, Mustang Two earned a favorable reputation throughout the oil patch. It was known as the rig for the 'slow hole'.

Jed Sands was its 35th driller.

The brisk night air blew off the Lake and rushed up Jed's nostrils. It penetrated his lungs like the paddles of a medic, reviving a victim of cardiac arrest.

His fellow 'rig rats' greeted him raucously, as they made their way up the plank.

"How was short change, boss?" asked Slim Jim, one of the pimply-faced roughnecks. "Did ya go into Edmonton?"

"Yep, but, as usual, it was way too short." Jed shook his head and then spit over the guardrail.

"I guess that's why they call it fuckin' short change

eh?" Big Al, the *chain spinning* motorman cursed, as he adjusted his hard hat.

Jed laughed at Big Al's figurative language. "Feelin' alright there, Big Al?"

Big Al swore again. "Fuckin' A!"

Tough talk and loud laughter echoed throughout the derrick.

Jed looked at the drill tongs that were suspended by his driller's station.

He cleaned off some grease that was likely left by one of the roughnecks, on day shift.

Then, something else caught his attention.

He looked up.

The winds had subsided.

He looked around.

The air did not feel as cold.

Jed took off his hard hat and placed it on the rail, by the *dog house*.

He ran his fingers through his sweaty hair.

The air felt good on his head.

He wasn't certain, though, if the sudden change in weather were a good omen or a warning of something not good.

He recalled, from his 'off shore' drilling days, that calm winds meant one of three things: a warming trend; a storm; or sharks.

He looked up at the black, star-filled sky.

He pondered its magnificence.

Then, without warning, the winds, suddenly, returned.

Like Bob Marley, they wailed.

Amidst the sounds of the hungry winds and the swearing riggers, Jed heard something else.

It sounded like cracking ice.

It didn't sound natural.

He turned to look at the draw works.

He studied the frozen, shiny cables. They looked like vines, hanging by the entrance of a haunted house.

Jed took a breath.

Along with the winds, the cold air had returned.

Jed tightened the Velcro collar of his rig jacket. He looked at the drill pipe. It was struggling as it churned its way, through the stubborn hole, in the platform.

The drawl, of the engine, was mesmerizing. Jed thought that it sounded like a wild animal, caught in a trap, howling in pain – struggling to get free.

He looked down.

He felt something slimy, beneath his boots.

Blue and white mud was oozing onto the platform.

Something wasn't right. There was more mud than there should be.

It was also extraordinarily thick.

It slithered its way down the guardrails.

It dripped onto the stairs.

For a moment, Jed lost himself to its creative flow.

He thought of a painting he had once seen, on a cave wall, during one of his assignments, in the Caribbean. The colors, of the mud, reminded him of that painting.

He followed the mud as it moved like an anaconda, along the floor and down the stairs.

Then, something else captured Jed's eye.

At the foot of the stairs, looking like a lost puppy, stood Marty, the rig cook.

Along with everything else, Jed thought that this was most unusual.

He left his driller station and approached the landing.

He called out to him.

Marty had one foot on the bottom step. He appeared to be ready to ascend.

Then, suddenly, everything disappeared.

There was no more wind.
No more laughter.
No more cracking ice.
No more swearing.
No more drawling engine.
No more cold.
No more Marty.

- CHAPTER 5 -

THE CALL

The phone rang, as Lana was getting ready for work.

Her digital read: 7:06 a.m.

The *"Bear 107"* disc jockey greeted sleepy Edmontonians, with a hearty "Good morning!" Lana thought that he was trying to sound like Robin Williams, in the movie '*Good Morning Viet Nam*'.

The voice, on the other end apologized for waking her up.

"Jed, is that you?"

The response was distorted, by static.

"No, Lana, this is Marty. Jed's been hurt. We had an explosion. A blow-out."

"Is Jed all right? Where is he?"

"The *Stars* chopper flew the guys *outta* here, late last night. It was pretty bad, Lana. I think Jed will make it, though. He took a blow to the head."

Through the static, Lana could hear that a drill pipe had hit Jed. He had been waiting by the draw works, when it happened. A runaway pipe pole-vaulted and hit him, in the back of his head.

Apparently, at the time, Jed was not wearing his hardhat.

"Jed and Al were unconscious when the chopper took them away. Slim Jim and Stewie were conscious but burned up, pretty bad, Lana."

"Marty, it is getting difficult to hear you. The static is cutting you off at the end of every sentence. Where is Jed, now?"

"The helicopter brought them all into Edmonton. They're at the Center."

"Okay. I got that."

"Sorry for starting your day like this, Lana."

"No, no, Marty. I appreciate the call. Thanks. I'll talk to you, later."

She hung up.

It was too early for Lana to notify her school that she would be late.

Fortunately, she did not have a teaching assignment. Her assistant principal responsibilities occupied her time so erratically that teaching a class, on top of everything else, would be too much.

"One of the advantages of being an assistant principal," she, at one time, had shared with Jed, *"Was that if, for whatever reason I'm late, I won't have students waiting loudly and impatiently by my classroom door."*

Jed, *kind of*, understood what she meant.

Lana tied back her hair.

She pulled on her overcoat and ran down the stairs.

She forgot to lock her front door.

She jumped into her Jeep and tore to the hospital.

Traffic was heavy.

"Typical."

When she arrived, parking was at a premium.

"Typical."

She cursed the volume of cars and the dearth of space.

"Damn."

The snow banks impeded her vision.

As she struggled to find a parking spot, she felt like a

25

rat, entrapped in a maze. "Settle down," she disciplined herself. "Settle down."

She held on tightly to the steering wheel. She thanked her trusty blue Jeep.

Finally, after circling the lot and finding nothing but cars, trucks and SUV'S, she left.

She settled for a vacant spot, two blocks away.

She ran to the hospital.

She disciplined herself, again. "For Pete's sake, Lana, calm down. He'll be all right."

As she approached the reception area, she paused to collect her thoughts. She reminded herself that Jed would be all right.

- CHAPTER 6 -

THE CALYX

Jed appeared to be awake when Lana entered the room.

Appearances, she knew, could be deceiving.

The top of his head was covered with a white bandage.

It looked like he was wearing a turban.

Lana said "Hello."

Jed turned her way but did not respond.

She asked how he was doing.

Again, there was no response.

She sat down on a chair that was beside his bed.

She touched his hand. It felt rough—rougher, than usual.

"Can you hear me Jed?"

Again, there was no response.

"He can't speak right now, Miss," an unfamiliar voice announced from behind.

Lana turned to see from whom it was coming.

"I'm sorry if I startled you, Miss, my name is Doctor Yen. Bill Yen. I am Jed's doctor."

In the dim light, Lana squinted to see a slim figure, standing before her, wearing a white lab coat.

It did indeed look like a doctor.

Dr. Yen approached the bed.

He extended a hand and formally introduced himself.

Upon closer scrutiny, Lana saw that Dr. Yen was of Asian descent and likely in his late fifties or early sixties.

Lana shook his hand. She introduced herself.

Dr. Yen pointed at Jed.

"He is in a trance right now, Miss. He is sedated. He should be okay in a day or two."

"In a day or two?" Lana was surprised and disappointed.

Dr. Yen nodded a shiny baldhead. "He is strong."

He tugged at short, gray, chin whiskers.

"Yes! A day; two at the latest."

He examined Jed's bandage.

"He is a fighter. He will bounce back."

"What is wrong with him, Doctor? He seems like he is awake. His eyes are open, but when I talk to him, he just stares."

"Yes." Dr. Yen leaned forward as if he saw something in the light of Jed's staring eyes.

"The medication has that kind of effect."

He touched Jed's cheek.

Jed did not flinch.

"Patients appear to be lucid, when, in fact, they are not."

He adjusted the pillow beneath Jed's head.

"Our man, here, is in a coma.

He is sleeping with his eyes open."

"Sleeping with his eyes open?" Lana frowned.

"What does that mean? What kind of medication does that?"

Lana's questions sounded accusatory.

Dr. Yen turned to face her. He told her that he empathized with her frustration.

"Relax, Miss."

He raised his hand.

He tried to calm her.

He paused.

He reached over and poured himself a cup of water, from a jug that was on Jed's bedside table.

He raised the cup as if he were making a toast. He brought the cup to his lips. He took a big gulp.

He wiped his lips.

He looked at Lana.

He smiled. He held out the cup. "Would you like some?"

Lana shook her head. "No, thank you."

"I must emphasize, Miss, that I am not a witch doctor."

Lana frowned.

Dr. Yen continued smiling. "I am Jed's medical doctor." He stressed the word *medical*. "You must remember that."

Lana tilted her head. She was still frowning.

She stood up. "I didn't say that you were a witch, Dr. Yen." Lana was at least six inches taller than Dr. Yen.

"I simply asked for some clarification and for the name of the medication." She walked over to the other side of Jed's bed. "You must understand, Doctor." Lana pointed at Jed. " I care about this man."

"Yes, I understand. Now, please."

Dr. Yen walked over and stood beside Lana.

He reached out and took her hand.

The gesture was made with good intent; nevertheless, it did not make Lana feel comfortable.

She pulled away.

Again, she walked around, to the other side of Jed's bed.

She turned to face Dr. Yen.

With hands on both hips, she asked: "What kind of medication did you give him, doctor?" Her tone was now administrative.

She looked directly into Dr. Yen's glass-covered eyes.

He sat down on the bed.

"Did you do a test, Doctor? Could he be having an allergic reaction?"

Lana looked at Jed.

Dr. Yen raised his hand, again. Lana thought that he looked like a timid schoolboy.

She didn't give him the opportunity to speak.

Then, as if he knew his nurturing approach was not working, he stood up. He walked over and quietly shut the door.

When he turned to face Lana, he did not look as meek as he did when he was on Jed's bed, nor when he raised his hand.

He pointed.

For a second, Lana thought that he looked like *Uncle Sam,* pointing an admonitory finger.

"Settle down, Miss."

"I am settled, doctor." Lana took a breath.

"Then will you please let me speak?" He walked over to Jed's bedside table.

With lifeless eyes, Jed continued to stare.

"That's kind of spooky, Jed." Lana spoke to him, as if he could hear.

Dr. Yen reached for the jug and poured himself another cup of water. He took a sip. Then, he looked at Lana.

"Listen to me for just one minute, Miss Lana."

He paused.

He took another sip. His throat made a gurgling sound.

Lana noticed that the corners of his mouth were dry.

He licked his lips.

He scratched his whiskers.

He looked at Lana, again. He took a deep breath.

"I gave him 20 milliliters of a drug that has worked wonders with patients who, like your Jed," he pointed at Jed, "have encountered serious head injuries. It is a drug called the *Haemostatic Calyx.*"

He paused.

He walked over towards the window.

He held the Styrofoam cup close to his chest. He looked like he was ready to make a speech, at a cocktail party. Lana could see that Dr. Yen was, now, in his comfort zone. She thought that with every move and with every word, he was gaining confidence.

He appeared to be pleased with himself.

He was in charge – the way he liked it.

He had Lana's attention.

"The haemostatic is a styptic agent, which stops internal bleeding."

He sipped his water.

He put the cup down on the window's sill. He removed his glasses. Then, with a handkerchief, which he pulled from the upper pocket, of his lab coat, he cleaned them.

Lana thought that he looked younger without them.

As he cleaned, he spoke:

"It is a fiber from the *calyx* or outer covering of the hemp flower. New Canadian drug but old Chinese secret."

He looked at Jed.

"Your Jed will be just fine." He smiled at Lana.

She noticed that his teeth were exceptionally white. Then, he leaned over to have a closer look at Jed.

He put his glasses back on.

He touched the knuckles of Jed's hand.

He asked him some questions in what sounded like a foreign language. Lana assumed that he was speaking Mandarin or Cantonese.

He looked into Jed's eyes with an instrument that he retrieved from his side pocket. It looked like a miniature pool cue.

He told Jed to close his eyes.

This time he spoke in English.

Jed let his eyelids slowly drop.

"That's amazing, Doctor!" Lana moved in to get a closer look.

"I think your man wants to sleep. The calyx has put him into a deep trance."

Dr. Yen looked into Jed's ear.

"There is no sign of suffering or internal bleeding."

He stood up.

"We must let him rest."

He paused.

He looked at Lana.

"By the way, did you inquire about the other gentlemen?"

The question caught Lana off guard.

He looked at her with judging eyes.

She shook her head.

"No doctor, I came straight here. Do you know how they're doing?"

Dr. Yen poured himself some more water.

"As far as I know, Miss, they are in stable condition. Two are in our *Burn Unit*. Our bone specialist is looking after the other gentleman who was brought to this unit, along with Mister Jed." Dr. Yen sipped his water.

"Dr. Young should be casting him as we speak."

He placed the cup down on the table and gestured for Lana to leave with him. "Please, Miss, if you would come with me, now. I must show you something else."

Lana looked at Jed.

"He'll be fine, Miss." Dr. Yen understood how Lana was feeling. "You can visit him later." He took her by the arm and accompanied her, out the door. Lana felt a little uncomfortable with that. Nevertheless, she went with him. "I feel as though my visit, with Jed, was incomplete, Doctor."

"There is nothing more that you can do for him, Miss, at this time."

Dr. Yen looked at Lana.

He repeated. "Nothing more, at this time." He emphasized the words: **this time**.

Lana reluctantly agreed.

They walked down the hallway of the I.C. unit. Their pace was steady and quick.
Dr. Yen did not let go of Lana's arm.
For Lana, the feeling was foreign.
Ordinarily, it was she who did the escorting, down hallways, at a steady and quick pace.
"Where are we going doctor? What's the rush?"
"I know how you are feeling, Miss. I do. I understand.

I would like to introduce you to my partner. She is the one who is endowed with the highest mental gifts on whom Buddha has showered insights, to twenty-first century medicine."
Lana was interested.
Dr. Yen continued.
"Her name is Caly, like the Calyx serum, of which you have just witnessed its effects."
Dr. Yen cleared his throat.
"She and I have been partners, for two years."

As Lana and Dr. Yen made their way towards the elevator, Lana tried to envision his partner. Her uneasiness was beginning to lift as he continued to describe Caly.

Lana imagined a tiny, softly spoken Asian lady who might also be wearing a white lab coat and, like Dr. Yen, thick wire-rimmed glasses. For some reason, knowing that Dr. Yen had a partner made him less threatening.

When they entered the elevator, Dr. Yen studied the floor-button panel as if it were the controls of a complex ship. "Now, let me see." He adjusted his glasses. "Ah yes, there it is B-1.

I'm still getting used to these bifocals."

The elevator ride was quick.

Before Lana could think of something to say, she and Dr. Yen arrived on B-1.

The first thing that Lana noticed was the lighting. The floor was illuminated by tiny signal lights, like the emergency direction lights in a theatre or on an airplane. The walls were painted in various shades of soft blues and grays. There were no overhead lights, however, small oriental lamps, with low wattage bulbs, lit the hallway. Dr. Yen was definitely, at home, in this environment. Lana could see how his gait slowed and his demeanor relaxed. He ushered Lana towards a green door that was at the end of a narrow corridor.

"And now, Miss, you will meet my Caly. I trust you will find her in good spirits. She is friendly and always enjoys meeting new people."

As they made their way through the door, Lana was immediately greeted by a tall slim black man with long dread locks in his hair. He was wearing a pink shirt and jean shorts. He smiled and asked Dr. Yen who the nice lady was. He had a thick Caribbean accent.

"This is Miss Lois. It is Miss Lois, is it not, Miss?"
"Good memory, Doctor. Lana will be fine."
"Clem, this is Miss Lana. She is here to meet our Caly."
Lana extended a hand.
Clem reciprocated.
"Irae man, so you be here to check out de coolest cat in de country... well I tink dat Caly be close by. Just wait and me give her a call, man. Caly!" He called out. "Where ya be at my slinky feline?"
Slinky feline? For Lana, the image was puzzling.
Lana's bewilderment, however, was short lived as her eyes beheld a startling and unusual sight. From behind a

counter that doubled as an island, appeared a big black and gray cat. It was not a domestic cat. Its size and markings revealed the call and look of something beyond domestic and yet, it did not look threateningly wild.

"She," Dr. Yen informed, "is a two and a half year old Canadian Lynx. She was abandoned at birth and left by the poachers. She is also a marvel of modern medicine!"

Dr. Yen pointed at Caly. He spoke like a proud father.

Caly, then, devotedly, stood by his side.

"She has greatly helped me and Clem with our Haemostatic Calyx Project."

Dr. Yen petted Caly's furry head.

"You see mam," interjected Clem, "When de Caly be found, she nearly be dead, sufferin' from dem achin' head."

"Yes," acknowledged Dr. Yen. "A serious hemorrhage and internal bleeding."

Clem joined Dr. Yen and Caly for the head petting and ear scratching.

"Dem evil forces set a trap to ensnare dis little *loup-cervier* or, like de good doctor say, de North American wild-cat." Clem walked over and leaned against the island.

Lana continued to stare.

Dr. Yen sat down in a chair that looked like an antique.

Caly slumped down, comfortably, at his feet.

"At that time," Dr. Yen continued, "Caly was very tiny. The trap clamped her like a vise." He gestured with closed fists—one on top of the other.

"Her head and neck and not dat paw, as dem trappers intend, be badly damaged." Clem opened a cupboard door. He pulled out a couple of crystal glasses.

"Can I get you someting to drink, Miss Lana?" He peeked at her from behind the cupboard. "Maybe some fruit punch?" He smiled.

Lana nodded. "Thank you. That would be nice."

She noticed that Clem's teeth were as white as Dr. Yen's.

"I'll have some punch too, Clem." Dr. Yen stood up. He resumed his account of Caly's history.

" Her coat and ears were in rough shape. When Clem found her, she was nearly dead. Isn't that right Clem?"

Clem nodded as he poured the punch. "Yes, Doctor. Some bad shape, man!"

"You see Miss," Dr. Yen knelt down, on one knee, beside Lana. "The large prominent ear-tufts, of the Canadian Lynx, mean dollars to the hunters and traders."

He called for Caly.

She came immediately.

Lana crept slowly back towards the island.

"It's okay, Miss. Caly be cool!" Clem joined Lana, as she coward against the counter. He was holding two full glasses of punch.

Dr. Yen asked Lana to come and sit down. He pointed to the antique chair.

"The hunters would have taken what they wanted and then either killed her or left her to die." He pointed out how precious Caly's ears were.

"Her ears look fine doctor." Lana, slowly and carefully, sat down. "She is friendly, isn't she?"

Caly moved in closer to investigate the newcomer. She pressed her smooth, streamlined body against Lana's leg.

"She is therapeutic, Miss Lana. I will be using her to assist with your Jed's rehabilitation. He, too, will soon be meeting our special Caly."

Lana petted Caly's head and the top of her neck. She petted gently and carefully. It was as though Caly knew how Lana was feeling. She began to purr.

"How does she help with the Calyx Project?"

Dr. Yen smiled. He was happy to respond to Lana's question.

"In 1991, when the Haemostatic Calyx was still in its embryonic stage, the serum had not yet been administered to animals. Clem and I were, undoubtedly, convinced of its effects." He took a sip of his punch. Lana did the same with hers.

Clem entered the room with his own glass of punch. He raised it, gesturing a toast, then, brought it to his lips.

The room fell silent as they all indulged their pink, ice-filled refreshment.

Dr. Yen continued.

"In the early sixties, we were successful with one patient who was victimized by a gunshot wound, to his stomach. It wasn't until recently, when I had my practice up in Fort McMurray, not far from the wilderness and the site of Caly's entrapment, that I decided to apply the Calyx to Caly."

He pointed at her.

She was still sitting by Lana's leg. Lana scratched the side of her ear. The purring grew louder. It was soothing, for everyone; especially for Lana.

Caly sensed that.

Dr. Yen was now standing in the middle of the room. As he did, when he was standing by the window in Jed's room, he looked like he was making a formal address. He could have been speaking at a medical convention or at a doctor's cocktail party.

"Lana, our man Clem here was on a trail ride with an outfit that was based in Fort McMurray. As good fortune would have it, he came upon the suffering Caly, scooped her up in his arms and upon returning to the Fort, brought her to me, for treatment. The rest is history!"

Dr. Yen finished his punch.

He smiled.

Again, Lana was struck by the whiteness of his teeth.

She stopped scratching.

Caly stopped purring.

Dr. Yen went over and knelt beside her.

"Here we are; two and a half-years later and, at your feet, is a result of the effects, of the Calyx wonder drug."

He smiled, again.

Clem returned to the kitchen. "Can I get ya some more punch, Miss Lana?"

"No thank you Clem. I must get going." She looked around the room and then at Dr. Yen. "This is quite a place you have here."

Dr. Yen smiled. "It's not mine."

"Mine neither, Miss." Clem called out from the kitchen. For the first time, since she and Dr. Yen met, Lana smiled.

She tilted her head.

Dr. Yen pointed, at Caly. "It's hers!"

Lana's smile turned into a frown.

Then, she looked at her watch. "Gentlemen, I must be off to work."

Dr. Yen nodded. "I understand."

"May I go and see Jed again, Doctor? I would like to say goodbye, before I head to the school. I just want to see him. You know."

"Absolutely Miss. I understand. I will accompany you."

"You go to school, Miss?" Clem called out from the kitchen, as he rinsed a glass.

"Lana smiled. No, no. I mean, yes. Well, I work in one." She was embarrassed by her ambiguous response.

"Cool!" Clem continued rinsing.

Dr. Yen escorted Lana to the door.

Lana thanked Clem and then, bid farewell.

"I'll catch ya later, Miss." Clem poked his head out from behind the kitchen wall.

"I will walk you to the elevator, Miss Lana. From there, I think you will be able to find your way back to Mister Jed's room. He is on C floor. Our floors, here, are alphabetized. Do not press C-1 or C-2. Simply press C." Dr. Yen looked serious. Lana assured him that she knew where Jed's room was. "The receptionist, on the main floor, clearly spelled it out to me, earlier, this morning, upon arrival." She looked at her watch, again.

Then, she looked down at Caly. She was nestled up against Dr. Yen's leg.

Caly looked up at Lana.

For a moment, Lana thought that her eyes looked human.

Then, Dr. Yen pressed the button, for the elevator.

- CHAPTER 7 -

FOCUS

When Lana arrived at her school, there were numerous phone messages. One was from Dr. Yen. She returned his call, immediately. She was anxious but not optimistic. Jed's condition, hopefully, had not worsened. Before she left the hospital, she checked in on him. There was little change.

Dr. Yen was unable to come to the phone. He was, apparently, with another patient. Lana left a message. She said that she would be at the hospital, later. She would, hopefully, touch base with him, then.

She sat at her desk.
It was difficult for her to stay focused.
The regular demands of a January Monday were awaiting her.
There were, what looked like, a hundred little yellow *sticky notes*, stuck to her phone and scattered about her desk.
Some days, the demands seemed never ending. Today, they seemed never ending and trivial.
She told the office staff about her unusual and frightening morning. Everyone was sympathetic and supportive. Her secretary, Laura, consoled her.
Lana, then, confided in her principal, Mr. Door. He said that the whole thing sounded bizarre.
"I've never heard of that kind of treatment." He shook his head and with his tongue, he made a tsk sound.

Lana thought that he wasn't being very sympathetic.

"And the idea of a cat," he criticized, "And an underground Chinese sanctuary? What is that?" he mocked.

"I'm certain the hospital staff knows what it's doing," defended Lana.

"And besides, I have all the confidence in the world, in Dr. Yen."

Lana knew that she was sounding defensive. She didn't care. The best offense is defense, she told herself. Then she asked herself, "*Why am I worrying about what he thinks?*"

She returned to her office.

She sat down at her desk.

She looked at the array of little yellow *stickies*.

She pulled one that was stuck to the receiver. It read: *Ossie called. Will call back.* Lana looked at it for a moment and then called Laura who was usually in earshot, of her frequent requests.

"Yes Lana?"

"Do you have a minute?"

"I'll be right there."

Laura appeared in the doorway, of Lana's office.

She was a pretty lady with bright blue eyes and short blonde hair. She was always pleasant. Today, she was exceptionally pleasant.

"How can I help you?" she smiled.

"Hi Laura, thanks for these." Lana pointed to the display, on her desk. Then, she rolled her eyes.

She held up the note about Ossie.

"Do you remember when this call came in?"

Laura looked at the paper.

She reflected.

"I believe he called about 9:30."

Lana looked at the clock.

It was now 10:50.

"Thanks Laura."

"By the way," Laura paused, "He was very polite. I remember he asked for you by your full name, including your middle name." She shrugged a shoulder.

"I thought that was kind of different." She raised her eyebrows.

Lana smiled.

"Yes, that is unusual. But if you knew Ossie, you would understand. He can be overly formal. He is a unique kind of guy."

Laura smiled. "Maybe I'll get to meet him, some day."

Lana gave her a look. "Maybe." She returned Laura's smile.

"Here is another message that you might find interesting." Laura pointed to a yellow sticky that was near the edge, of the desk.

Lana picked it up. It read: *Long distance call from Cuba. Lee.*

She looked at it for a few seconds and then thanked Laura. She did not comment about that note.

Laura asked if there were anything else.

"Not at the moment but don't go too far. I'll probably need you for something just as soon as you return to your desk." They shared a friendly chuckle.

Laura asked if she wanted her door closed.

Lana replied that it was okay to leave it open.

Just as Lana was about to check another message, her phone rang. The display indicated that the call was coming from an outside line.

"Hello! Lana Lois here."

"Hi Lana! It's Ossie."

"Ossie! I got the message that you called earlier. Where are you?"

"I'm in Miami. I was doing some consulting for the 'Partnerships' and I got a call from Lee saying that Jed had been hurt in a blowout. What's going on?"

"How did Lee find out?" Lana was puzzled. "Who told him?"

There was a pause at the other end. "I don't know," responded Ossie.

"I thought you called him."

"Why would I call him?"

"Well, because of Dr. Yen, I thought."

"Doctor Yen? What do you mean? How do you know about him?"

Another pause.

"Lana? How **is** Jed?"

"Well, I saw him about an hour ago. He is in a coma."

"A coma?" Ossie was concerned.

"What did you mean about Jed's doctor phoning Lee, Ossie?" Lana was suspiciously curious.

"Why would he do that?"

"I'll fill you in on those details, at another time.

I'm going to try to catch a flight out of here. I want to see Jed. I'll probably go through Toronto. If all goes well, I'll arrive either late tonight or early tomorrow morning."

He paused.

Lana paused.

She didn't say anything.

She stared at the notes, on her desk.

"Are you still there, Lana?"

"Yes, sorry, Ossie. I'm here. I just got lost for a second. I was thinking about something else."

"Okay! I'll keep you posted. I'll call when I get in. If you're busy, don't worry, I'll take a taxi." Lana thought that Ossie sounded like he was in a hurry to hang up.

"Talk to you later, Lana. Got to go! Adios!"

Lana remained motionless, for a few minutes, holding on to the phone receiver, listening to the dial tone.

She thought about her conversation, with Ossie.

She was certain that he had avoided some of her questions.

Then, her eyes fell upon the little note that stated she had received a long distance call, from Cuba. She reflected upon that, as well.

She looked at her watch. Then, she adjusted it to the same time as the clock, on her wall. She reminded herself that it was a two-hour time difference between Edmonton and Miami. She jotted down a quick note in her *daytimer* recording when the second call came in, from Ossie. Then, she called for Laura.

"Is there any coffee left in the staff room?"

Laura responded, affirmatively.

"I'll get you a cup, Lana. I was headed that way, anyway. I've got to do some duplicating."

Lana thanked Laura and once again looked at the array of little yellow notes, scattered about her desk.

She turned to her computer.

The 'screen-saver' was splashed with moving windows, fading in and out of sight. She lost herself to their hypnotic rhythms. With her index finger, she left clicked the computer mouse. She waited for the prompt indicating that it was ready, for her, to log on.

Laura arrived with the coffee.

"You're lucky, Lana. Here is the last cup, from this morning's pot."

Lana swiveled to face her. "Oh, thanks. You're a dear."

- CHAPTER 8 -

IMAGERY

The visions inside Jed's head were deep and penetrating. He struggled, in vain, to bring himself, to the surface. He felt like he was submerged in water, weighted down with scuba tanks—filled with nitrous oxide.

> He could smell perfume.
> It smelled familiar.
> It smelled strong.
>
> He heard a voice.
> It was a woman's voice.
> It sounded far away.
>
> His mouth was dry.
> His eyes hurt.
> His head hurt.

"Hello Jed, can you hear me?"
Jed heard the question but was unable to respond. His vocal chords were jammed.

"I am Nurse Rogers, Jed. Dr. Yen has sent me to help you."
Again, Jed tried to respond but to no avail. The smell of the perfume, though, elevated him, from beneath the warm water.

"Take your time Jed. There is no rush. You will be able to speak when you have more strength. I can see your eyes moving, behind those bubbling lids."

Jed listened to footsteps as they made their way out the door and down the hall.

Then, there was silence.

The smell of the perfume lingered.
It was not an unpleasant smell.
On the contrary, it helped Jed remember another place and time.

It was in a place where he could feel the sun's warmth, on his face.
It was at a time when he was lost but then found—below but then above, the surface, of the lime green ocean.

"I must be on the sand now," he told himself, *"waiting for her. The sand feels smooth like silk."*

His memory, of that day, on a secluded Cuban beach, assisted in lifting him from the depths, of his coma.

It was the smell of the perfume that really helped.
"It was the same as hers, above and below the water."

He recalled the feelings that he had felt, for that special lady, with the sweet smelling perfume.

Her name was Rachel.

"I can smell her perfume even when I am here and she is in the water. I hope she comes back soon."

Jed was still deep.

"Did she call herself a nurse? Why would she do

that? Her last name wasn't Rogers? It was Lee; like her dad's."

Even though Jed was now, a little closer to the surface, than he was before, he was still well under and would be, for a while.

His thoughts were distorted.
The coma held a firm grip.
Nevertheless, he struggled to climb.

"That smell," he reminded himself, *"It's Rachel's smell."*
He reassured. Then, he doubted.
"But, she called herself Rogers. Nurse Rogers? Was it? Or was it Nurse Rachel?"

He began to sink, again.
He slid – this time, deeper and deeper and deeper.
"Her skin is smooth, like a dolphin's."
Jed continued to slide – up and then, down again.

Outside, the Edmonton sun was losing its own battle.
Dark, puffy clouds were rolling in.

Jed no longer felt the warmth.
He no longer felt the sand.
He no longer smelled the perfume.
He no longer heard the voice or the footsteps.

- CHAPTER 9 -

TEMPUS FUGIT

Marty arrived.
He appeared anxious and paranoid.
He pleaded a weak case, to the receptionist, and explained that his tardiness was due to the chaos, at the rig. The receptionist was indifferent, to his feeble excuses.

She was, however, adamant about where Jed's room was. She told Marty to go straight to the room and nowhere else. She also told him that Jed was improving. He was out of his coma and not in critical condition, any more.

But, Marty was not to pester him, too long.

It had been two days since the blow out.

Marty thanked the strict receptionist and quickly made his way to C hall.

When he entered his room, Jed turned Marty's way.
"Hi Jed! You're awake!"
Jed smiled.
He nodded.
"I'm awake. Yep! At least, I think I am?" He pinched his left arm.
"My throat is sore, though. It's difficult to speak."

"Are you doin' okay, Jed?"

Jed took a frustrated breath. "I guess so. Once I get a grip on what the hell happened, I'll be better."

He pointed to the chair. He motioned for Marty to sit down.

"How are **you** doing, Marty?"

"I'm okay. I'm okay." Marty looked at the intravenous tube and followed it up to the bag, above Jed's head. He swallowed.

Jed could see that Marty was uncomfortable. "Hospitals ain't my favorite place, either, man."

"Sorry I'm late, Jed. I called yesterday and they told me that you were in a coma. I was worried." He shook his head. "I was scared, Jed."

Jed looked out the window. The sky did not look friendly.

He turned to Marty. "They told you I was in a coma? That's odd. Who?"

Marty replied that he didn't really know but that it was some chick's voice and he figured it was the receptionist or a nurse. He shrugged a shoulder.

Jed looked out the window, again.

"How's the rig?"

"It'll be okay."

Marty was relieved that he was able to respond to a question that he knew something about.

"The fire is out and the damage is not as bad as we originally thought."

Jed continued to look out the window. "What the heck happened that night, Marty?"

Marty stood up. He walked over and stood by the window. He looked out at the dark, grumbling sky. "We're in for a storm." He turned to Jed.

Jed thought that he looked sad.

Marty shook his head.

Jed studied him, for a few seconds, and then broke the silence.

"Everything was okay, Marty, before *short change*, right? There was no sign of pressure or leak. Was there?"

"How would I know, Jed? I'm just the fuckin' cook."

Jed lifted himself a little higher, against his pillow.

"That's a slow hole, Marty. There's lots of time to bull shit. You're always at the derrick, honing in, on the conversation. Did you hear anything?"

Jed winced. He rubbed his throat.

He continued. "A blow out like that just doesn't happen when we're torkin' out. Not at that speed."

Jed flinched. His head ached.

"You okay, Jed?" Marty approached the bed.

Jed ignored his question. "Somebody must have *dicked* around with something."

He looked directly at Marty.

Marty turned away. Then he looked up at the purple intravenous bag.

Jed caught sight of the lapel on Marty's jacket. He examined the logo: **Mustang Rigs**. He studied the white bucking horse and the backdrop of the bright red derrick.

Marty walked to the window, again. He looked outside. It was as if he were looking for the answer, to Jed's questions, in the cold, black sky.

Finally, he turned towards Jed. "I've been wrestling with so much, Jed. Remember, I'm just the cook."

Jed rolled his eyes.

Marty returned to his chair.

He slumped down.

He sighed.

"Fuck, maybe we'll never know, Jed. Maybe it's just one of those fuckin' things that occur without rhyme or reason."

Jed asked if he wanted some water. He pointed to the full pitcher on his bedside table.

Marty poured himself a cup. He poured one for Jed.

"Thanks."

Then, as if Marty had been struck by divine enlightenment, his eyes brightened and he sat upright, in his chair.

"You know, Jed, some people claim that poltergeists have their hands in and on things. I don't know. I'm as clued out as you are." He drank some water. "Ooh, that's good!"

Jed shook his head.

He was frustrated.

Under his breath, he whispered, "You just don't get it, do you?"

He was exhausted. He closed his eyes.

"Oh, I see you have another guest!" Dr. Yen broke the silence.

Jed opened his eyes and looked in the direction, of the doorway.

Doctor Yen's arrival was timely. The quiet, in the room, was making Marty edgy.

"And who is this young man?"

"Hi." Marty stood up. "I'm Marty, Jed's cook, at the rig."

"You must feed him very well, Mr. Marty. Jed, here, is recovering fairly well."

"You are what you eat, eh doc?" Jed extended a hand.

"You **are** my doctor aren't you?" Jed asked, assuming the obvious.

Dr. Yen responded with friendly affirmation.

"Yes, Mister Jed, I am your doctor…and happy to be."

Jed tried to sit up, a little higher. Dr. Yen moved in quickly.

"Take it easy, Mister Jed. You want to be careful not to be moving around too much."

He adjusted Jed's bed.

"Ah, that's better. Thanks."

"Now I don't feel like such an invalid. I can sit up like this and converse like one of the boys." He patted the bed.

He looked at the intravenous tube that was taped to his arm. Its contents contained a liquid that resembled grape cool-aid.

He shook his head. "This is a bummer, guys." Jed looked at Marty.

"You know that I don't like being imprisoned, like this. But, I guess it's better than bein' dead, eh?"

Marty looked at Dr. Yen. "Jed's not one to be trapped."

"I kind of figured that." Dr. Yen examined Jed's bandage and checked his pulse.

Marty seized the opportunity to make his exit. "I'll leave you two to take care of medical business." Dr. Yen did not discourage him, from leaving.

"I'm going to go for a coffee or something." He stood by the door. "Is there anything I can get either of you?"

"No thanks. Thank you just the same." With his miniature pool cue, Dr. Yen looked into Jed's eyes.

"I'll have a cold one, Marty. Preferably a Bud." Jed was half serious.

Marty laughed. Dr. Yen turned to face him. He placed his little eye instrument into the upper pocket, of his white lab coat. "They only sell Vietnamese beer, in this hospital, Mr. Marty."

Marty frowned. "Really?"

Dr. Yen laughed.

Jed shook his head. "Well, I guess that'll have to do."

"Actually, he can only have this stuff."

Dr. Yen held up the pitcher of water. "For a few more days, that is." He gave Jed a stern but friendly look.

Jed ran his fingers up and down his throat. "Oh, but Doctor, Bud's the only thing that eases my pain."

Dr. Yen smirked. "I'm sure."

"Later, guys." Marty left.

"And so, how are you doing, Mr. Jed?" Dr. Yen looked serious.

"Well, my eyes hurt and I'm just so damn tired."

"The Haemostatic Calyx does have those *minor* side effects."

Dr. Yen pointed to the intravenous tube.

Jed followed it up the wall and fixed his eyes upon the bag that was hanging, by the drip meter. It was about the size and shape of a rugby ball. It was half full.

Dr. Yen adjusted his glasses. He cupped his hand along Jed's forehead to check his temperature.

"We should have this dressing changed." He pointed to the bandage. "I will notify Nurse Rogers."

Jed looked up at the mention of her name.

"One of the minor side effects, Mister Jed," Dr. Yen continued, "Is, as you have described: fatigue and visual discomfort."

"That's two," Jed teased.

Doctor Yen didn't react.

"It is going to take a few days, Mister Jed. I hope you have patience." He paused. He sat down, in the chair.

"You will have the opportunity, however, to spend some time with one of my partners." He leaned forward. "You will find her to be very special. She will be helping you with your healing."

"She?" Jed raised his eyebrows.

"You mean Nurse Rogers?"

"No, No, No!" Dr. Yen shook his head.

He pointed an admonitory finger.

Then, he stood up and headed for the door.

Jed noticed how quietly he moved. His feet barely touched the floor.

He turned to Jed. "I will look in on you later and more frequently, Mister Jed." Then he mentioned that he had met Lana. He didn't say when or how. Jed was interested to know but before he could ask, Dr. Yen put up a hand.

"And oh, by the way." He paused. He tugged at a chin whisker. "She is not as tall as Nurse Rogers."

Jed frowned.

"My partner, Mister Jed." He took a step forward. "My special partner!" He stressed the word 'special'.

Jed thanked him for the clarification and then asked about Lana.

Dr. Yen smiled and replied with only two words: "Nice lady!" Then he left.

Jed rested his head against the pillow.

He looked up at the ceiling.

He thought about Dr. Yen.

He thought about Marty, Lana and Dr. Yen's *special* partner.

"What made her so special, anyway?"

He looked down at the intravenous tube.

He thought about the drug that was seeping through his veins.

His eyelids grew heavy.

His thoughts faded.

He drifted.

His last image, before passing from thought to sleep, was about the rig.

"It should never have happened," he told himself. He remembered taking off his hard hat.

He slept.

Seconds ticked.

Minutes moved.

Hours rolled.

Days changed.

When Jed opened his eyes, he wasn't certain if it were day or night.

He looked out the window.

Even though it was dark, a little light struggled to illuminate the room. From where the light was coming, Jed could only guess.

"Maybe it's a full moon." Jed strained to look out the window.

"Maybe it's the sun rise."

He panned the sky.

Then, from behind a cloud that was shaped like a lynx, appeared a bright full moon.

Jed followed its light, as it beamed through the hospital window carving a thin line along the distant, hospital floor.

It stretched across the linoleum making its way along the wall and resting at the foot of the door and at the feet of a silhouetted body, leaning against the frame.

Jed looked up.

He squinted.

"You're still alive, I see." A familiar voice emanated from the approaching figure.

It was a friendly voice.

It was an equally friendly figure.

"It's a good thing you've got a hard head, Jed."

Ossie looked tall as he stood by Jed's bed.

"Ossie?" Jed leaned on an elbow. "Ossie Lee?" He tried to sit up. "You're here!"

"Yours truly. In the flesh and in the west." He lifted a leg and placed a shiny new boot, on the edge, of Jed's bed. "New cowboy boots, with decent sized heels."

He pointed to the heel.

"No wonder you look taller than I remember."

"It's good to see you Ossie but what are you doing here?" Jed was surprised.

"I'm visiting the sick." Ossie moved in closer. His heels solidly, gripped the floor.

"Well, I am honored Ossie, I truly am, but?" Jed sat up.

"How did you get here? I mean." Jed shook his head.

"When did you get here?" He rubbed his eyes. "How did you know?" Jed had so many questions.

"Lee told me." Ossie sat down. "I was in Miami when I got the call. He told me that Mustang Two fell." They shook hands.

"Then, I called Lana." He paused. He looked at Jed. "And then I caught a flight. Two actually. I had to go through Montreal."

"Holy crow, Ossie! So, you're here. That's great! Thanks." Jed smiled. "It's good to see you."

"You too. But you have looked better." He pointed to the bandage. "Nice hat!"

They shared a laugh.

"Yep! You bet. So, don't turn on any lights. I might scare you away when you see what I really look like."

They spoke about the rig, the hospital, Jed's doctor and whether or not there were any hot nurses. Jed couldn't share much. Since the blow out, he had spent most of his time sleeping and dreaming – or, at least, that's what he thought.

"I'm as thirsty as hell, though." He asked Ossie to pour him some water. "Help yourself, too."

Jed asked about Ossie's father.

Ossie took a sip of his drink and responded that Lee was doin' okay. He hadn't seen his dad, though, for a while, since he had been spending a lot of time in Miami and off shore drilling.

"Lee, as you know, doesn't drift too far from his home."

Jed agreed.

As the moon moved slowly and westerly, across Alberta's *Big Sky*, it took the thin ray of light with it.

The room was darker, now.

The floor was no longer illuminated.

Ossie got up.
He tiptoed towards the door.
Jed couldn't hear his heels.
Ossie looked out into the hall and then, seeing that the coast was clear, he gently, shut the door.
The room was now, virtually, pitch black.
Ossie returned to his chair by Jed's bed.
He sat down.
He moved in, a little closer.
Jed was curious.
Ossie leaned forward. "I don't want to speak too loudly, Jed. The two-hour time difference has got me all lagged out and I'm getting kind of tired. I should be headin' out soon, but before I go, I want to share something with you."
He leaned back.
He took a deep breath.
Jed studied his moves.
In the darkness, Ossie managed to reach out and retrieve his cup, from the bedside table.
He took a sip.
Then, he returned it, to the exact same spot.
He leaned forward, again. "I'm going to be crashing out, at Lana's."
Jed thought that was a good idea.
Both his eyes and Ossie's were adjusting to the darkness.
Jed could see Ossie's face a little better, now. He looked more serious, than he did, when he first arrived.
"I've got to tell you, Jed." He looked around the room ensuring that they were still alone.
Jed was still curious.
"It's been on my mind since your blow out." He looked

at the table. He saw the pitcher of water. He asked if he could have some more.

Jed said "Of course. Me too."

Ossie poured two fresh cups."

He looked up and down the walls, searching for a clock.

"What time do you think it is right now, Jed?"

"What? Time? Hell, I don't know." Jed shrugged. He thought that Ossie's question was weird.

"No. Seriously! Jed?" Ossie repeated. "What time do you think it is?"

"I don't know. Who cares? I'm not wearing a watch." He looked out the window.

"Based on the sky, I would say that it's about 2:00 a.m." He looked at the wall. "I guess I didn't get a room with a clock."

Ossie looked at the window. "Nice view, though."

Jed shrugged.

He looked over at the closed door. "How did you get in here, anyway, Os?"

"I walked in. I told the lady, at the front desk, who I was and where I came from and she directed me to your room. She didn't guarantee that you'd be awake, though."

Jed pondered. "Interesting."

"Jed?" Ossie touched Jed's arm—the one with the intravenous tube.

"Somebody might know something, Jed."

Jed frowned.

"Somebody on or somebody connected to the rig—and somebody might know you know something you shouldn't."

And the clock, on the wall, downstairs, in Nurse Rogers' station, read exactly: 2:02 a.m.

PART TWO

THE 'COPS'

- CHAPTER ONE -

SUMMER RENDEZVOUS

On a hot August morning, in the summer of 1982, 27 miles south west of the Cuban shoreline, Jed Robert Sands met Ossie Jack Lee. The two men were employed with Cuban Oil, working on a rig called: Mustang Rig One. At the time, Jed was a 'motor man' spinning engines and chains. Ossie was supervising the site, representing Cuban Oil Partnerships or 'COPS'. He was 26 years old and Jed was 25.

It wasn't long before Jed and Ossie struck up a friendship. Through the exchange of their common ages and experiences, they were both taken aback by how similar their pasts were.

Ossie, like Jed, celebrated a November birthday. He was born the only son to a young couple, living in a small oil town and never remaining in one place long enough to call home. Jed experienced the same kind of youth. Both were relatively new to their positions, without any meaningful friendships or relationships.

Mustang Rig One was a triple rig that was dredging through mud and rock, deep beneath the white caps of the Caribbean Sea. The gallons of gas that it was attempting to liberate were copious. According to Ossie, "The barrels could energize Cuba, Jamaica and Barbados, for the ensuing three decades." Jed thought that was impressive.

The summer shift was tough but simple. The day crew worked a twelve-hour, fifteen-day cycle, beginning at

8:00 a.m. The night crew covered the *graveyard*. The riggers were free to leave the ship provided they were back on deck, thirty minutes before shift change.

Their relentless toil was well balanced with generous meals and friendly skies. The island of Cuba, however, was another story. It, paradoxically, featured beautiful sandy beaches patrolled by noisy, ominous police boats. It celebrated an economy that castigated the *Yankees* yet wanted to get its hands on their U.S. *bucks*.

Ossie owned a tug that he had purchased from the 'COPS'. He used it to commute from the island to the rig. Whenever he and Jed were *on leave*, they would faithfully head for the flats to take in the Latin sites and sounds, of the Caribbean's largest island.

Ossie and Jed made use of the tug on numerous occasions. It was on one of these ventures that Jed met Lana.

- CHAPTER 2 -

QUÉ PASA

There was a club in Havana called the ***Que Pasa***. It was a beachcomber's watering hole that was frequented by both locals and tourists. It featured an outdoor patio with a covered bar filled with tropical plants flanked by statues and torches.

The dance floor was made of old barn wood.

It told a story.

Beer stains and cigar burns disclosed a history of hard celebrating, rowdy crowds and late reckless nights. The walls were splattered with paraphernalia, from both World Wars. Graffiti was written in Spanish, English and German.

The artwork was colorful but some of its messages were dark.

The machine guns and helmets, hanging from the ceiling, emblazoned the club with a look that appeared older than it actually was. Jed said that it reminded him of a setting in a *Humphry Bogart* film. Ossie thought that it was more like an *Indiana Jones*.

That summer, Lana and her friend Sally were on vacation, in Cuba. They were seizing the opportunity to take a breather from their boring summer jobs and even more boring university courses. They had just returned from a *Tropical Fish* snorkeling trip. While perched on the front steps of the Que Pasa, they exchanged impressive but exaggerated fish stories.

Jed and Ossie were beginning a seven-day—much deserved—*long change*. They agreed that a visit to the ***Que Pasa*** was the only way to commence their break.

The music that was emanating from the bar was soothing and inviting. As they walked up the boat plank, Jed commented on the music.
"The music, Ossie, like the clientele, is awaiting you." Jed winked.

Lana saw Jed first.
She was immediately struck by the color of his skin. His rosy cheeks brought out the blue in his eyes. He had fair hair that was only slightly visible, jutting out from beneath his Montreal Expos baseball hat.
Like a catcher, behind the plate, he wore his cap backwards.

Lana thought that he looked like Chuck Norris.
Sally disagreed.
She said that he was more of a Dennis Wilson.
Lana frowned.
"You know, the drummer of The Beach Boys!"
Lana shrugged.
Jed's white t-shirt was exceptionally bright. It was contrasted by the gold, of his toned and tanned arms. On the shirt, there was a Mustang Rig logo. It was a horse and a derrick, with a backdrop, of the Canadian flag.
Lana and Sally greeted the boys with friendly hellos.
Lana asked Jed about his Canadian origin.
Sally did the same with Ossie.
He informed her that he was born in the U.S.A. and not in Canada. He was also emphatic when he stated that his family now lived, on a little island, south of Cuba.

Cervezas led to dinner; dinner led to dancing and dancing led to a tugboat cruise, around Havana's harbor.

"This is wonderful!" Lana pointed at the lights, of Havana.
"Look!" She pointed. "It looks like they're glittering."
Then, she looked down, at the water.
"And dancing!"
"Yes." Agreed Jed. He liked it how much Lana appreciated life's simple treasures.
The three quarter moon spilled part of itself, on the sea, beneath them.
Jed looked at Lana. " That's neat!"
"What?" She was embarrassed.
"I can see the reflection of the water, in your eyes."
Lana liked that. "Thank you."

She was at home with Jed.
She felt safe with him.
He was kind. He was warm. She liked those qualities, in people.
"I feel as though I've known you for years."
"Maybe you have." Jed felt the same way about Lana.
He liked her enthusiasm.
He smiled at her wit.
He was moved, by her spirit.

He leaned against the rail.
Lana leaned against him.
They counted stars and outlined the Big Dipper. Then—the Little Dipper and then—the Milky Way.
From a distance, they heard the rhythms, of the Cuban calypso.
Meanwhile, Sally and Ossie were doing their own outlining.
Ossie was teaching her how to operate the helms of his

reliable COPS tug. He and she were considerably more academic, though, than the two romantics, outlining stars, on the deck below.

The water was calm.

The boat seemed to be hardly moving.
As Sally navigated, along the shoreline, the hours of the night turned the colors of the sky into a magical array of morning pink and purple.
Sally and Ossie remained focused.
She kept the tug on a steady course.
He rested his hands, on hers.

Lana and Jed remained focused, too.
Their focus, however, was slightly more playful.

They bid goodnight, in the lobby of the girls' hotel.
The plan was to meet at noon, later, that day, on the steps of the **Que Pasa**.
Twelve o'clock would sneak up on them quickly, though, as the hands of the front desk clock, held firmly at 4:00 a.m.

Jed and Ossie returned to the tug.
In the east, the West Indian sun was peeking over the horizon.
It was a cool morning but the sunrise beheld the promise of a warm day. Just before they drifted off into a short but deep sleep, Ossie told Jed a story about his father.

In a few days, Jed would get the opportunity to meet Ossie's father. Only then, would he recall Ossie's story.

- CHAPTER 3 -

LANA IN HAVANA

The mid-day sun was perched high and mighty, in the bright blue, Caribbean sky.

Its penetrating heat reddened the tips of Jed's ears.

Ossie's pace had slowed since the last time he ascended the twelve steps, of his favorite haunt.

Sally told him that he looked a little rough but still 'kinda' cute.

"The 'hung over' look suits you, there, Ossie."

"You mean the achin' head look." He held his forehead.

His short brown hair was cow licked in front. His sharp jaw and high cheekbones enhanced his piercing dark eyes. To a stranger, Ossie could be mistaken for a member of the militia. Despite his apparent fatigue, he was ready for another adventure, with his henchman, Jed, and his new, Canadian friends, Lana and Sally.

"Hurtin' a bit, boys?" Lana adjusted her sunglasses.

"I'll be okay." Ossie attempted to smile. "I will, however, watch my liquid intake and request that y'all speak in a lower key." He sat down on the fifth step.

Jed poked a friendly jab at Ossie's shoulder.

"That'll teach ya for drinkin' and drivin' a 'COPS' tug."

"Oh ya. Look who's talkin'. At least I kept the tug afloat. In the head space you were in, we would have been grounded, for sure."

Sally laughed.

Lana rolled her eyes.

And Jed just smiled. "Oh ya?"

Despite their lack of sleep and aching heads, they were all happy to be together, again.

The symmetry, between Ossie and Sally, was a healthy mix, of academic interest.

The chemistry, between Jed and Lana, was a steamy blend, of harmonious trust.

Ossie appreciated Sally's interest in the tug, in the island of Cuba and in his family's home, on Juventud.

Sally, in turn, was impressed with Ossie's work experience, his attention to detail and his love of the sea.

Ossie was not accustomed to such appreciation and support.

Until now, most of the people, in his life, had been judgmental, guarded and uptight.

Jed liked Lana.

It felt right being with her.

As they walked along the boardwalk and up and down the docks, his desire, for her, grew more profound.

He wanted to hold her, to kiss her, to touch her and to be touched, by her. He reached out to hold her hand; something that he was not accustomed to doing or ever wanted to do, with anyone.

He asked himself, *how, in such a short period of time, could he feel so close to somebody?*

Like Romeo and Juliet, he thought, *was it possible that the stars had crossed for him and Lana? Perhaps it was just the setting! Perhaps it was the Big Dipper. Who knew?*

As they made their way onto the tug, Jed reminded himself of the island's reputation: *it was famous for strengthening one's desire but weakening his control.* He thought that *maybe, just maybe, his feelings for Lana, were a result of that 'island' pull.* At the same time, he saw their relationship as something real, something that could last and something that could be fun. *It already was.*

Her lips invited him to kiss.

As he gently drew her body closer to his, he could feel her heart beating in her attractive, firm chest.

It was a kind beat.

The warmth of her skin, the freshness of her fragrance and the tenderness of her touch – they all enveloped him like a wave, curling over the falling surfer.

His legs were losing grip.

Lana ran her fingers along the back of his neck and along his shoulders.

For Jed, the floor, of the tug, felt like sponge.

When he was growing up in Brooks, Alberta, Jed flirted with adolescent love. At high school dances, weekend ski trips and Friday night drive-ins, he was kissed, in what he would later describe as in only fun and infatuation. The passion that emanated in those days, though, was a mere candle, next to the fire that burned from Lana, in Havana.

"Virgin Punch anyone?"

Sally's question sounded like it was coming from afar. It startled Jed.

It awakened him, as if he were in a deep sleep or trance.

"That sounds great," Lana, momentarily removed her lips from Jed's.

Jed could only nod. Words escaped him. He was relieved that Lana, on the other hand, was able to respond.

"How ya' doin' Jed?" inquired Ossie, poking his head through the kitchen porthole.

"I'm okay! You?"

"Life is good, Jed. Life is real good!" He gave a thumb up.

- CHAPTER 4 -

THE ALBATROSS

Labor Day, in Canada, as in most parts of the world, marks the 'unofficial' end of summer. It is celebrated on the first Monday in September and pays tribute to the working people. The following Tuesday represents *day one* of classes for most students, at most schools and at most levels.

Lana and Sally were scheduled to begin their final year at the University of Alberta on the first Tuesday of September, 1982.

The 30th of August was going to be the last day of their Cuban vacation. It was the day before they would take flight, back home, to Canada. It was destined to be a very significant day. It would represent the last day that Lana and Sally would see Jed and Ossie for a long four months. It would also be a day that would change Jed's life, forever.

Jed was not feeling his usual self. Both his and Ossie's *long change* was quickly coming to a close. He would have to be on tower, at midnight, the eve of Lana's and Sally's departure. He did not want their break to end. He did not want to bid farewell to Lana. Although, he didn't mind his job, at the rig, he wasn't quite ready, to return to the sea.

Ossie, too, was feeling less inclined to return to work.

To mend their pains, Ossie recommended, a little cruise, around the Caribbean.

His parents owned a piece of property, on a tiny island, south west of Cuba. It was called the ***isla de la Juventud***.

It was like Prince Edward Island, in size, but more like Cape Breton Island, in shape. It lay cradled in the arms of *Comrade Cuba*, basking in the warm waters, of the Gulf of Bataband.

It had a population of just over 70,000. It was technically another Cuban municipality but the islanders considered it to be their own province.

Although, the island had its own shops and markets, the Cuban city of Guane was Juventud's most widely used city, serving the islanders, with their provisions and dry goods.

At the Guane Market, following a lengthy and a rather conspicuous telephone call, Ossie purchased a few domestic items. Lana and Sally did some last minute shopping picking up souvenirs—and Jed—Jed bought a bottle of Havana rum.

He also treated himself to a $2.00 cigar.

He claimed that he was going to puff on it, while sailing to the island.

At noon, the tug left, for its two-hour cruise.

The Caribbean weather was friendly, for their late August mid-day sail. The sea was its usual aqua-blue. It revealed the appearance of a thousand emerald gems, scattered about its rippled, sandy floor.

As the tug chugged at a steady 25 nauts, Jed and Lana stood transfixed, at the bow, leaning on the rail and leaning on each other. They didn't need to talk. Words were spoken in other ways.

The wind, the sky, the sun and the surf said it all.

Ossie and Sally were perched, in control, in their usual

spot, as well. They weren't saying much, either. Like Jed and Lana, they were holding on to the helms- and to each other.

Jed looked back.

He looked up.

He couldn't help but notice how focused Ossie was.

He was generally a person given to smiling, teasing and acknowledging the presence of others. Today, his expression was stoic – his eyes looked straight ahead.

Sally looked content but, like Lana, was weighted by the same Albatross that was hovering high and invisibly, above their heads.

- CHAPTER 5 -

THE COMRADES

Ossie's father, Mr. Lee or 'Lee', as he preferred to be called, met the 'COPS' crew, when it landed on Juventud.

He, like Ossie, was not tall but, like his son, was fit with sharpened features and a confident demeanor.

His graying hair was receding but his tanned forehead was not unpleasantly pronounced.

He wore a white t-shirt with blue overalls. From a distance he looked like a landscaper, but upon closer scrutiny, his appearance was more professor-like. His eyes were deep with intellect and thought.

He drove a red '62 Dodge that was splashed with patches of fiberglass and primer. The radio station, blasting from its dash, sounded like it was intentionally, lost in the sixties.

Like the truck, the music and the Spanish speaking disc jockey, Lee was a 'throw back' to a decade, of guns and roses. Even the package of Camel cigarettes, strategically tucked under his rolled up sleeve was the look of a beatnik turning hip.

After friendly greetings and informal introductions, Lee chauffeured the group through the swamps, plains and fields, of the Isla de Juventud.

The roads were not good.
The ride was bumpy.

The beautiful scenery, however, cushioned the journey.

Jed commented on its appeal.

Lee appreciated that.

He made it clear, to all, that he was very proud of his *special* island.

Like the eyes of a camera, Jed panned the fields and the farmers as they tilled the soil in the baking sun.

The truck finally bounced into a more densely wooded area. Jed commented that the palm trees had a protective appearance. "They look like statues," he pointed, "Carefully carved, by a protective hand."

Lana smiled at Jed's perception.

"They're intentionally designed like that to stand guard like sentinels." Lee turned to Jed.

"Not many notice that," he nodded. "Good eye!" Jed could see that Lee approved of his observations. The changing landscape was a good omen, Jed felt – but for exactly what, he could not be certain.

Upon arriving at Lee's home, Ossie's mother, Mrs. Lee welcomed the group and gave Ossie a warm, motherly hug. Jed's first impression, of her, was that she was a friendly woman who made those, in her presence, and in her home, feel genuinely, welcomed.

She greeted Jed like he was a celebrity.

She made a fuss over him.

"Ossie has spoken so highly of you, Jed. When he called, he said that you were the best."

Jed smiled and asked "Oh ya, the best?"

Jed looked at Ossie. "The best at what?"

Ossie raised his eyebrows.

Jed thought that Ossie looked mischievous – like he was up to something. He was relieved to see that Ossie was more relaxed, now, than he appeared to be, on the tug.

Like Lee, Mrs. Lee was not a large woman but her round face and wide smile gave one the impression that she was bigger than she actually was.

It was obvious that she was energetic but Jed could see that she was restless.

She could not sit still.

She repeated how happy she was that Ossie was home and that he had such nice friends.

As she spoke, she fixed her hair and adjusted pictures that were hanging, perfectly straight, on the kitchen wall.

Jed presented her and Lee with the bottle of rum that he had purchased, at the market, in Guane.

At his request, Jed and Ossie joined Lee, in the den, for a smoke and a beverage. He, too, appeared to be restless. Jed attributed his anxiety to the excitement of having Ossie back home and to having a group of strangers, in his home.

The den resembled a study that Jed once saw in a 'Sherlock Holmes' mystery.

Lee asked Jed if he were interested in reading. Jed responded that he was. He looked at the book-filled shelves.

"I can see that you are."

Lee ignored Jed's presumption.

He invited him to browse and then told him to take a seat.

Jed sat in a chair that was close by the door.

"No, no. Sit here." He pointed to a chair, in the corner. Jed thought that it was kind of far away. He sat in it, anyway. "Thanks."

Ossie remained standing.

Lee offered Jed a cigar and then filled two glasses, with the rum, that Jed had earlier presented, in the kitchen, as a 'thank you' gift. He placed Jed's glass down, on the coffee table, near his chair. It made sense, now, for Jed, why Lee wanted him to sit where he had instructed. The chair was near the table.

Lee turned to Ossie who looked, faithfully, familiar with the routine.

"Ossie. Go and fetch us some punch, will ya'. It's in the fridge." He looked at Jed. "Unless you want to drink that straight?" he pointed to Jed's glass.

Jed shook his head. "No, no." He looked at Ossie. "I'll have some punch. Thanks."

Ossie left the room.

Lee lit Jed's cigar and then took a step back. He puffed at his own smoke and then leaned against the bookshelf.

Jed thanked Lee for the cigar and for lighting it.

Lee did not acknowledge Jed's gratitude. For a moment, the room was ritualistically quiet. Lee just puffed at his cigar and studied Jed like he was sizing him up.

He finally broke the silence.

"Are you a philosopher, Jed?"

Jed sighed. He responded that he thought that all people, to a certain extent, were philosophers.

Lee asked him again.

"But are **you** a philosopher, Jed?"

Jed nodded. "I guess so." He then clarified that he had never studied the subject.

Lee asked if he were interested in politics.

Jed said that he was but that he was not an expert on that subject, either.

Ossie returned with the punch.

He handed it to Lee who then proceeded to pour some into Jed's glass of rum.

He didn't add any to his drink, though. "I like it

straight up." He raised his glass. "Cheers!" Jed raised his. "Salut!"

"You're not havin' one, Os?" Jed was surprised.

Ossie shook his head. "I'm okay." Jed thought that he was more content in playing the harbinger.

His demeanor appeared to be a little uncomfortable but Jed attributed it to a respect for his father and a mutual respect for his father's favorite room.

Jed smiled.

Ossie, sort of, returned his smile.

He could see that Jed was confused.

"I prefer to listen, Jed, rather than get caught up in a philosophical or political debate."

Jed responded that he understood. He looked at Lee for his reaction. He was still standing, on the far side of the room, leaning an elbow, against one of the shelves.

"Tell me Jed," Lee cleared his throat. "What do you make of the current relationships between the U.S. and Cuba?" Like Ossie had done earlier, Lee mischievously, raised his eyebrows.

Jed took a sip of his drink. It tasted strong. It also tasted pretty good.

"Ooh, that's got a kick to it!" He paused. He looked at Ossie and then he looked back at Lee. He answered the question.

"I think it is unfortunate that the two countries, being geographically so close to one another, are so distant in their principles and ideologies."

Lee slowly approached Jed. He stood directly in front of him.

"And what, specifically, Jed, would you define as the principles, of the U.S.A.?"

Jed took another sip.

He smiled. "You like this stuff, eh Lee?" Jed assumed that Lee was enjoying the opportunity of having a fresh mind to pry and to challenge.

He decided to go with it.

"That's a good question, Lee! In theory, the U.S. is a democratic country, grounded in the belief that all men are created equal." Jed was amused by his own sophisticated response. He stood up. He looked over at Ossie and then walked towards him. He held on to his drink. Then, he stopped in the middle of the room.

He took a breath.

He turned around to look at Lee.

"And all men are entitled to certain freedoms. Freedom of speech, freedom of..."

Jed's intended list of *freedoms* was cut short by Lee's interruption:

"Freedom of opportunity?" Lee frowned.

"Yes," agreed Jed. "Absolutely! Especially freedom of opportunity! Every American can aspire to become the president." Jed sipped his drink.

Lee smirked. "That's quite a prophetic statement, there Jed." His smirk turned into a grin – a sardonic grin. "Who would have thought that a poor boy from Maine, with no formal education, based solely on his strength of intellect and force of character, would rise to the highest position in the world?" Lee walked over and sat down, in Jed's chair, in the corner. He raised his glass.

He looked like he was going to make a patriotic toast. Instead, he just studied the clear liquid that was encircling the bottom of his glass.

"Who was that? Ford? Carter?" Jed squinted.

"No, amigo." Lee finished off his drink. "Not those guys." He shook his head. He licked his lips and then wiped them. "Gerald Ford was not from Maine, but Lincoln was."

He looked up at the ceiling. He took a long puff, of his cigar.

Ossie walked over and refilled his father's glass. Then, he topped up Jed's.

"Thanks Os." Jed held up his glass. "This is good punch."

Lee continued to stare at the ceiling.

"The sixteenth president of the U.S.A." He appeared to be lost in reverie.

"Abraham Lincoln! Slave emancipator!" He sipped some rum. This time, he did propose a toast. "To Lincoln!"

Jed was not certain whether he was being sincere or sarcastic.

"You know your history, Lee."

"It's not my history, Jed. But I do know Lincoln's and I like what he did for the African Americans." Lee stood up. He walked over and stood beside Jed. He placed a hand on his shoulder.

He paused.

He looked directly into Jed's eyes.

Jed looked into his.

Lee smiled.

Jed swallowed.

He recalled a story that Ossie had recently shared with him, in the wee hours, of a cool August morning, in the bowels of the COPS tug. Before they drifted off to sleep, Ossie told Jed a story about his dad.

Something in Lee's eyes triggered Jed's memory, of that story.

"What about Kennedy?"

"What?" The question caught Jed off guard.

He sipped his drink.

"Do you know much about his history?" Lee was still smiling.

He puffed at his cigar.

He squinted.

He asked the question again.

Jed couldn't respond. All he could think of was what Ossie had shared with him, that morning.

The cigar smoke drifted upwards, towards the ceiling.
Jed began to feel a little faint.

He needed to sit down. He returned to his chair, without his punch. He shook his head. He shrugged.

"Not really. I know a little bit about Kennedy but it sounds like you wish I knew more."

Lee leaned against the shelf.

Jed rubbed his eyes. The cigar smoke was getting to him.

Lee continued.

"Well, yes, Jed, I am interested in your thoughts pertaining to the Bay of Pigs."

"The Bay of Pigs?" Jed was shocked. "Is that why you asked me about Cuba and America?" Jed looked for his drink. Ossie brought it to him. He had left it on one of the shelves.

Lee nodded, with approval. He looked like he was pleased with Jed's question and with his struggle to contend with the smoke.

"To some degree," he paused, "But I was interested in how you might predict our political futures." He paused, again. He took a drink. He stood by Jed's chair.

"Both together and apart?"

"I'm flattered, Lee," Jed leaned on the arm of his chair, "That you would value my opinion that much." He looked up at Ossie. "No more punch for me, Os. It's twisting my brain."

He looked up at Lee. "Remember, Lee. I'm only a *rig pig*."

"Precisely!" Lee pointed a finger. " That is precisely why I am asking you, Jed. I respect rig pigs and besides, Ossie told me that you had some brains – and not twisted ones." He smiled. Jed noticed the whiteness of his teeth.

Jed looked at Ossie.
Ossie looked at Lee.
Lee looked at Jed.

"That's enough." He said. He made his closing statement like he was claiming *check- mate.*

"The hours of your afternoon are slipping away." He devoured his drink. He turned to Ossie.

"You should take your Canadian friend, here, on a stroll, about the place."

Jed agreed. "Good idea! I could use some fresh air."

He stood up. He thanked Lee for the drinks and the smoke.

"No, no, Jed. It is **you** that I must thank." He escorted Jed towards the door.

"I thank you for our discussion. I found our political debate to be most philosophical."

Jed frowned. "Debate? I hardly…"

Lee interrupted.

"We have covered years of history and centuries of people." He clarified. "Important people."

Although he was a little confused, Jed thought it was best to simply agree.

"Let's go out on to the verandah, Jed. I could use a little fresh air, myself. It's too smoky, in here." Ossie led the way.

Jed agreed. "That's for sure! All that toasting to former presidents can get to a guy." He smiled. He was feeling a little better now that he was walking.

Lee laughed. "I'll meet you two outside. I want to check in on your mother and the girls. Maybe I can scare up a political debate with one of them." He headed for the kitchen. Ossie and Jed headed for the front door.

When they arrived on the porch, they were surprised to see Lana and Sally.

Lana was sitting in the swinging deck chair and Sally was stretched out on the top step. "Enjoying the warm weather?" Ossie sat down, beside Sally.

Jed joined Lana on the swing. "How's it going?" Lana

looked at her watch. "It's getting late and we've got a plane to catch. I think we had better start making tracks."

Jed sensed tension.

"Is everything okay?"

"Oh ya. I'm fine." Lana shrugged. "It's just that the clock is ticking and we've still got to get across the bay."

"Everybody enjoying themselves?" Lee arrived on the porch. He stood by Jed.

Jed leaned back. He rested his head against the back of the chair. "Ooh, this could rock me to sleep, in no time." He held on to his forehead. "That was powerful punch, Lee."

Apparently, Lana had a couple of glasses, herself. "I know what you mean. I couldn't finish my second glass."

"Me neither. Or was it my third?" Jed paused. "What do you have in that punch, anyway?"

Lee laughed. "Glad you liked it. It's my *Lee Harvey* special." Jed looked up at the mention of the name *Harvey*. It didn't faze Lana, though. Ossie reacted but Sally remained horizontal. She looked like she was in a state of blissful warmth. Lana stood up. She extended her hand. She thanked Lee and said that it was a pleasure meeting him.

Just then, Ossie's mom poked her head out the door. "Can I get anyone, anything else?" She was looking at Ossie. Jed could see that she didn't want him or his friends to leave. The inevitable, though, was close at hand.

Ossie explained to her that they had to be heading back. She said that she understood. Like Jed, Lana detected that, although she understood, she didn't want them to leave.

"Well, time to go." Jed stood up. "Thank you both, very much. Great hospitality!" He smiled at Ossie's mom and then he looked at Lee. "I'm going to need a nap, though, before I'm back on tower, tonight."

Sally dragged herself, from the step. "It's that time, is it?"

Lee walked towards the Dodge. "I'll go and fire up the truck. I'll give you guys a ride back to the docks." He looked at Jed. "You can sleep while I drive." He shook his head. With tongue in cheek, he added: "And, I thought you rig pigs were tough."

Jed laughed. "No, but we're smart, though. Remember?" Lee opened the driver's door. Jed cupped his hands around his mouth. He called out. "But not tough, Lee."

Lee opened the door and sat in the driver's seat. He rolled down the window. He shook his head. He stared at Jed.

Ossie said goodbye to his mom. He hugged her and told her that he would call her, in a couple of days.

Although he was the most reluctant to leave, he agreed, with Lana, that they all were in for a busy night. He apologized for leaving, so soon.

Lana and Sally expressed their gratitude and said that they enjoyed their visit. They also added that they hoped to be able to visit, again.

As the truck sped away, down the dusty drive, Jed looked back. Through the rolling dust and spinning stones, he could not help but notice the look on Ossie's mother's face. She looked sad. Jed thought that she was crying.

She was waving a bright red handkerchief. The action looked like it was from a scene, in a movie – an old movie—either 'Gone With The Wind' or 'Oklahoma.'

Jed stared.

The arm continued waving.

Jed thought of the significance, of the color red.

Wasn't it the color of a rebel?
The color of a communist?
And, the color of blood?

Standing and peeking from behind a grapefruit tree was a tall, slim black man.

That, too, caught Jed's eye.

He thought that he must have been doing yard work or gardening.

He was not certain, but, as the dust settled and the air cleared, Jed thought that their eyes met.

It would be weeks before their eyes would meet again.

- CHAPTER 6 -

THE RETURN

School began in a flurry of long line-ups and long cheque writing.

Lana was able to register in some, what she believed, would be useful courses. Sally, on the other hand, was not as lucky or optimistic. In the chaos of school start-up, she lost patience. She refused to wait in line. Consequently, she was compelled to take courses, in which she had little interest and little or no background. Her academic advisor tried to console her. "These things happen, Sally."
She was not one to be pacified.

Her petite appearance was not to be mistaken for a petite mind. Sally was big in heart, big in soul and big in wit. Her medium length, shaggy brown hair was also not to be mistaken for an unkempt character. There was nothing sloppy about Sally—except her hair, of course—which was *neat*, in its own *messy* way.

Sally was fun but, at the same time, serious.
She was unselfish but not patient.
She was trustworthy but trusted few.
She was ambitious but not greedy.

Lana knew how fortunate she was to have Sally as a friend.
Despite her unattractive timetable, Sally attended her

classes and learned things that, as she put it, "Might, somehow, help me, when I arrive in the *real world*."

Years later, that prediction became a reality when, in 1985, she was offered a position as an elementary school generalist, working in one of Edmonton's largest schools.

Life, on the rig, was in a bit of a flurry, as well. September and October were busy months for offshore drilling. The autumn shifts followed a rigorous schedule of 21 days, 21 nights and 21 well-deserved days off. For all the riggers, the three weeks break was greatly appreciated and desperately needed to recuperate from the demanding 42-day cycle.

The climate, on the sea, was erratic.

During the fall season, it changed rapidly. The days were moderate, like in the summer—the nights, on the other hand, were the contrary. After the sun sank into the western horizon, the air and water temperatures, quickly, dropped 10 to 20 degrees. The winds accelerated, without warning and the waves, sometimes, reached heights of 25 feet.

Jed and Ossie concentrated more on their work than on their friendship. At mealtime, they spoke about the weather and the sea. They talked about valves and pipes and sumps and pumps. Occasionally, they mentioned Lana and Sally but only in casual conservation and only when the other riggers were out of earshot.

Jed missed Lana – but with each passing day, the ache subsided.

He was not certain how Ossie was feeling about Sally, though.

Was he missing her?

There was a private side to Ossie that Jed had not seen before.

He told himself that was probably normal. *Everybody has a private side.* He knew that, at times, even *he* needed space. *After all, who doesn't?*

But, Jed sensed that there was a distance, now, between him and Ossie – a distance that he had not felt, in late August, when he and Sally were flitting and flirting around the Caribbean.

Had something happened? Jed wondered if it had anything to do with Lee.

Did he say or do something that might have made Ossie feel uncomfortable?

Jed was perplexed. And so, he decided to give Ossie what he deemed as his *needed space* – a space that, at that point in time, seemed necessary and crucial.

Jed spent more time alone and sought comfort in his own thoughts and reveries.

Even in his busiest and most dangerous moments of chain spinning and tong tightening, Jed would let his mind drift to thoughts of home and family, life and death, Lee and Lana.

He missed Lana – that was certain. But he wondered if she were missing him.

When he thought about that, he told himself to stay strong.

It may have just been an island fling.

He wanted to talk to somebody about Lee. *That was quite something meeting him.* But, at the same time, he felt that it was best to leave the subject alone, for now, anyway.

He wondered if Lana knew who Ossie's father really was.

While working the graveyard shift, Jed would look up

at the moon and wonder if Lana were looking up at the same moon, having the same kinds of thoughts, in those Canadian skies, thousands of miles away.

He did a lot of thinking.
He did a lot of reading.
He did a lot of planning.

Mid October arrived with a breath of fresh and friendlier air.

It brought with it a 21-day break from the wind, the rain and the rig. Jed and Ossie returned to Cuba, spending only one night at the Que Pasa and then leaving the next morning for, hopefully, a quiet and relaxing three week break in the sun and warmth, of Juventud.

Jed was looking forward to reading some literature that was on the shelf of Lee's study. Ossie spoke of how good it would be to listen to the sounds of the birds and insects as opposed to the thuds of rig motors and drill pipes. They both spoke of letter writing and phone calling. Jed cringed as he speculated what his phone bill was going to look like. They both vowed to play more chess, against each other and against the old men in the Nuevo Gerona Square. Jed treaded with caution but humored Ossie by declaring that he would even allow Lee to entice him into solving the political problems between the United States and Cuba. Ossie laughed at that. Jed was happy to see him smile.

"Good luck," he teased, as he held on to the helms of the COPS tug. He looked out at the water and made a comment that Jed thought was both significant and heartfelt.

"The political problems between the U.S. and Cuba should not exist." Ossie paused.

He looked at Jed. "But they do." He stopped smiling.

He continued to hold on tightly to the helms.

"You choose to stay away from political debates with your dad, eh Os?"

"Lee and I have had our battles," he stated flatly.

Jed nodded.

"There's Juventud," he pointed straight ahead.

"It looks nice!"

Ossie nodded. "It is nice.

It's a treasure!"

- CHAPTER 7 -

SAM THE MAN

Their arrival, this time, on the Isla de Juventud was different than the last.

A young slick talking Cuban, by the name of Sammy Giancana, met Ossie and Jed, at the dock. He, unlike Lee, drove a bright red sports car, with a loud engine and an even louder stereo. Jed thought that the speakers were in need of either more bass or more treble. He wasn't certain but he knew that something wasn't right.

Sammy told Ossie that Lee was busy.

Lee had asked him to run the pick-up errand for him.

Sammy said that he didn't give a shit and besides, it had been a while since he had seen Ossie. "What the hell, right Os?"

Ossie thanked him. Then, he offered him a cigar, which he, literally, grabbed out of Ossie's hand.

He offered him a light. Sammy refused. "I'll light it up later, man."

He tucked the cigar into his upper pocket. "I'll save it."

"How have you been, Sammy?" Ossie asked the question hoping to establish a little camaraderie, for Jed and for their trip back to Lee's.

"I'm rich, Os, and getting richer." He looked at Jed. He sported a conceited grin.

As the car squealed away from the pier, Sammy started bragging about his father, the infamous *Sam Giancana* and how his so called *blood money* was paying for his gas—and his hash. Jed laughed. He figured that Sammy was kidding and just acting tough.

Jed knew the type.

"Nice to have connections, eh Sammy?"

"Those I have, gringo." He spit out the window. "Those I have."

Sammy Giancana, as he was formally introduced to Jed, was, indeed, the son of Sam Giancana, the former head of the Chicago Mafia. Even though Jed thought that he was just talking big – he was – but truthfully so.

"My father killed people." He looked at Jed, in the rear view mirror. "He never had anyone do his killings, for him." He turned around. "He was no wimp. I'm like my old man," he boasted. "I do things my way. Me and Sinatra." He laughed. It was not a kind laugh.

"Sam Giancana was your father?" This time Jed's question was more serious.

"Is my father, man." He paused. "Is my father," he repeated. "He knew President Kennedy and now he knows that dude Carter. He knows everybody, man. Like me, ain't that right Os?"

"You're the man, Sam. You're the man."

Sammy liked the compliment.

"Fuckin right, man." He spit again. "Fuckin right."

He hit the dashboard with his fist. He laughed. This time, Jed thought his laugh was like that of madman's. *Maybe this guy's nuts?*

From the back seat and in the rearview mirror, Sammy's eyes looked like doll's eyes—dark and sunken deeply, into the crevices of his olive colored skin.

"You come from quite the family, Sammy!" Jed made an attempt at flattering him.

"I do," agreed Sammy. He was pleased with himself. He lit his cigar, from the car lighter.

"My father controlled betting, women and loan sharking. He did all that in **your** cities, man."

"Not in his cities," corrected Ossie. "He's from Canada."

Sammy ignored Ossie's correction. He went on to boast about how his father owned casinos, in Las Vegas and Reno.

"Where is your dad now?" Jed's question was innocent, enough.

"Here, there and everywhere; mostly in Havana." Sammy was evasive.

"Why? What's that to you?"

"Nothing really, Sammy. Just wondering, that's all."

"Wondering?" Sammy sounded angry. "What the hell is that? I call it being nosey. That's what I call it."

He laughed and then winked at Ossie. This time Jed noticed that he was missing a front tooth.

Jed made no comment.
He looked out the window.

As the sports car screeched into Lee's front yard, Sammy told Ossie to bring Jed to the *Oasis*.

"The Oasis?" asked Jed. "What's that?" He was puzzled.

This time Ossie and Sammy both laughed.

"Bring the *Canada Man* to the Oasis, Ossie. Should be a good crowd there, tonight." He laughed, again.

Jed and Ossie grabbed their bags, from the back seat and let themselves out of the car.

Then, Sammy sped away, in a cloud, of Juventud dust. His car radio was blasting.

As Ossie and Jed mounted the steps of his home, he turned to Jed. He placed a hand on his shoulder.

Jed stopped.

"Although he sounds like a bull-shitter, Jed, everything that he told you is the gospel truth."

"Oh ya?" asked Jed.

"And you believe in the gospel, Os?"

Ossie laughed.

"Only the true parts, Jed." He qualified.

This time it was Jed's turn to laugh.

"Ha ha—only the true parts.

I like that!"

They walked up the remaining steps.

- CHAPTER 8 -

AFTER MIDNIGHT

The graveyard shift was catching up with Jed.

After a brief but friendly visit with Ossie's mom, Jed asked to be excused. He said he needed to *crash out*.

"I'm exhausted. I can never get used to working nights."

Jed asked about Lee. His absence was evident.

Ossie and his mother, however, made light of it.

"He'll be happy to see you boys," she looked at Jed. "But first, you should go lie down and get some rest." She asked Ossie to show him to the guest room.

She smiled. "Lee will likely be here when you wake up. Go ahead, Jed. You have a nap. You'll feel better."

Ossie took Jed to the guest room.

"Here ya go! You can crash out on the top or bottom." He pointed to a bunk bed. "Your choice."

"Heh! A bunk bed! It's been years." Jed dropped his bag on the bottom bunk.

"Sleep well. We'll get caught up later." Ossie shut the door.

Jed kicked off his sandals and climbed up the ladder to the top bunk. He was too tired to change out of his clothes.

Although the temperature in the room was pleasant, Jed had a chill. He attributed that to his fatigue. He pulled up a blanket and adjusted the pillow.

He looked up at the ceiling. It was close enough to touch.

He checked the time. His watch read: 5:31.
He closed his eyes.
In seconds, he fell into a deep and dreamless sleep.

When he awoke, it was dark.
He pressed the night-light of his *Aqua Indi*.
It read 12:04.
Jed was disoriented.
The numbers appeared to be clear enough but his ability to grasp them was not.
He didn't know if it were 12:04 a.m. or 12:04 p.m. The watch didn't have that feature.
It was difficult to see.
He sat up. He hit his head, on the ceiling. He rubbed his forehead.
He remembered the bunk bed.
His eyes panned the darkness. *Oh ya. I'm in the guest room.*
He groped to find the ladder.
He descended.
He located his sandals. He slipped into them. He reached for the door handle.
He opened the door. *Aah! And then there was light!*
A lamp, on a tiny table, by the bathroom, lit up the hall. *That helps.* Jed could see.
He headed for the kitchen.
He was hungry.
He noticed a bowl, in the middle of the kitchen table. Inside it was a grapefruit.
In the dim light and deceptive shadow, the grapefruit assumed an unusual shape. It appeared to be bigger than it actually was and it looked like a bull, standing alone, in the middle of the ring.

Jed approached it.

He picked up the fruit.

Ordinarily, Jed would not be so forward. His growling stomach, however, made him uncharacteristically taunting, like the matador, in the bullring.

He left the kitchen and headed for Lee's study.

As he peeled, he walked.

He didn't know what to do with the peels, so he put them in his pocket.

Upon entering the study, he pulled the cord of a stand-up lamp. It was strategically placed, in the corner, behind a chair – the same chair that he sat in, 43 days ago.

The room lit up—a little.

The rest of the house, except for the hall, remained dark—but not empty.

Jed could feel the presence of sleeping humans.

Somebody was snoring.

It was kind of spooky for Jed, being in Lee's study—eating a stolen grapefruit and hearing sounds in the distant dark. Jed was not one to be snooping in people's houses and eating forbidden fruit.

He sat down, in the corner chair. It felt familiar.

Jed's looked up at the shelves, the books, the magazines and the pictures.

Along with the titles and the West Indian art, he could not help but notice the neatness of the study and how everything appeared to be arranged alphabetically – either by artist, title or year.

He saw a picture of Lee.

It looked like he was standing in front of an old barn or shed. The backdrop looked more American than Cuban. The picture might have been taken in the foothills of The Rockies or on the rolling hills of Virginia.

Jed stood up to have a closer look.

He removed it from the shelf. He needed more light. He stood by the stand-up lamp. He studied the picture. He read the inscription: *To Lee, Love, always, your friend, Caroline.*

On the same shelf and two titles to the right was a thin book, more like a novella than a novel or anthology. It was entitled: ***The Memoirs of C. Lee Bouvier***. Jed removed **it** from the shelf as well. He thumbed through the first few pages. It appeared to be an autobiography. The narrative voice was written in the first person. Jed continued to browse. He turned to the inside page of the back cover. There was a message, written in what appeared to be a woman's hand – likely, the same hand that wrote beneath the photograph of Lee, in front of the barn. *To Lee! Thought you might appreciate these. Thanks for your pains. Caroline, 1964.*

Jed returned the book to its place, on the shelf. He saw that it was flanked, on the left by a famous book: **MacBeth**, by William Shakespeare.
To the right – another famous book: **To Kill A Mocking Bird**, by Harper Lee.

It was **The Memoirs** that he was thinking about.

The other two, he had already read.

- CHAPTER 9 -

TWO SISTERS

"Buenos Dias, Senor."

Jed opened his eyes.

He had fallen asleep.

His thoughts about **The Memoirs** had pulled him back to the corner chair. He had never intended on falling asleep. In fact, what he really wanted to do was just relax in Lee's smoke-free room, with a clear head, void of any 'Lee Harvey Punch'. Until he was awakened by the unfamiliar voice and the friendly Spanish greeting, he had drifted away—literally and figuratively. He had drifted to Dallas and Washington; to Moscow and Havana; to Brooks and Juventud.

He thought about Lee and Caroline. He thought about the picture and the book. He thought about the shelves of Lee's study; he thought about the bunk bed.

But it wasn't the Spanish.

It wasn't the greeting.

It wasn't the voice.

It was the smell.

The smell was inviting.

The smell was arousing.

Although it was foreign, Jed was drawn to it.

He spoke:

"Hello. I was sleeping, sort of, I think. How are you?" He rubbed his eyes. "**Who** are you?"

In the dim light, Jed did not recognize the face. He did, however, notice that the woman in front of him was young and pretty. She looked Spanish or Russian. Jed wasn't sure.

She was wearing a see through blouse. It was unbuttoned, to her navel. Jed's eyes were drawn to the contours of her breasts.

"I am Rachel—Ossie's sister—Ossie's younger sister."

"I didn't know that Ossie had a sister," Jed rubbed his eyes, again.

He sat up. He had been slouched.

"Oh si, Senor! My brother Ossie has two sisters!"

"Two?" asked Jed. He was surprised.

"I didn't even know that he had one."

"Oh si," she affirmed, "I am his sister and I have a sister."

Jed watched her as she moved around the dimly lit room. Somebody must have pulled the switch turning off the stand-up lamp. The only light that was penetrating the room was coming from the outside. Jed pointed to the window. "The sun's coming up."

He looked back at Rachel. She was slim. Her clothes hung on her like loose silk.

She moved gracefully. She moved like a ghost. She sat down on the floor beside Jed.

The perfume lingered.

It filled the room.

It didn't smell too strong. On the contrary, Jed thought that it smelled kind of nice. He liked its fragrance. *I bet it's expensive.*

"Do you live here?" Jed broke the sensuous silence.

"I do, although, I was not here during your last visit. My sister, June, and I were in America, visiting the land of Disney."

"In Florida?" Jed asked the question, expecting the obvious.

"Si Senor, in Florida."

"Did you like it?"

"Disney, I enjoyed. The line-ups, I did not. I don't mind crowded places, Senor, but I am not one for waiting." She paused. "In line."

She moved in closer to Jed.

"Do you, Senor?"

"Do I?" Jed swallowed.

"Do you?" Rachel leaned against his knee.

"Do you like crowded places?"

Jed shrugged.

"I want to sit here." She patted the floor.

"Is that all right with you, Senor?" She looked up at Jed.

"I can see you better, from here—and besides, we should not speak too loudly." She pressed a finger against her lips. "My brother is sleeping, unlike you and I, Senor Jed."

"You know my name?"

"Sammy told me all about you. The **oil man** from Canada." She made a quotation sign with her index fingers.

Nice hands. Jed studied her hands as they remained suspended, in front of him, for, what he thought, was an inordinate length of time.

Rachel could see that Jed was looking at them.

He refocused. "Sammy?" His question, once again, begged for the obvious.

"Yes, my amigo—Sammy. He told me your name. I like your name...Jed...what does that name mean...Jed?"

"It doesn't mean anything." Jed shrugged, again. "It's just my name."

"Si Senor, Jed. It is just your name. Did my brother tell you about my father's name?"

Jed looked at Rachel. She smiled.

"His is just his name too, like yours, Senor Jed ... just his name."

Jed was confused. But, at the same time, he was intrigued.

Lee was, in fact, the man who Ossie said he was—paid off, by the U.S. government to keep his mouth shut and his feet off U.S. soil, forever.

Jed needed confirmation. "What do you mean, Rachel?"

He stood up, vacating the chair that he, at this point, was almost sharing with her.

He walked over and stood by the window. He looked outside. He recalled something that Ossie had said to him, one drunken morning, in the bowels, of the 'Cops' tug. He remembered that the words were smothered in alcohol but, nevertheless, he remembered.

Ossie had spoken about names.

The name Lee, to be exact!
What was it that Ossie had said?
Lee? Jed scratched his head.

He turned around.

He looked at Rachel. She had her father's eyes.

Lee? Jed struggled.

Rachel smiled. It was like she was reading Jed's mind.

Ossie had said something about his father preferring to be called by his first name only. He had also said that his father wanted only the one name – Lee—his first name to be his only name. Mr. Lee was only Mr. Lee or Lee. That was it. No other name. No surname.

It was important that Jed knew that for his own good

and for everybody's own good – and for everybody's safety.

"Rachel? What does that name mean?" Jed was direct.

"My name is biblical." She stood up. She walked towards Jed.

"I am told that Rachel was the second wife of Jacob." She snickered. "Just as I am the second sister of Ossie."

She stood in front of Jed. She looked over his shoulder. "The sun is coming alive. The early morning sky is brightening."

Jed turned to look out the window. He could hear birds chirping.

Rachel moved in front of him, blocking his view. She leaned back against the sill.

"Are you staying up, Senor, or are you going back to bed?" She licked her lips.

"Would you like me to take you for some breakfast?"

She pressed her palm against his stomach. "Hungry?" She paused. Jed did not move. "Breakfast or bed, Senor?" She removed her hand from his stomach and placed it against her own. Then, she slowly, buttoned her blouse.

Jed studied her fingers. With perfection, they closed each button.

"Breakfast or bed?" She put her hands on her hips.

Jed smiled. He knew that she meant business. "Breakfast!" He stated with authority.

"Bueno!" She nodded.

"I will take you to The Oasis." She extended a hand. "They make good Jamaican meat patties, there." Jed took her hand.

"Breakfast any time of day, Senor. Day or night." She spoke as if she had shares in the place. Jed thought. *Maybe she did.*

They left the study. They walked down the hall and headed for the front door.

"At this time of morning, it will not be too crowded. I like to go to The Oasis, at this time. Sammy is usually there." Jed looked at Rachel, at the mention of Sammy's name. "He is?"

Rachel clarified. "He is **always** there." She shrugged. "I think Sammy likes crowded places." She giggled. "He prefers Saturday nights, though, when the real fun is taking place." Before they reached the door, Rachel stopped. She looked at Jed. "Do you like fun, Senor Jed?"

Jed thought.

"Sometimes, I do. I guess."

"Then you should get your fill, as I drive you to The Oasis, in my father's truck. I can drive a standard shift, you know, but I am not good at it." She let go of Jed's hand. "I will be right back. I must powder my nose." She smiled. "And then, I will get my purse." As she walked towards the bathroom, she asked Jed if he needed to powder his nose.

Jed laughed.

Rachel disappeared.

Jed stepped out, onto the front porch. He looked over at the swinging chair. He thought about Lana. He recalled the last time when she was sitting in that chair. He remembered that she seemed a little restless. *A little antsy.*

He sat down.

Rachel swung open the front door.

"Can you drive a standard truck, Jed? I mean, Senor Jed." This time she emphasized the word Senor.

"Yes, I can, Rachel," Jed frowned. "Would you prefer if I drove?"

"I think I would like that, Senor."

"Do you think it will be okay with Lee—I mean Mr. Lee, your dad?"

"Oh yes, my amigo. Lee likes you."

Jed smiled. "Do you always call your dad by his first name?"

"How do you know that is his first name?" Rachel asked, as she threw Jed the keys.

Jed smiled, again.

Rachel winked at him, and then, as she took his hand in hers, she said: "Let's go."

- CHAPTER 10 -

SUNRISE AT THE OASIS

The Oasis was a dimly lit, smoke-filled room that, according to Rachel, was, at one time, a warehouse used for building and repairing army trucks. It had been, long since, renovated to resemble a Las Vegas styled casino. Now, it was not much more than an underground watering and gambling hole that was, roughly, the size of a school gymnasium.

Jed commented on how busy it was.

Rachel didn't think that it was all **that** busy.

People were seated at Blackjack tables, slot machines and Roulette wheels. Some were hanging out, at the bar and others were just hanging out.

The octagonal shaped bar was located in the middle of the room. It covered a large area that housed eight bar keepers—one at each tap.

"I'm surprised at how busy this place is. It's five-thirty in the morning and it looks like it could be ten at night."

Rachel held on to Jed's hand.

"People should be in bed, at this time, right, Senor?"

Rachel poked Jed, affectionately, in the side of his ribs. She pressed her nose up against his and stared into his eyes.

"Right? Senor?"

Jed smiled.

He didn't know what to say or do. He didn't pull or turn away.

He, simply, returned her stare.

Rachel, finally, turned her head. She looked around the room. She took a breath. "Do you like to gamble, Senor?"

Jed was indifferent. "Sometimes."

"Come here." Rachel directed him to the slot machines. "Along this wall," she pointed, "There are two hundred machines." She was proud. "Pretty good, eh, Senor?"

Jed scanned the long row of brightly colored machines. "Wow! Which one's a winner?"

Rachel laughed. "They are all winners, Senor."

"I'll need some change." Jed reached into his pocket and pulled out an American twenty-dollar bill.

"Si Senor. You can get change from that man who is standing right over there."

Rachel pointed to a short, stocky, looking gentleman who was wearing a black beret and a blue army shirt. Across his chest, he wore his belt and change purse, like he was sporting a gun or sword belt. He was standing, about four or five meters to the right of Rachel and Jed. He looked more like a guard than a change man.

Just as Jed was about to leave for some change, he noticed that something had caught Rachel's eye. "What?" He looked around to see who or what she was looking at. He saw only the same group of drinkers and gamblers. Nothing or nobody appeared to be unusual.

"On second thought, Senor, I don't want to gamble." Rachel tugged at Jed's arm. She pulled him back, and then dragged him over to the bar.

"Buy me a drink, Mister Oil Man, from Canada."

Jed frowned. "Why the sudden change of mind?"

Rachel ignored his question.

Jed shrugged. He decided to let it go. He changed the subject.

As they approached the bar, he turned to Rachel. "You didn't call me Senor."

She looked up at him.

Like a vixen, she made a face. She stuck out her tongue.

"You are a good listener, Senor, Jed." She nodded. "A very good listener."

She pressed her body against his. "I thought you would like to be called Mister Oil Man." She ran her fingers through his hair and then rested her hand upon his shoulder.

"Ya right." Jed smirked. "Guilty."

She took his hand in hers. "I am guilty, Senor."

She bailed herself out. "We are all guilty of something, Senor." She winked. "Now, buy me something to drink, Senor."

Jed shook his head. "Fine. You win. What kind of drink would you like?"

He looked up at the rum bottles, perfectly aligned and suspended from a rack, high above his head.

Rachel touched his chin. She pulled his face towards hers. She pressed her nose up against his and asked, "What kind of drink do you think I would like, Senor?"

Jed paused.

He smiled.

He tilted his head to one side as if he were studying her.

"You look like a rum drinker." He made his declaration with confidence.

Rachel giggled. "Good answer! Not only are you a good listener, Senor, you also possess a good eye for a woman's taste."

She nodded. 'You are right, Senor, I do like rum. And this morning, I would like you to buy me a special kind of rum."

"A special kind of rum?" Jed was curious. "I thought that there was only one of a kind?" He pointed upwards. "Cuban!"

Rachel made another face. She looked up at the bottles and then panned the array of blenders and mixes.

"I want my rum, this morning," she raised a finger as she stated 'this morning' "to have a splash of coffee in it." She nodded. She smiled at Jed. "Si, Senor. A splash of coffee, in it."

Jed raised his brow. "You mean like a Spanish Coffee or an Irish Coffee?"

Rachel looked at Jed. This time he thought that she looked more Russian than Spanish. "An Irish Coffee, of course, Senor." She growled. "A 'Fighting Irish' Coffee. You should know that, Senor."

She leaned against him and whispered in his ear. "I like the 'Fighting Irish', you know, Senor."

She smiled.

Jed tried to figure her out. He wondered what she might be getting at.

He turned towards the bar. He caught the bartender's attention.

He ordered Rachel's 'special coffee'.

"Aren't you having one, Senor?"

Jed shook his head. "I'll wait. It's still a little early for me. I may have a sip of yours, though."

"A sip?" Rachel mocked. "I don't think so."

Jed smirked. "We'll see."

Rachel agreed. "We will."

The drink arrived.

Jed paid for it with his American twenty. The gruff looking bartender examined the bill as if it were counterfeit. He slammed it into the till and counted out some change. He handed Jed a wad of dirty bills.

Jed counted out 14 American dollars. He kept 13 and left one on the counter. He thanked the bartender. He acknowledged Jed's tip with a quick nod. "Adios!"

As Rachel dragged Jed around The Oasis, she did most

of the talking. She was enjoying the Irish Coffee and the extra cherries, as she had requested, from the suspicious bartender.

They made their way from table to table. Jed was entertained by Rachel's control and confidence. She liked to move, to visit and then, to move on.

Jed didn't love being pulled so much, and at such a pace, but, he didn't pull his hand away, from hers, either.

Rachel knew everybody – or so it seemed. She was friendly but not phony. She was outgoing but a little guarded. She played innocent but wasn't naive.

Jed liked her. She was unique. In her own mysterious and mischievous way, she appealed to him.

Like the scent of her perfume, she left her mark, at each table and with each one of the drunks and their envious girlfriends.

Jed enjoyed the drama.

He felt like he was a character, in a play that starred a leading lady in whose hand, his was firmly gripped and relentlessly dragged.

They, finally, stopped at an empty table. It was close to another section of the bar.

Rachel turned and kissed Jed's cheek.

"I want another one of these, Senor." She held up her empty glass.

"This time, I want you to order it with more rum and less coffee."

She kissed him, again. "I will sit here and wait for you, Senor."

After the first kiss, Jed figured, *she was just making a pass but after the second,* he attributed her affection to culture, personality and upbringing. *After all, her mom was an affectionate person.*

He asked. "More rum and less coffee?"

Rachel smiled. "And lots of cherries; as many as you can get."

Jed headed for the bar.

He thought.

Those kisses are innocent enough. What the hell am I worried about?

Rachel was unique. Jed knew that.

There was something about her, that Jed had rarely, if ever, seen, in anyone, before.

He thought about Lana. He liked the way she kissed but *it isn't fair to compare the two.*

He liked the way she laughed but *Rachel's laugh is contagious.*

He liked Lana's scent but *they wear different perfume. They must?*

He liked the way Lana felt but...

Jed arrived at the bar.

He asked for an Irish Coffee.

This bartender, who introduced himself as Norman (it sounded like Nor-Mon) was more amicable than the other, suspicious bartender, who was still at the other side, of the octagon. As Norman prepared Rachel's drink, Jed requested that he go heavy on the rum and light on the coffee. He also asked about the cherries.

Norman assured Jed that it would include a double shot of Cuba's finest. He asked Jed where he was from and if he could speak Spanish. Jed told him that he was from Canada but that he could speak only *"un poco pedacito"*. Norman smiled and told Jed that he had a pretty good accent.

"Bienvenida a el Oasis."

Jed understood. *"Gracias, Senor Norm."* He paid for Rachel's drink. *"Adios!"*

Rachel thanked Jed. "Ooh, that one looks yummy." She took a sip.

She extended a hand, gesturing for Jed to help her up. He did.

They resumed their promenade around The Oasis.

Jed, finally, took control. He told Rachel that he needed to stop, for something to eat.

Rachel was reluctant. "If you must." She paused. "Why don't you have one of these?"

She held out her drink.

Jed gave her a look.

He rubbed his stomach. "Good patties, you claim?"

She brought him to the 'Patty Stand'. "Fine, fine." Rachel would be stalled—temporarily, that is.

After purchasing two meat patties and having the time to eat only one, the high-paced escort continued.

Rachel was almost bouncing, now, as she bopped, throughout the club.

The crowd was beginning to thin.

As the Caribbean sun heated up the outside, inside The Oasis, things were starting to cool off.

Jed noticed that most of the remaining faithful were male. Except for a small number, most were seated at the Blackjack tables. All were focused on their cards or those that were being shuffled by their cigar-smoking dealers. Both players and dealers possessed deceptive and squinting eyes.

It was late – or early, for some.

The handful of women that remained looked tired and bored.

Jed was, kind of, feeling the same way, himself.

Some of the women were draped over the shoulders of their chauvinistic mates.

Others just smoked and stood around – looking for action – looking for something.

Jed was not certain if the women were even interested in their men. *What are they doing here, anyway?*

Maybe that's just the way things are at 6:00 a.m. in The Oasis, on Juventud.

When Jed saw Lee, he didn't recognize him.

Jed was surprised. Lee was supposed to be at home, asleep, in his bed.

He was wearing a New York Yankees baseball cap and a sleeveless white t-shirt. Both garments made him look younger than what he was.

He wore the baseball cap backwards—*Like the Catcher in the Rye.* Jed studied him.

His t-shirt fit his tight and streamlined body like a glove on the fist of a lightweight boxer or a martial artist. He was wearing a black leather vest.

He greeted Jed and Rachel in a friendly and fatherly manner. Nothing seemed to be a big deal. He hugged Rachel and shook Jed's hand. After he shook Jed's hand, Rachel kissed him.

Under normal circumstances, that would not have caught Jed's eye. However, as Rachel kissed Lee's lips, it was confirmed, for Jed, that he was amongst a group of people that loved and shared their love differently, than what he was accustomed to.

Jed was okay with that.

He was learning something about the Latino culture.

It was refreshing!

It was a pleasure to see and be a part of a treasure that he would celebrate, for a long, long time.

Lee smiled and told Jed that he was glad to see him. Jed thanked him. They exchanged honest pleasantries.

Once again, Jed noticed the whiteness of Lee's teeth.

They appeared to be exceptionally white! Unnaturally white!

"Rachel's lipstick brings the shine out in those pearly whites, of yours, Lee."

Jed was trying to make light conversation.

Lee didn't respond nor did he react.

Instead, he just looked at Jed as if he were waiting for him to say something else.

Then, he disappeared. Jed figured that he went for a drink – or to gamble.

The dim lights of The Oasis were being snuffed out by the sunlight, penetrating from the outside. For Jed, the past hour had been spent mostly in the clutches of Rachel's controlling hand. She had led him from table to table and from one group to another. It was evident that she knew a lot of people. It was evident that she was at home in the untamed Oasis.

Jed had gone along.

But, for a moment, he did not feel as comfortable as he did when he was practicing his Spanish, with Norman, the friendly bartender.

There was something that didn't feel right. Jed looked around.

Maybe it is someone and not something.

Another hour, he told himself, *and that will be enough.*

That hour, however, would prove to be a short and ugly one.

When Jed first encountered the slick talking Sammy, he could see that he was drunk. At first, Rachel thought he was amusing.

But, Sammy got loud. He became obnoxious. He grew angry.

Rachel tugged at Jed's arm and then, whispered in his ear.

"Watch this. This is going to be fun." She approached Sammy. "Heh, Sammy. What's up?"

Rachel asked her question and then, turned to Jed. She kissed Jed's earlobe.

Her lips felt dry.

It was more of a nibble than a kiss.

"What is your Canadian ass doing with my lady, man?"

Sammy pointed his finger.

Before Jed could reply, Rachel interrupted.

"I'm not your lady, Sammy. I'm nobody's lady."

She made a face. She curled her upper lip.

Then, she stuck her tongue out at Sammy and turned to face Jed.

She winked.

"Take it easy Rachel," cautioned Jed. "This isn't a game."

"What do you mean no game, Gringo?" Sammy stepped forward.

"This is The Oasis! Everything here is a game."

He took a swig of what Jed figured was a rum and coke.

"You don't play games where you come from?" He scowled.

"What about that crazy thing you guys do on ice? What is that called again?" He looked at Rachel. "Hackey?"

He laughed and then shoved Jed, aggressively. His toothless grin was repulsive and his push was even more so.

Jed turned to Rachel.

"Let's go. Let's get out of here." This time, it was his turn to pull her.

As Jed attempted to move, Sammy blocked his way and grabbed his shirt.

"After I drive you and Ossie from the docks, this is the way you thank me?"

Jed could feel the spray from his spit.

It felt slimy.

"You come into my club and pinch my lady's ass, all over the place.

And now, you want to leave? I don't think so."

He spit on Jed, again. This time, it wasn't just his spray.

Jed could smell the liquor, on his breath and on his body.

He, slowly and carefully raised a hand to wipe his face.

Then, as he brought it down, he pressed it firmly, against Sammy's chest.

"Back off Sammy, you're spitting on me and you're crowding me."

Sammy moved in closer. His face was almost touching Jed's.

"Take it easy, Sammy," Rachel tried to help.

"You're drunk and you're acting like a fuckin' jerk."

Jed looked at Rachel. He was surprised at how she spoke.

"Leave us alone and we'll leave you alone." Rachel didn't want to back down.

Jed didn't take his eyes off her. He was in disbelief. Sammy didn't take his eyes off Jed. He was in disbelief.

He did, however, remove his hand, from Jed's shirt, long enough to slap Rachel, on the side of her face.

"I'll deal with you later, bitch. But now, I'm going to kick this Canadian's ass."

Rachel raised a hand to return Sammy's slap.

Jed shouted "No!"

Sammy leaped at Jed, attempting to push him, to the ground.

Jed swerved, avoiding Sammy's leap and then blocked a kick from his exploding leg. He was not, however, as lucky in maintaining balance, when Sammy unsheathed a hunting knife.

The sight of its shining metal caught Jed by surprise. The dim lights, of The Oasis, reflected its edge.

Jed squinted. He was shocked.

"What are you doing, Sammy?" Jed stepped back to avoid Sammy's pumping arm.

He tripped over a misplaced chair.

At the moment of Jed's fall, Sammy was restrained.

"No, Sammy. Not here and not now." Jed looked up. He saw Lee and a tall black man, with arms that were as long as drill pipes. They were suppressing Sammy.

Jed stood up.

He asked Rachel how she was.

She responded that she was okay.

Jed could see that her eyes were watering and that there was a red mark, on the side of her face.

"Are you sure you're okay?" Jed put his arm around her.

"I'm fine. It's not like it's the first time."

"What? You mean that creep has hit you before?"

"I don't want to talk about it." She turned away. Jed thought that she was embarrassed. He let it go.

He caught the eye of the tall black man and nodded in appreciation, thanking him, for his help.

"No problem, man." He called out to Jed.

"I be here, at The Oasis, to keep everybody cool."

He looked at Lee who was standing, by the black man.

Jed saw that he was holding Sammy's knife.

The 'change man' arrived on the scene. He stood by Lee.

Lee concealed the knife, under his beer stained vest.

He escorted Rachel and Jed to the nearest exit and apologized for Sammy's behavior. Jed shook his head and told him that there was no need to apologize.

"These things happen," he said. "What doesn't kill us makes us stronger."

He smiled. "Right, Lee?"

Their eyes met.

At that moment, Lee knew that Jed knew more than just the name of his favorite drink: *The Lee Harvey special.*

He knew that when Jed mentioned something about: *what doesn't kill us*, he knew that Jed knew that he didn't die, in Dallas, Texas, at the hand, of a thug named Ruby – Jack Ruby – to be exact.

Lee gestured a thumb-up.

He opened the side door, for both Jed and his daughter.

He opened his arms.

Rachel snuggled. "Thanks, dad." She looked at Jed. "Lee's my dad."

Jed nodded. "I know." He paused. "That's good." He looked back.

He saw Sammy.

He was leaning against the bar.

He looked like he was boasting, to some of his friends.

Jed caught his eye.

He was certain that Sammy caught his.

In the next second, he blew Jed a kiss.

Jed turned and shook his head. He took Rachel's hand.

"Can you believe that guy, Rachel? He just blew me a kiss."

"Who? Lee?" She asked in disbelief.

"No, no, no. Not Lee! Sammy!"

As they headed for Lee's truck, Rachel stopped and asked Jed to do the same.

"What?" Jed looked at her.

She pulled his body closer to hers.

She looked into his eyes.

"He blew you a kiss, Senor?"

Jed smiled. "Ya. Whatever."

He confirmed "Ya. He blew me a kiss."

Rachel held Jed's jaw. Her hand felt nice. "And do you know why, Senor?" She caressed his chin. She pressed her lips against his ear.

She whispered. "Because you are kissable, Senor."

She pushed her tongue inside the folds of Jed's ear.

She moved it up and down and then, slowly, in a circular motion.

- CHAPTER 11 -

THE TREASURE ISLAND

Jed and Rachel left The Oasis, in Lee's truck and drove in an easterly direction, towards the shore. This time Rachel was behind the wheel looking very calm, with one arm hanging out the window.

"Where are we going?" inquired Jed.

His tone was steadfast.

"To the beach," responded Rachel.

Her tone was blunt.

As they rolled through the flats of Juventud, Jed, once again, admired the beauty of the island's landscape and its clear blue sky.

Rachel was quiet.

This was out of character for her.

Jed figured that she was likely in need of some 'down time' to clear her mind of the troubling encounter, with Sammy.

He broke the silence.

"You lied to me, Rachel." The accusation sounded more serious than Jed had intended.

"Oh," she replied, looking straight ahead. "And, in what way, Senor, did I speak falsely?"

"You told me that you couldn't drive a standard truck." Jed, affectionately, pinched her arm.

"By the way you're handling this vehicle, it appears that you've had plenty of experience."

"Oh no, Senor. I did not say that I was incapable of driving a standard truck." She paused. "But, I do recall saying that I was not **good** at it." She looked at Jed. "Especially not at five o'clock, in the morning." She turned to concentrate on the road, ahead.

"It is daylight now, Senor. I am much better in the daylight."

Jed smiled and nodded. "Oh, I see."

"Much better at driving, that is." Rachel smiled and shook her head.

She took her eyes off the road, again, for just a second, to look at Jed.

"Actually, Senor, I am much better in the daylight, in other ways, too. You'll see."

Jed was still smiling. "I have yet to be with you in the daylight, Senorita." His attempt at Spanish was poor. It made Rachel laugh.

"You would definitely not have been comfortable with me driving, at dawn."

Jed raised a brow.

"You didn't exactly lie then, you simply withheld the whole truth. Was that it?"

"Precisely, Senor. Just like gangsters and politicians. They withhold the whole truth. You know about that, right, Senor, Jed?"

Jed knew that she was teasing but, at the same time, he felt that she was trying to tell him something; like dropping him a hint or a clue about something she wanted to say but couldn't – not yet, anyway.

He sat back.

He thought that it might have something to do with Lee or Sammy—or both of them.

Jed studied the road ahead and the palm trees to its side.

He closed his eyes.

"Senor?"

Jed heard a voice.

"Senor?" Rachel touched his arm.

Jed opened his eyes.

The truck was parked. Jed looked at Rachel. She was sitting right beside him – almost on top, of him. "You fell asleep."

Jed yawned. He sat up. He rubbed his eyes. He looked ahead.

Rachel nudged his arm. "What do you think, Senor?"

Jed couldn't believe his eyes. "Wow! What a view!" He looked to his side. He looked behind. "Where are we?"

"You know Senor, that most of the people who live on Juventud, live in the northern part of the island." Jed looked out the window. "Really? But this place looks deserted."

Rachel chuckled. "That is because we are on the eastern shore, Senor."

Jed looked ahead, at the beautiful, lime-green, Caribbean. "It's beautiful."

"And warm, Senor." She leaned against him. "Did you know," she continued, "that this island, or I should say my father's island, used to be a hideout for pirates?"

Jed shook his head. "No I didn't."

He scratched his whiskers. "When was that?"

"During the time of Francis Drake and John Hawkins."

Rachel's response was scholarly.

"Wow!" Jed was impressed. "You sure know a lot about this island."

"Of course, I do, Senor. I read books. I look at my father's books. Just like you, Senor."

Rachel looked at Jed with a reassuring smile.

"I must also tell you, Senor, that Lee has a book, on his shelf that was written by a man named Robert Louis Stevenson. Have you heard of him?

His book is called, 'Treasure Island'."

Jed nodded. "I think so."

Rachel continued. "He wrote it after he spent some time on this island that we, so proudly, call our home!" Rachel reached for Jed's door handle. "Come, let's explore." She pulled on the handle and opened the door.

"Juventud?" Jed stepped out. "Great name for an island!" He reached for Rachel, to assist her, as she stepped down, from the truck. "What does it mean?" Jed was interested.

"What do you think it means, Senor?" Rachel handed Jed the keys.

"Should we lock up?"

Rachel shook her head. "It is not necessary, Senor."

Jed shrugged his shoulders and twisted his lip.

"Okay! Give me a hint, teacher, and we'll see how I do."

"A hint?" Rachel smiled. "You ask for a hint?"

They walked in the direction, of the water. Jed tucked a strand of hair in, behind Rachel's ear.

Rachel held on tightly to Jed's hand. "A hint, Senor?" She repeated. "You need a hint to know what Juventud means?" She looked up at the sky. "How **juvenile** of you, Senor; my smart man, from Canada."

Jed gave Rachel a look, reacting to her comment, about his Canadian intellect.

"You flatter me, Rachel. You hardly know me and you assume that because I am from Canada, I am smart and that I am your man?"

Rachel nodded, assertively. "Yes!" Then she leaned forward as if she saw something on the ground. The gray, cracked pavement, beneath them, was giving way to a steeper, rockier path. "We must be careful, Senor, from here and for the rest of our trek; the route can be difficult."

In harmony, like the footpath, the waters of the sea were becoming more treacherous.

"You can really hear the water, now, eh Rachel?" Jed looked out at the encroaching sea. "Where does this path lead?" Jed cupped his free hand to cover his eyes. "The sun is so bright."

Rachel agreed. "Oh yes, Senor – and, like the water, very powerful."

As they made their way down the narrow, primitive path, Rachel informed Jed that he was en route to a 'special' place. "I am taking you to Punta del Este. There, you will see some Indian cave paintings."

"Punta del Este? Sounds interesting!"

"You will like it, there, Senor. You will also discover why Senor Stevenson was so inspired to write a book about this island—the island that is and was so inviting to delinquents. That is, **juvenile** delinquents, Senor. Hint. Hint."

Jed smiled. "Good hints, Rachel. I get it now. Juvenile! Juventud!"

"Well done, Senor." Rachel asked Jed to lead the way. She preferred to hold on, from behind.

Jed agreed. "Okay, but I don't know where I'm going."

Rachel poked him. "Down, Senor. You are going, **down**."

The path looked like it had been traveled many times. Rachel explained to Jed that the area had, at one time, years ago, been popular, with both the tourists and the locals. But, now, it was only visited, by a select few – "A very 'special' select few."

The stones were worn to a smooth surface. The ground was hardened clay.

Jed and Rachel paused, on occasion, to take in the beauty of the sky, the richness of the land and the power of the spray. The water was exploding, on the rocks, below.

"You like the water, Senor?"

"It's awesome, Rachel!"

"You know, Senor, that Juventud is not only inviting to delinquent juveniles, it is also a hideout for pirates, gangsters, and **assassins**."

"Assassins?" asked Jed, taking his eyes off the path and the water, to look back at her.

Rachel nodded. Jed stopped.

"Si, Senor," she smiled. "You have heard people say that life is," she tilted her head to one side, "Like this island, Senor—full of surprises. Do you like surprises, Senor?"

Jed shrugged. "Sometimes." He looked down, at the water.

"That's good, Senor. Because at Punta del Este, there is a surprise waiting for you." Rachel motioned, for him, to resume the trek.

"Not only are there picturesque caves, the sandy beaches are also beautiful. And the water, Senor, is so warm and invitingly blue." She paused. "Like your eyes, Senor—warm and invitingly blue."

"And don't forget, deep, too, Rachel."

"What, Senor? Your eyes?"

"The water," stated Jed. He looked out at the sea.

"This place reminds me of a lookout I used to visit, on the east coast, of Canada, on Cape Breton Island."

The name Cape Breton didn't mean anything to Rachel, but she said that it must have been quite a spot.

They arrived at the caves.

The entrance was unique!

There were no signs or significant landmarks. With the Caribbean sun positioned highly and easterly, in the early morning sky, the rock formations above and to the sides, looked like big cats, ready to pounce, on the unsuspecting visitor. Jed managed to catch sight of some words that were chiseled, into the jagged entrance. They read:

"Bienvenido Amigos ... Caverns Punta del Este."

"Holy crow, Rachel! This place looks gothic! "

"And spooky too, amigo. After you." Rachel gestured with her hand.

She nudged Jed, playfully, as they walked through the entrance.

It was dark.

It was damp.

"Keep your head down low, Senor," she cautioned. "Take short steps and do not let go of my hand."

"Are you sure that you don't want to lead, Rachel?" Jed was wary.

"No, not now, Senor. We are not at The Oasis anymore."

Jed looked back. He could barely see.

She teased. "You can be the boss, in here."

Jed just shook his head. "You're one of a kind, Rachel. One of a kind."

They slowly made their way through the entrance. Jed could feel Rachel's grip tighten as they moved deeper in.

She had one hand in his and the other was clamped, like a vice, to the back of his belt.

"Watch out for the wild parrots, Senor. They live in these caves and sometimes have been known to swoop down on the green visitor."

Jed stopped. He looked at Rachel. His eyes were adjusting. He could see that she was smiling. " Now, I know you're pulling my leg."

"No, Senor, I am pulling your belt." She tugged.

Jed ducked and raised a hand to cover his head just in case Rachel's warning was not, totally, in jest.

"And you know what else we have in our caves, Senor?" She paused. "Turtles and iguanas."

Jed continued walking. He saw some light at the far end. He hoped that was an indication that their cave visit was nearing an end.

"And what do **they** do to the green visitor?" Jed figured that he might as well play along.

"You need to ask, Senor?"

He laughed. "I should say so!"

The damp, thick air, tickled Jed's nostrils.

"I can smell the sea, Rachel."

"Of course you can, Senor. Most of these caves are located beneath the heavy waters, of our Caribbean."

Jed could see more clearly, now. He noticed that some of the walls were covered with claw-like crevices, imparting pathways, for the trickling water.

"It sounds like the walls are talking to us, Rachel. Like they're trying to tell us something."

"They are, Senor. They are beckoning you to turn this way."

She quickly pushed Jed to one side, turning him in the direction of another entrance.

It was a low, narrow entrance. It compelled him to crouch. Jed covered his head. They entered a room. It was a large room.

In contrast to the previous space, it was well lit.

The natural light filtered through the cracks. The sunbeams poked, like lasers, through the ceiling.

Surrounding them, were a thousand tiny images. They looked like Indian hieroglyphics.

"Wow," Jed pointed. "Look at these colors, Rachel. They're all so vibrant!" Jed scrutinized the walls. His eyes discerned a spectacular array of blues and reds—splashed against a background of iridescent yellows and whites. The more Jed looked, the more the paintings came alive. They consumed him. They transported him from a world of darkness, dampness and concern to a world of mystery, color and enlightenment.

"Come with me, Senor. I have a very special painting that I want you to see."

Rachel escorted Jed to a little room, around the corner.

"This room is my favorite!" She squeezed his arm.

"It is my little bower."

Jed thought that it might have been an add-on. He told Rachel that it reminded him of a boudoir or a private chamber, in a medieval castle.

Rachel commented on Jed's comparison. "Precisely, Senor. You are correct!" She pointed to a display of rainbow colored streaks. It was on a wall that appeared to be more modern than those located in the darker corners, of the cave. Jed noticed how the artist's brush had captured the spirit of Juventud's land and water. In the middle of the kaleidoscope there was a small painting that beckoned Jed to move closer. At first, he was unable to decipher exactly what the artist was conveying. He noticed that the strokes had formed a vortex, revealing an image of a man hiding behind a rock. The rock looked like it was protecting the man from a huge tidal wave. Upon closer scrutiny, Jed noticed that the wave was shaped and painted with the colors and markings of the American flag. The man positioned behind the rock was wearing a red short-sleeved T-shirt and red overalls. On his arm, was a little tattoo. Although the tattoo was very small, Jed was able to ascertain that it was the image of a hammer and a sickle; the same that was on the Soviet flag.

"This is very interesting, Rachel."

"It is!" She moved in closer, too.

They stared at it, in silence.

Rachel held on to Jed's hand.

"And do you know what it is called, Senor?"

Jed shook his head.

Rachel pointed to words that were scribbled, at the bottom.

The letters were difficult to construe. They were immersed into the blues and grays of the wave's curl.

Jed read and sounded the letters out loud: "C A B E Z A DE T U R C O."

Rachel laughed.

"That's funny, Senor. It is pronounced Cabeza de Turco."

Jed laughed at himself. "Your Spanish is definitely better than mine. You'll have to give me lessons. I'm beginning to like the language, Rachel." Jed was curious.

"What does it mean?" He pointed to the painting.

"It means *The Patsy*. You know, the fall guy, *El Scapegoat.*"

Jed looked closer. He studied the artwork.

"Can you tell me some more about it?" He looked at Rachel.

"Of what significance are the words and how do they relate to the picture?"

"So formal, Senor? Really!" Rachel shook her head. "Save that question for the artist, Senor."

Rachel pointed to the man hiding behind the rock.

Jed squinted. As his eyes panned slowly across and down, he noticed three letters and a number. They were located at the bottom, right-hand corner.

They were the letters L.H.O.—beside them was the number '67'.

"This painting is almost fifteen years old!"

Rachel nodded. "Si, Senor. I was present when it was being painted." She spoke with pride.

She let go of Jed's hand and took a step back. "I observed every stroke of the artist's brush." She put her hands on her hips.

"You would have been very young at the time." Jed tilted his head.

"That is correct, Senor! I was only seven years old but I remember it like it was yesterday."

"How long did it take the artist to complete it?"

"Approximately, two months."

"Two months? That's a long time for a seven year old girl to be alone in a cave watching an artist at work."

"Oh, I was not alone, Senor. I was with Lee."

"Lee watched the artist, too?"

"No, no, Senor. Lee was the artist."

Jed looked at the painting, again. He viewed it, this time, with a more understanding eye. He reread the words Cabeza de Turco.

"Lee painted this?"

He ran his fingers slowly and carefully across the painting. He stopped at the spot where the man was hiding behind the rock.

When he turned to Rachel, for her response, she was gone.

- CHAPTER 12 -

THE DOLPHIN AND THE SHARK

Following his unsuccessful attempt to find Rachel in the cave, Jed left to resume his search outside.

The brightness of the sun, once again, forced him to squint.

He didn't have his sunglasses. They were in his backpack, sitting on the bunk, in the guest room, at Lee's. *Typical.*

The sky was clear—crystal clear.

Although its light was overbearing, the sun's warmth was soothing compensation—especially after the dampness of the caves. It, immediately, lifted the chill from Jed's back and shoulders.

The sand was white – *exceptionally white,* Jed thought. The sun's intensity must serve to whiten this beach's grains—at least that was his deduction.

He heard Rachel before he saw her.

"Come in, Senor. The water feels wonderful."

Jed was barely able to identify the person, who was calling out to him, from the sea.

Her hair was wet and slicked back.

She must have been on her knees.

She wasn't out that deep.

The water, however, was up to her neck.

Jed wasn't certain whether or not she was wearing a bathing suit.

"Is that you, Rachel?" he called out.

"Come in, Senor." She repeated.

She gestured with her arm for him to join her.

Jed kicked off his sandals. Beneath his feet, the sand felt warm.

He walked to the water's edge. It looked inviting.

He cupped his hands around his mouth. "Why did you leave the caves?"

"It was time, Senor." She shrugged a tanned shoulder.

Then, she dove under the water. When she surfaced, a couple of meters closer, she asked, again, for Jed to join her.

"Are you coming in, Senor?"

"Well, yes, but I don't have a bathing suit."

"Bathing suit?" Rachel laughed.

"You do not need a bathing suit to swim here. And besides, there is nobody around."

She pointed at the empty beach. "Do not worry, Senor. I will not peek."

She floated on her back and kicked at the water, attempting to splash Jed.

Jed removed his shirt and shorts. He thought about keeping on his 'boxers'. Then, along with his shirt and shorts, he threw the 'boxers' on the same piece of driftwood, where Rachel's clothes were strewn.

"It is alright, Senor. No one will steal them."

"Heh," laughed Jed. "I thought you said you weren't going to peek."

With that, Rachel plunged into the water performing a series of impressive dolphin dives.

Finally, she surfaced and, like a mermaid, floated on her back. She exposed a full body tan.

Jed ran into the water. When it was deep and safe enough to do so, he dove under and swam towards her.

Under the water, Jed could see her legs. They looked nice. He wanted to reach out and hold them.

Instead, he surfaced. Rachel teased him about his tan lines.

Jed smiled. "Thanks. It's a rig pig's tan." He splashed some water at her. Then, he ducked, again. Upon surfacing, Rachel was gone. *Disappeared again?* Jed looked around. Finally, after what seemed like minutes but, in fact, were only seconds, Rachel leapt out of the water and jumped on Jed's back, pulling him down.

Jed struggled to come up for air. "That was pretty good." He took a breath. "I didn't even hear you coming." Rachel straddled Jed's back. He dropped to his knees.

"Did you like the paintings, Senor?"

Jed had to think for a second. "The paintings?" He looked at the beach. "Oh yes! I loved them—especially the last one."

Rachel whispered. "Si, Senor, it **is** a very special painting."

She slithered from his body. She dove into the water and remained beneath the surface for what, Jed thought, was an extraordinarily long time. When she, finally, came up, she was out quite deep. *Too deep*, Jed thought. He considered swimming out to join her, but chose to remain where he was, chest deep, with his knees firmly planted, on the sand.

He watched as she moved, gracefully, on and in the water. It was obvious to Jed that Rachel had spent most of her life, by the sea.

She was in her element.

Like a shark, Rachel was fast and sleek.

Like a dolphin, she was smooth and graceful.

Jed called out saying that she was out too deep. "Come back in, Rachel. Come here!"

"Can you tread water, Senor?" Her voice carried well. "It is **really** deep out here, Senor," she teased. "Come out and join me." She motioned with an arm.

" Come out and swim with the fish."

At first, Jed thought that Rachel was referring to herself. Then he figured it was the tropical fish to which she was referring.

He couldn't resist.

He swam towards her.

As he got deeper, the temperature of the water got cooler.

"It's a little bit cooler out here." He shivered.

Finally, he reached Rachel.

He seemed to be working harder than she was at treading water and staying afloat.

He looked down.

He could barely make out the ripples on the sand, below.

The bottom appeared to be a good two meters deep.

"Would you like me to warm you up, Senor?" Rachel didn't wait for Jed's response. She swam towards him and then stopped, in front of him, close enough to touch him. She continued slowly and gracefully, treading the water.

As Rachel pulled the water inward and then, pushed it away, from her body, Jed followed the treading motion with respectful eyes. The shapely curves, of Rachel's figure, amidst the colors, of the sparkling water, glistened in the sun-speckled salt. Rachel moved, in rhythm, like a ballerina. *She must have been carved, by the hand, of a patient sculptor. Her skin – smoothly polished and choicely colored.* Jed wanted to tell her how nice she looked.

But, before he could speak, she swam behind him.

She ascended his back. Jed felt the smoothness of her skin.

In contrast to his stalwart roughness, her silken pliancy enveloped his body, securing it and warming it. Like two magnets, at opposite poles, they were united.

Rachel kissed Jed's back.

He could feel her fingers caress his ribs and tingle his spine.

Then she wrapped her legs around him.

The weight of her body compelled Jed to tread rigorously to keep them both afloat.

"It is okay if you lose your strength, Senor."

"Oh, yah?" Jed laughed. "If we do, then we will sink." He panted.

"That's okay, Senor. I will resuscitate you."

With that, like a playful kitten, Rachel climbed onto Jed's shoulders and elevated herself, into the air.

She forced him down, beneath the water.

Jed did not resist.

He was not afraid.

He knew that, at any time, he would be able to free himself from Rachel's playful restraint.

In a way, it was a relief, for Jed, to stop treading water.

As he was under, he wondered about Rachel's next move.

He succumbed to her playful aggression, but soon, he knew, he would need air.

Inside his head, he could feel and hear the beating of his heart.

It was time to surface.

Just as Jed was about to extend his arms to free himself, to pull upwards, Rachel slid down and moved in front of him. She touched his lips. Then, she pointed to her own.

The pounding in Jed's head grew more profound.

Rachel pulled him close to her chest and then pressed her lips tightly against his.

With her tongue, she forced his mouth open.

With confidence and control, she held the back of his head, with one hand, and, with the other, she held his chin. She blew air, slowly and precisely, into his mouth.

As she blew, she stroked the back of his head.

It was comforting, for Jed—different—but, nevertheless- comforting. The pounding of his heart subsided.

She withdrew.

She held him beneath the water.

Jed did not resist.

He looked up. From below, Jed could see that Rachel was drawing deep breaths, from the air above, before joining him, once again, beneath the surface.

Her body looked and felt beautiful.

Their mouths were, once again, united.

Jed couldn't believe the sensation. *Where did she learn how to do this?*

He didn't want Rachel to stop. *This is unreal.*

Her air was invigorating.

Her lips were stimulating.

Her hands were captivating.

Rachel knew what she was doing. She knew Jed was enjoying it.

She repeated the life-saving act several times and then she stopped.

She signaled for Jed to join her, above the water.

"That was unbelievable, Rachel. I could have stayed under for hours."

"I know. That is why I think we should stop."

Jed looked at her.

"I was starting to enjoy it, too, Senor."

She turned and looked at the beach. "Race you in." She dove under and before Jed could get his bearings, Rachel was already walking on the sand and heading for the driftwood.

As he stumbled, on the sand, attempting to get his other leg into his 'boxers', Rachel sat on the driftwood combing the knots out of her hair.

"Do you need to borrow this?" She held out the comb.

Jed shook his head.

"I'm alright. Thanks anyway."

Jed looked at Rachel.

He tried to figure her out.

He wasn't certain but, again, he felt that just as things were really starting to jell, they came to a complete stop – a sudden turn around.

"I've never felt anything like that, before, you know."

Rachel kept combing her hair. "Me neither."

Jed scratched his head. He tilted it to one side. "Rachel?"

"Senor?"

"Is everything okay?"

She stood up.

She walked over to him.

She took his hand in hers.

"I told you that there was a surprise waiting for you at the beach, Senor."

Jed nodded.

She adjusted the strap on her wrap-around skirt.

"You like adventure, Senor?"

"Is that what this is?" Jed raised his brow.

"Well, you see, Senor," she buttoned the top of her blouse.

"Sometimes in life, it takes two people to keep one person alive."

Jed frowned.

"Alone, we die. Together, we live." She looked into Jed's eyes.

"You understand, Senor?"

Jed nodded. "You look beautiful."

"Thanks." She kissed his cheek. "Shall we?" With his hand still in hers, she turned to leave.

They walked towards the cliff path.

They held on to each other's hands as they made their way back up the hill in the direction, of the truck.

Unlike the descent, the ascent was quiet.

Periodically, they turned to look back at the water and the sky.

Jed commented on their color and their beauty.

Rachel simply nodded.

Jed thought about the water experience, with Rachel.

When they reached the top, they both turned to take in the beauty of the sky and the unending Caribbean Sea.

Rachel gently turned Jed's head towards hers and looked into his eyes.

"It's like making love, Senor. Would you agree?"

Jed smiled. He leaned forward to kiss her on her lips.

She lifted her head and offered him the front of her salty tasting neck.

"We are not in the water anymore, Senor."

Jed nodded.

"You're right."

He paused.

"You are also very special."

He smiled at her and then, he kissed her neck again.

"Thanks," she whispered.

"And so are you."

She put her arm around his waist as they walked to the truck.

- CHAPTER 13 -

ACTIONS SPEAK LOUDER THAN WORDS

The drive back was different than the drive to the shore.

This time, Jed was behind the wheel. Rachel was in the passenger seat.

"Where do you want to go, now?" Rachel asked, as she placed both feet, on the dashboard.

"Well, I guess Lee's going to want his truck back."

Jed shrugged his shoulders. "After all, we didn't even tell him how long we were going to be away."

"He will not want his truck, Senor. He is sleeping." Rachel tucked her hair behind her ears.

"On the days after his nights at *The Oasis*, he passes out, on his hammock, in the front yard. The afternoon sun is like a blanket for him. But, suit yourself, we can head home."

She closed her eyes and rested her head against the seat.

"It's my turn, to have a snooze, now, Senor. All the swimming and climbing has made me tired."

"Go ahead," Jed encouraged. "I'm not tired, any more. You rest."

While journeying back to Lee's, Jed took three wrong turns.

As a result, the drive took longer than it should have.

Jed figured that wasn't so bad. The scenery was great and it gave Rachel more time to sleep.

Finally, they arrived.

Jed turned the key. The engine stopped.

Rachel opened her eyes. She looked out the window.

"We're back?" she sounded disappointed.

Lee was awakened by the sound of the truck when it pulled, into the drive.

He had been, as Rachel predicted, passed out, on his hammock.

He waved a lazy arm.

"How are you doing, Lee?" Jed approached the hammock.

"I'm asleep." He squinted. He covered his brow.

"Sorry, if I woke you." Jed apologized.

"No problem." Lee sat up. "I've slept enough."

Rachel said a quick hello and then went into the house.

As she approached the verandah, she turned and called out to Jed.

"I know you like the taste of salt, Senor. But, I must wash it from my body."

She walked up the stairs.

Jed laughed.

Lee looked at him. "You went for a swim?"

"Yep. Rachel brought me to the beach, by the caves, at Punta del Este."

"That was a good idea!" Obviously, Lee approved. "It must have been a nice break from Sammy and the smoky crowd, at The Oasis."

"We had a nice day," Jed smiled.

"You might want to know," Lee stood up, "that our hot-tempered Sammy is at home, right now, sleeping like a baby."

He stretched. "Do not take him too seriously, Jed.

You're not the first person who has had to contend with him."

"Ah, that's okay, Lee." Jed shrugged. "I know what people can be like after a few beers. Sammy was loaded, that's all. Plain and simple."

"Beers?" Lee laughed. "Yes, he was loaded, Jed. He was loaded with booze and filled with jealousy." He raised a finger. "That, my friend, is a deadly combination."

Jed nodded.

He wanted to change the subject.

"Rachel showed me your painting. That's quite a painting. You're very talented."

"Oh, she showed you one of my political admonitions, did she?" They walked side by side, towards the house.

"One of them?" asked Jed. He wanted to be careful.

Lee nodded. "I have painted others." He clarified. "But, only one at the caves, though."

Jed asked if he had a minute. "Could we just take a break, here, on the porch to sit and talk?" Jed chose his words, carefully. "Something has been on my mind."

Lee was fine with that. He enjoyed discussions. "Absolutely." He sat in one of the deck chairs. Jed sat in another.

Jed took a breath. "Can you tell me a little more about the painting, at the cave, Lee?"

"Oh, like what?" Lee sat back. "What would you like to hear?" He folded his hands, behind his head.

"Well, to begin," Jed leaned forward. "I was hoping that you could tell me a little bit about the man, hiding behind the rock."

"That's easy." Lee crossed his legs.

"The man is me—and the rock." He paused. He looked around the property. "The rock that the man is hiding behind," he unfolded his hands and opened his arms as if he were going to embrace the land. "The rock is Juventud!" He smiled. "You understand?"

Jed didn't say anything. He nodded. He scratched his head.

"Interesting!" He continued. "And the wave, of course, is the American flag. Correct?"

"Correct." Lee rolled up the short sleeve, of his t-shirt, to the blade of his shoulder.

Jed noticed that slightly below the right shoulder was a tattoo.

Lee pointed to the tattoo and apologized, saying that it was a little faded.

"After all, it's been a few years; fifteen, to be exact. But this hammer and sickle," he pointed to his arm, "Are the very same as those that are on the man in the painting, hiding behind the rock. On **his** arm, however," he raised a finger; " I placed them a bit lower. I guess they call that an artist's creative freedom, right Jed?"

Jed noticed the whiteness of his teeth.

He nodded. "Yep. I guess so."

"So, my sister took you swimming?" Ossie emerged from the house. He stood, on the porch, beside Jed.

"It was quite a swim." Jed extended a hand. "Good to see you, Os."

"Yes, my sister sure can swim!" Ossie shook Jed's hand. "Good to see you, too."

"So how do you like the island, Jed?" Ossie sat down on the top step.

"It's very special, Os." Jed meant it. "It's very, very special."

"You've got that right," agreed Lee. He stretched his arms towards the sky. Then, he rubbed his eyes.

"I'm heading inside. It's getting too bright for me, out here." He looked at Jed. "You must be hungry. Do you want something to eat?"

Jed said that sounded good.

Ossie stood up. "I'm just going to hang out, relaxing,

in the shade, of that big old palm." He pointed to one of the trees, supporting the ropes, of Lee's hammock.

He started down the stairs. "Enjoy!"

Jed and Lee went into the house. "See ya in a bit, Os."

When they arrived in the kitchen, Ossie's mom was putting the finishing touches on some chicken salad sandwiches. Jed saw the plate of sliced tomatoes. "Ooh, those look good!" She claimed that the tomatoes were fresh and that the "virgin fruit punch" was delicious. "It's cold and wet. It should serve to quench both your thirsts." She smiled.

Lee helped himself to a glass and offered one, to Jed.

"Thanks, Lee. The salt water can make a guy pretty thirsty."

"Two glasses of this stuff will hit the spot." Lee poured some more punch.

Jed sat down.

"Go ahead." Lee said. "Dig in."

Jed reached for a sandwich.

He was hungry.

He gobbled it down, in seconds. He livened it up with the splash from three, juicy, tomato slices.

Lee said that he was glad to see that Jed was enjoying his food. Then, he picked up his plate and said that he was going into the study. In one hand, he had his plate. In the other, he carried his punch.

"Feel free to join me for some political *chit chat*, Jed."

Jed thanked him and said that he would be there shortly. He reached for another slice of tomato.

He looked over at Ossie's mom. She was busy clearing, cleaning and rinsing.

"Help yourself to the other one, Jed." She pointed to the last sandwich.

"Are you sure? Isn't anyone else eating?"

"No, no. Ossie already ate and Rachel is in the shower. I can make something for her, if she is hungry. Please." She moved the plate closer to Jed. "Finish it off."

Jed accepted her offer. She smiled at him and then, she left the kitchen. Jed wasn't certain where she was going. As she walked down the hall, Jed listened to her fading footsteps.

As Jed chewed, he thought.

He thought about the painting, the tattoo, and what Lee had said about an author's creative freedom. He thought about Rachel, Ossie and Ossie's mom.

He also thought about a book that he had seen, before he fell asleep, earlier, that morning, in Lee's study.

The title of the book, he recalled, was **The Memoirs of C. Lee Bouvier**.

He had not given it much thought, until now.

He finished the sandwich.

He decided that he would ask Lee, about the book, when he joined him, in the study.

Maybe, Lee will lend it to me. Jed got up. He put his plate, in the sink.

Rachel entered the kitchen.

"How was lunch?"

"Delicious!" Jed was happy to see her.

He smiled, at her. She smiled back.

"Where is Ossie?" She looked out the window.

Jed told her that he was outside.

Rachel left the kitchen. She went outside.

Jed left the kitchen. He went into the study.

Lee was slouched, in the corner chair. His eyes were closed.

Jed tip toed around the room and looked at some of the pictures and authors, on the shelves, surrounding him.

He looked at things differently, now.

He stopped in front of C. Lee Bouvier's book.

He took it from the shelf. He leafed through the first few pages. Then, he closed it. He looked at the cover. His eyes focused on the name *Lee*. He put the book back on the shelf between **MacBeth** and **To Kill A Mocking Bird.**

He left the room and went out on to the porch.

The first thing he noticed was that Ossie was not lying, on Lee's hammock. Instead, he was leaning on one of the porch posts, talking to Rachel. She was sitting in the swinging chair.

"Hi guys." Jed waved. "How's it goin'?" He sat in one of the chairs.

Rachel and Ossie looked at him.

Rachel spoke first. "You are choosing not to visit, with Lee?"

Jed shook his head. "He's asleep."

Ossie laughed. "He's getting too old for those late nights."

Rachel looked at her brother.

Jed stood up. "You know what?" He walked over and stood beside Rachel. "While I was eating lunch, I was doing some thinking."

"Since when can you do two things at once, Senor?" Rachel teased. She winked.

Jed smiled. He knew what she meant. He thought about their water experience.

Ossie looked confused.

Jed continued. "I need to spend some time, alone." He was direct.

Ossie left the post that he was leaning on and walked down the steps. Jed thought that he was either mad or disappointed. He stopped on the bottom step.

He turned and looked up at Jed. "So is it something we said?" He was smiling. Jed was relieved.

Ossie understood. "I know what you mean. Sometimes a guy," he looked at Rachel "And a girl, just need to get away."

Jed appreciated his thinking. "Thanks. I just need a timeout. That's all." He walked down the steps and stood beside Ossie. "You know, a chance to just chill."

"Say no more." Ossie put up his hand, signaling for Jed to stop. "I understand."

"You can stay on the tug and take care of it, for me, until we need to get back on tower."

Jed was surprised. "Really? That's a generous offer, Os. The tug will be a great escape for me. Thanks. That's awesome."

Jed looked up at Rachel.

"Before I get my gear and all, I need to ask you, something." Rachel tilted her head. "Are you able to drive me to the docks?"

Jed gave Ossie a quick glance.

"It is not that I don't want your company, Os, I just want to spend a little more time, with Rachel. I want to thank her for the great tour she gave me and, well," he paused, "You know? No offence, though."

"None taken." Ossie smiled.

"I'll go and get the keys for the tug." He touched Jed's arm and told him, again, that he understood.

Jed was grateful.

Ossie went back up the stairs and headed for the front door.

Jed followed. He walked over and stood beside Rachel. "You have a good brother, Rachel. He's a good man."

Rachel pulled her hair back as if it were in need of a hair tie. "He cares." She stood up. "But **you're** a good man, Senor." She stood in front, of Jed.

Jed frowned. He thought that she looked tired.

He asked her if she were okay with driving him to the docks.

"I would love to accompany you to the docks, Senor. I like your company. Where are the keys, to the truck?" She extended a hand.

Jed looked back at the truck. He remembered that he had left the keys in the ignition.

"They're still in the truck. I hope!"

Jed leaned against the post.

"I'll be gone for nineteen days." He reached for her hand.

"Enjoy yourself." She sounded sincere but Jed detected a hint of melancholy, in her voice.

"Just don't go sailing around the world, Jed. I mean, Senor, Jed." She moved in closer.

She hugged him.

Jed hugged her. "I won't go on any trips, Rachel." He looked into her eyes. "At least not in the true sense of the word."

She walked down the steps and headed in the direction, of the truck.

She opened its door.

She climbed in.

She shut the door.

She opened the window.

Jed was lost, for a moment, watching her every move. Then, something caught his eye.

He looked up at the sky.

He saw a lone bird soaring high above. The bird was silhouetted against the bright blue sky. He covered his brow in an attempt to shield the light and get a better look. He wasn't certain what kind of bird it was. He thought it might be a seagull. He watched it glide.

He called out to Rachel. "I won't be long."

"Take your time." Her head was resting against the seat.

Jed looked up at the sky. The bird was gone.

There was also something about that soaring bird that motivated him.

He went into the house.

Upon entering, he, immediately, headed for the study. He walked over and stood beside Lee. He, gently, tapped his shoulder. He whispered. "I've come to say goodbye, Lee. Sorry, I know you're sleeping."

He apologized for waking him up a second time, in the same day.

The snoring subsided.

Lee opened his eyes.

"Sorry, Lee, but I'm heading out soon and I wanted to ask a favor."

"No problem. I was just resting my eyes." He stretched. "How are ya?"

"I'm okay – you know?" Jed was a little nervous.

Lee nodded. "Go ahead," he rubbed his eyes.

Jed took a breath.

"You have a book on your shelf, there," Jed pointed, "That I'm very interested in reading." He paused.

Lee was more awake, now. He looked up, with curious eyes.

"I would like to borrow it from you, Lee." Jed put up his hand. "Don't worry. I will return it to you as soon as I'm finished reading it. I hate borrowing, but…" Lee stopped Jed, in mid sentence.

He put up his hand. He looked at Jed as if he were reading his mind.

He stood up.

He smiled.

He walked over to the exact spot, by the shelf that housed Jed's desired book.

He stopped. He turned to look at Jed.

He smiled. "I bet I know which book you want."

Jed tilted his head and squinted. "Oh ya!" He placed his hands on his hips. " How much do you want to bet?"

Lee reached out and removed a book, from the shelf.

He held it in his hands. He snickered.

Then, with extended arms, he held it out for Jed, as if he were offering him a sacred covenant.

Lee told him that he shouldn't make such risky bets.

"I don't want to take your hard-earned *rig pig* money."

Lee carefully placed **The Memoirs of C. Lee Bouvier** into Jed's hands.

"Enjoy it. It's a good read."

Jed thanked him.

Then, their eyes met, again, for a silent, telepathic moment.

Lee broke the silence warning Jed about not folding any page corners.

Jed obliged. "Don't worry, Lee. I don't believe in that, either. Especially with such a precious manuscript."

He looked at the book.

"Thank you." He turned to leave.

Lee put out a hand stopping Jed. "How do you know it's so precious, Jed?" He sounded like a lawyer. His question was accusatory but not unkind.

Jed paused. He wasn't nervous, any more.

He looked down, at the book.

He looked at Lee.

He said nothing.

The response in his eyes, however, was enough to satisfy Lee's curiosity.

"Good." Lee returned to the corner chair.

Jed left the study, with book in hand. He went into the kitchen. There, he saw Ossie's mom. She must have known that he was coming – or going. She was sitting at the table—as if in prayer. Her hands were tightly, clenched, on the table, in front of her. Jed thought that she looked concerned. He said hello.

"I overheard." She looked up at Jed. "I am sad to see that you are leaving." She was sincere. She spotted the book. Jed knew that there was nothing phony about this lady. She was true! But, there was something she wasn't saying – or couldn't say.

She smiled.

Jed smiled. He could see the similarity between her eyes and Rachel's.

She got up and hugged him. "Ossie will be here, in a minute."

"Oh?" Jed was curious. "Where is Ossie, now?"

She ignored his question.

"You be careful, now, on that tug." She straightened out the collar, of his shirt.

"I'll be fine."

Ossie, finally, appeared in the doorway. He was holding Jed's backpack.

He looked at his mother. "Before Jed leaves, mom, I think he might be interested in knowing your first name."

Jed reached for his pack. He looked at Ossie's mom.

"My name is Marina!" She sounded apologetic. "But thank you for calling me, Mrs. Lee.

Jed nodded. "I know. I mean," he corrected himself. "I had an idea." He smiled. "That's a nice name." Jed scratched his whiskers. "But, Mrs. Lee is a nice name, too."

"You are welcome, in my home, any time, Jed." Marina repeated.

She hugged him, again. "Any time."

Jed slung his pack over his shoulder. He looked at Ossie. He was nodding.

He held up the book. "Should be a good read!"

Ossie approached him. He handed Jed the keys, for the tug.

"Thanks." Jed put them in his pocket.

Ossie poked Jed's shoulder. "Don't sink it."

Jed gave him a look. Then, he left the kitchen. He headed for the front door.

Just as he was about to reach for the handle, he stopped. He looked over his shoulder. He sensed that someone was watching him.

He saw Lee standing, in the doorway, of the study. His arms were folded, across his chest.

"In case you were wondering," his volume was high. His tone was serious. "I never met her sister or her famous husband."

Jed was confused.

He squinted, the same way he did, when he was trying to follow the soaring bird.

"Pardon? Whose sister?"

Lee unfolded his arms. He pointed to the book.

"The author's!" His volume was still high. Jed did not hear anger in the volume, though. He heard sincerity – certainty – honesty and concern.

Jed looked down.

He looked at the name Bouvier.

When he looked up to see Lee, he was gone.

Jed waited for a moment. Lee didn't reappear.

Jed opened the front door.

He looked at the driveway and the trusty red truck that had taken him and Rachel on such an unforgettable adventure. Rachel had moved over and was, now, sitting in the passenger seat.

He called out. "Are you ready?" He walked towards the truck.

She tilted her head and responded sarcastically. "Well, Senor, I am sitting here on this lonesome seat and the keys are there, like you left them, in the ignition, awaiting your, sluggish arrival. Yes, Senor, I **am** ready." She ran her fingers through her hair. "The question is—are **you** ready, white boy, with the tan lines?"

When Jed opened the driver's door, he saw that Rachel

was wearing, what looked like, a new blouse. It was bright yellow in color and, like her other blouse, see-through. It was also, not surprisingly, low cut and unbuttoned to just below her breasts.

"Nice blouse. It's you!"

He closed the door. He placed **The Memoirs,** carefully, underneath his seat.

"Thanks for waiting. I guess I'm driving."

He threw his pack into the back.

"Do you remember the way, Senor?" Rachel moved close beside him. "It's simple. There is only one main road—many turns, though." She teased.

Jed smiled. "I know. I took a few of them, earlier, today."

"You must take only one turn to get to the docks, Senor." Rachel's instructed, with her usual charm.

"Only one turn—the *off ramp*." She shrugged. "It's the only turn for the docks. No other turns. Okay, Senor?" She winked.

Jed looked at her, with an intuitive eye.

He leaned an arm against the opened window.

"I thought you were asleep, way back there when I was making all those wrong turns."

Rachel grinned. "What turns, Senor? What are you talking about?"

She rolled her playful, brown, eyes.

Jed shook his head.

"You're one of a kind, Rachel!"

He turned the key to start the engine.

As they made their way off the property, Rachel asked Jed why it took him so long to leave the house.

He waited a few seconds, before he answered.

He wanted to respond, honestly, but not to go into too much detail.

"I asked Lee if I could borrow one of his books." Jed sounded nonchalant.

"And did he lend you one?"

"Yes, he did." Jed nodded, with assertion.

"And, I promised that I would take good care of it, too. I intend on returning it with the person who drives Ossie, in a couple of weeks, back to the tug."

"That person might be me." Rachel touched Jed's knee.

"Or it could be Lee." She shrugged.

"Or," she teased. "It could be Sammy!" She looked at Jed, for his reaction.

"Imagine that, Senor!" She poked his ribs.

Jed laughed. "Ooh, be careful, Rachel, you're liable to make me take a wrong turn, poking me, like that."

Rachel, then, touched Jed's arm. "That might not be so bad, Senor."

Jed turned to look at her. She licked her lips.

Jed looked ahead. "Whew! Oh boy!" He took a breath. Then, he pointed to the landscape.

"What a beautiful island, you have! Wow!"

He stayed his course.

He stayed in control.

"I would prefer it if you drove Ossie back to the tug, Rachel. In fact, I hope you do."

Rachel smiled. "Well, Senor, we will just have to wait and see." She settled comfortably into her seat.

"You like my father's library, Senor?" Rachel asked, with, what Jed thought, an ulterior motive.

"Yes, Rachel, I do. It has some very interesting and unique books."

"What is your favorite book, Senor?" She sat up.

"Well, my favorite book is actually a play called **Hamlet**, by William Shakespeare."

"I know the play, Senor. I know about **Hamlet**." She nodded.

"I like it, too.

Is that the one you borrowed, from Lee?"

"Actually no, Rachel, it's not."

"Oh no, Senor? You didn't ask to borrow your favorite book?" Rachel sounded surprised.

Jed turned his head to look at her. He thought that she looked pretty. He reached down beneath his seat and felt for the book that he had so carefully placed.

"I have something here," he took a breath, "that I am concealing, for safe keeping."

Rachel leaned over to have a look.

When Jed brought his hand up from under the seat, he revealed a thin, black covered novella that was not much bigger than his hand. He placed it on Rachel's lap.

She took it into her hands. She studied its title and examined the picture of the pretty lady, on its cover.

"**The Memoirs of C. Lee Bouvier!**" She smiled and nodded her head.

"I should have known, Senor, that this and only this would be the book that would catch your attention."

"That it did," acknowledged Jed. "It caught my attention. That's for sure!"

Rachel looked at its cover. She studied it, for a moment.

"Have you read it?" Jed asked, breaking the pensive silence.

Rachel did not answer.

"This is my father's favorite book, Senor. You two have similar tastes."

She looked up. "Here is our turn, Senor." She pointed ahead.

"Already?" asked Jed. He was surprised.

"Now you can see, Senor, the sign says: *El Muelles*." She pointed to an overhead sign.

Jed shook his head, "Heh, you said that it would say *The Docks*."

"I did? No, Senor. Did I say that? Really?"

Jed scratched his head. "I don't know." He turned on the indicator light.

"Senor! *El Muelles* means *The Docks*, in Spanish, of course, Senor. You have forgotten where you are, amigo."

Jed smiled.

"I guess sometimes, I do, Rachel. Especially when I'm with you."

He turned to look at her.

"Sometimes," he swallowed, "When we're together, I forget where I am—above and below the water."

She touched his hand. "I understand. Me too."

Her hand felt nice.

Jed told her.

The arrival, at the docks, leaped upon them more quickly than Jed had anticipated or desired.

He told Rachel that he was enjoying the drive and the opportunity to spend some more time with her. She nodded and admitted the same.

"I would be happy to keep driving, Senor. There are other places that I would like to show you."

Jed, slowly, pulled the truck into the lot, by the pier.

He turned off the engine.

He handed Rachel the keys.

"Thanks, Senor." She slid them down between the lower part of her tummy and the top of her jeans.

"You don't use pockets, Rachel?" Jed reached over to retrieve his backpack.

Rachel opened the passenger door. She stood outside. She had her back turned, to Jed. She asked him if he could see any pockets.

Jed took a look and then shook his head. "I've never heard of pants without pockets," he claimed. Rachel smiled. She put her hands on her hips. She wiggled. "We've heard of them, in Juventud."

Jed laughed. "You've got the moves, Rachel."

Jed slung his pack over his shoulder. He carefully placed the book, in the zipper pouch. He walked around to the passenger side.

"Thank you for coming." He leaned over to kiss her cheek. He knew that lips were 'off limits'. That was just the way it was.

"It was nice spending time with you, again, Rachel." Jed paused. "That's why I wanted you to drive me."

"You drove, Senor."

"I know but, what I meant was," Jed was struggling. He looked at Rachel.

She bailed him out. She placed a finger, on his lips. "It was my pleasure being your navigator, Senor. It was nice being together, again."

Jed nodded.

"In such a short period of time, we've experienced a lot and we've become good friends."

"Friends, Senor? Friendship takes longer than what we have had." Rachel leaned against the side of the truck. "Love, on the other hand." She emphasized the word love. "Love can happen in seconds. And lust, too!" She pulled Jed closer. Their noses touched.

"Si Senor, and lust. Maybe, lust takes even less time; imagine that! Lust is even quicker than love and friendship. Oooh!" Rachel dragged her hand up and down Jed's arm.

Her hand felt warm.
The sun felt warm.
The air was calm.
The late October sky was still bright and cloud-free.
For a moment, time stood still.

Jed moved back. He looked out at the water.

"The seagulls look like statues," he said, "sitting motionless, on those rope posts and buoys." Rachel reached out and held Jed's hand.

"What do you want to do, Senor? If I go onto the tug, I may not leave until morning. Do you think that is a good idea, Senor?"

Jed didn't say anything.

Hand in hand, they walked, slowly, towards the tug.

He looked out, again, at the water.

Rachel stopped. She turned his head.

"Do you want me to stay, Senor?

If you answer yes, then I will stay."

Jed thought about Lana.

He looked into Rachel's patient eyes and smiled.

He didn't say anything.

Rachel understood.

"Close your eyes, Senor." With her index fingers, she gently closed his eyes.

"Count down from ten to zero, Senor, and do not open your eyes until you get to zero."

She blew a warm breath into Jed's face.

"Count slowly, Senor. It is very important that you count slowly."

Jed laughed. "Why?"

Rachel pressed a finger against his lips and whispered. "You're a good man, Senor. I knew that. Your lady friend, in Canada, is lucky."

Jed opened his eyes. "How did you?"

"Hush." She closed his eyes, again.

"Don't open your eyes until you get to zero, Senor.

Now start counting.

Count slowly, Senor."

Jed began at ten.

He swallowed, as he reached number seven.

At six, he heard a door shut and the sound of a truck engine drowned out the sound, in his head, of the numbers five and four.

The sound of the vehicle faded, as he counted down to the last two numbers.

At zero, he didn't open his eyes.

He took a deep breath and then turned towards the sun.

He remained, like the sea gulls, motionless, on the plank, of the wharf.

When he finally did open his eyes, the reflection of the sun, on the breakwater, made the rocks, in the water, look like diamonds, shining in green glass.

The smell reminded him of being beneath that water, holding on to Rachel's lips, inhaling her air.

Her lips and air, Jed thought.
The enigmatic Rachel!

He walked, slowly, up the gangplank, towards the deck, of the **COPS** tug.

PART THREE

IRAE MAN

- CHAPTER ONE -

SERIOUS LAUGHTER

"Somebody might know something.

Is that what you said, Ossie?" Jed squinted.

"Did you say somebody on or connected to the rig? What do you mean?"

Jed was concerned.

Ossie nodded.

"I think you know what I mean, Jed. I have dark thoughts about it."

"Dark thoughts?" The statement took Jed by surprise.

Ossie nodded.

Jed pondered.

A scene from Shakespeare's **Hamlet** entered his mind.

It was the image of the tragic hero seeking refuge and truth, in feigning ignorance and insanity. Like Hamlet, Jed wanted to know the truth. Like Hamlet, he needed a method. Like Hamlet, he was alone in his quest. At least, that's how he was feeling, at this point, in time.

A*mnesia*! Jed told himself to let on that he couldn't remember things – well, not everything.

Jed's thoughts were like warning lights and caution signs!

He told himself to slow down—*remain guarded*.

He didn't want to be blurred by paranoia and confusion.

He looked at Ossie. "What kind of dark thoughts?"

Ossie stated that he didn't like the smell of things.

Jed asked. "What smell?"

Ossie laughed and replied that he was speaking metaphorically.

Jed thought that his laugh was forced.

He closed his eyes.

The room fell silent.

Minutes later, he looked up. Ossie was still sitting by his bed.

Jed reached for a cup that was on the side table. It was flanked by a large pitcher, filled with water and a stack of cups, faced down, beside it.

Jed asked if Ossie would pour him some water. He told him to help himself. Ossie accepted and thanked Jed.

Jed pointed to the bed, the room and at some of the hospital paraphernalia.

"For me, all this is like a metaphor, Ossie; more like a dream." Jed shook his head.

Ossie nodded. He did not speak, though. Instead, he just sipped at his water.

Jed decided, in those few seconds, as he watched Ossie's Adam's apple, rhythmically moving up and down that he was going to take direction from Shakespeare's Hamlet. Until he was certain that it was safe to let down his guard, he would heed to the *warning lights* and *caution signs*.

The room was still dark.

Jed was surprised at how well he could see, in the dim light, of his room. It was as though his sense of sight had improved, both literally and figuratively.

He was thirsty.

He drank some more water.

The water tasted good.

He felt that it was not just his sense of sight that had sharpened; his taste buds were enlivened, too.

He told Ossie that he was finding it difficult to get a handle on things.

He said that he couldn't think straight.

Jed said that his thoughts were in a maze of darkness and, at times, even blindness.

Ossie, again, didn't respond. He continued sipping and nodding.

"I know people when I see them," he explained, "like you and Marty, but Ossie, I did not remember you, until I saw you."

Ossie laughed. "Who's Marty?"

Then, before Jed could answer, Ossie told him that he was probably just tired and that the painkillers must be making him confused.

"Give me some of those drugs you're on Jed. I wouldn't mind being in a maze of darkness, myself. It could be fun."

Jed continued playing the role. "What pain-killers?"

Ossie tilted his head.

Jed looked at the shadow of his head and shoulders, as they moved slowly, on the far wall. Then, he looked directly at Ossie.

Ossie saw that Jed was studying him.

He leaned forward.

He whispered.

"Jed, tell me what you remember, of the blow-out?"

Jed felt that Ossie's question was untimely and that it bordered on doubt.

He told himself that whatever answer he were to provide, it would probably not be the right one; not the one that Ossie wanted to hear; not the one that Ossie should hear; not the response that anyone, at this time, for that matter, should hear.

He pretended to be looking for the answer in a confused and troubled head. "I can't remember a thing, Ossie. My mind is totally blank."

"Seriously?" asked Ossie. "You can't remember a thing?"

Jed thought that Ossie sounded somewhat pleased with his admission of amnesia.

He decided to go on the offensive.

"Why is it so important that I provide you with the details of an incident that I can't remember? I feel like you are treating me like I made a mistake. You sound like the rig police."

For effect, Jed raised his voice a little.

"You respond with the word *seriously,* when I tell you something.

Other times you don't respond at all. You just nod your head. What is that?"

Jed took a sip.

He swallowed, slowly.

His throat was dry and sensitive.

He shook his head.

He returned his glass to the table.

He looked at Ossie.

He continued.

"That blow–out should not have happened. That's all I know."

He paused. He looked over at Ossie's shadow that was still on the far wall. It was starting to fade. The struggling moonlight was giving way to the morning sun.

"It was deathly quiet, Ossie and then bang. The next thing I know, I am lying in this hospital bed with a sore head and heavy eyes. Nothing is making sense.

Not even you." Jed pointed a stern finger.

Ossie stood up and went over to the window.

He looked to the right and then to the left. Then he looked up at the sky.

Jed waited for him to say something. He just turned

away from the window and faced Jed. He leaned on the sill.

Jed continued. "Why the hell am I so thirsty?" He reached for his glass.

"For all I know, that explosion could have been intentional.

What do you think of that, Ossie?"

Ossie dragged a chair and sat beside Jed.

He reached over and took the pitcher from the table. He topped off his glass and replenished Jed's.

"The drugs, they have you on, make you thirsty."

Jed looked over at Ossie. "How do you know that?"

"Look at how much you're drinking."

He pointed at the water. The pitcher was almost empty.

"Your nurse has to keep filling it."

Ossie sat back.

He sighed.

"Trust me, Jed. I know. We'll get into the details, at another time."

Jed studied Ossie's eyes. They had never changed.

He told himself that Ossie could be trusted. He always could be trusted. After all, Ossie was a good man. Unlike Ossie's eyes, Jed' s mind was changing.

The room was beginning to brighten.

Jed waited for Ossie to say something.

Jed chose to speak.

"Ossie! It's starting to come back to me." He told himself that he had to be honest – with somebody. *That person should be Ossie*. "I can recollect more now than I did when we first started talking. I guess I can attribute that to becoming more alert."

Ossie looked at Jed. "Or all that water." Ossie pointed. He smiled.

"Sorry, if I caught you off guard with my questions and questioning techniques.

I didn't mean to mess you up.

I'm here as a friend but also because I have concerns about what really happened to the rig.

There's been some shit happening on Lee's rigs back home, too.

We're concerned that it's not just a coincidence. But I'll talk to you more about that later."

He looked at Jed's head, with a sympathetic eye.

"You took quite a blow. That must have hurt."

Jed shook his head. "Don't remember!" He paused. "Honestly!" He smiled.

Ossie took a drink.

Jed did the same.

"I can still be trusted, Jed." He stood up. "You know that."

He went to the window.

"Do you mind if I open this window a little. I could use some fresh air."

Jed agreed. "Good idea! It is kind of stuffy, in here. I could use a little air, myself."

Ossie repeated that he could be trusted. "However," he took a breath, "That may not be the case with others. Do you know what I mean?"

Jed leaned on an elbow. He tried to sit up.

"I have some troubling thoughts about it all, too, Ossie. You've got to tell me more about what you think happened here and what is happening down south."

Ossie returned to his chair.

Jed continued. "Did you have a blow-out, off shore?"

The door, of Jed's room, suddenly opened.

Both he and Ossie looked towards the door with wide and startled eyes.

They reacted like delinquent schoolboys, guilty for talking after curfew.

"What you be doin' in there, Mista Jed man? Everyting Irae?"

"Who are you?" Jed squinted as he tried to decipher the slim figure that was standing in the doorway.

"It is I, man, Clem. I be hoping dat everyting be cool with you, at dis time, Mista Jed.

Everyting Irae, man?"

"Clem? I don't know anybody named Clem. Are you a doctor?"

"A doctor?" Clem laughed. "Yes man, almost man. You know Clem. Everybody know Clem. Ain't dat right, Ossie?"

"You know this guy?" Jed pointed.

Clem approached the bed.

Ossie stood up.

He smiled.

He and Clem shook hands.

"Yes Jed, I know Clem. I have known Clem, ever since he moved to Juventud, a long time ago. Good to see you, Clem." "Long time, man, long time." Clem nodded, in nostalgic thought.

"How's Mista Jed?" Clem asked the question, as if he and Jed were old buddies.

He examined Jed's bandages.

"So, are you my other doctor?"

"No man, I ain't your doctor; your doctor be Doctor Yen, man. Bill Yen! He be cool man. Ya man. Dr. Yen, man. He be your doctor. Ya man. Everyting be cool."

"I've met Dr. Yen. But listen. Listen just for a minute. Please, just stop."

Jed put up his hand.

"What's happening here?

Can one of you two guys enlighten me as to what I owe this little friendly but confusing reunion?"

Jed looked at Ossie.

"Enlighten me, Ossie. Who is this guy? "

Ossie looked at Clem.

"Should I tell him Clem, or do you want to do the honors?"

"Tell him all man, tell him all.

Ya man Irae." Clem sat in Ossie's chair.

Ossie took a deep breath and then, he sat down. This time he sat on the edge of Jed's bed.

Jed leaned back, on his pillows.

Ossie began.

"Clem and I go back a long way." He paused. "A long way." He shook his head.

"Our first encounter, like ours, Jed, took place in Cuba."

He asked Clem to pass him his glass of water.

"Thanks." He drank. "Clem's father worked on one of Lee's rigs, out in the high seas, south of Cuba, near Jamaica. He and Lee struck up a friendship. When Clem's mother passed away, Clem's father needed a place, for his only child, to live, while he was off-shore."

Ossie paused. He stood up and adjusted his pant leg, over his boot. He sat down, again, on the edge of Jed's bed.

"There's more." He continued.

"Clem lived with us, from the age of nine, until he was seventeen.

For eight years, he lived between Juventud and Jamaica. When his dad was on long-change, the two of them went back to Negril.

When his dad was on tower, Clem stayed with us: my sisters and me. He became, what you might call, our half brother."

"Ya man, brothers man," Clem smiled. Jed noticed that he had exceptionally white teeth.

"Me and Ossie man—we be jammin' man.

Ya man, cool runnin'. Everyting Irae, man—Everyting Irae."

Jed looked at Clem.

Clem looked at Jed.

For a second, Jed thought that he had met those eyes before.

They were distant but familiar eyes.

Jed asked if he had ever met Clem before.

Clem smiled at Jed's question. He didn't respond, though. He just kept smiling.

Jed figured that he was just a happy and friendly sort, always upbeat and liked to smile.

His faith in Ossie had been restored. Now, he was starting to trust this new guy – a stranger—well, maybe not that much of a stranger, after all.

Although he wanted to trust and be honest, he decided that he would, nevertheless, remain *somewhat* guarded.

Ossie continued.

"Your doctor, Doctor Yen, was Clem's mother's doctor.

In 1977, she died of a brain hemorrhage but not before Doctor Yen did all he could to save her.

Like you, Jed, she was hit in the head. It was not a drill pipe that struck her, though. It was a car windshield. She had been in a serious car accident, in Jamaica.

Anyway, Jed, although Clem replies honestly when he tells you that he is not your doctor, he is, however, studying under Dr. Yen, to become a doctor."

He paused.

He finished off the water.

The jug was now empty.

Ossie looked at Clem.

"Like Dr. Yen, Clem is specializing in unique medicine."

"So you're almost a doctor," declared Jed "Okay! I'm getting it, now…kind of.

"Almost a doctor, man. Ya man, dat's it. Almost a doctor!

I still gots a ways to go, man.

But Dr. Yen, man, he be helping me out like he always done."

Clem pointed to the empty jug. "I'll go and get us some water, man"

Jed thanked him.

Ossie stood up.

He took a breath.

"Dr. Yen practiced in Negril, for ten years, after Clem's mother passed away.

Like Lee, Dr. Yen took Clem under his wing. He helped him with his schooling and his entrance into medicine, here in Edmonton, at the university hospital."

Ossie paused.

"Not at this hospital, though. This hospital is different. It is different and very special. It is Dr. Yen's special place."

Ossie smiled. "Like you, Jed. Dr. Yen's *special* project."

Jed raised his eyebrows.

"You see, after Dr. Yen was transferred from Jamaica, he came to Canada.

He took Clem with him, at that time, to help him fulfill his dream."

"So Clem and Dr. Yen are going to cure me of all my pains?" interrupted Jed, with tongue, in cheek.

Clem returned. He placed a jug, full of, what appeared to be *ice-cold* water, on Jed's table.

"Just some of your pains man; ya man; just some of your pains. Now ya'all be cool."

Jed was surprised. "How did you hear that?"

Clem just smiled. He said that he had to go but encouraged Ossie to tell Jed more about his famous doctor.

"When you see me again, man, I'll be with the Canadian Lynx.

Ya man, the Lynx man."

Clem left the room, purring like a cat.

Ossie stood beside Jed's bed, with his arms folded, like a bouncer.

"Oh by the way, Jed, I neglected to mention one more thing." He cleared his throat.

"Along with being Clem's mother's doctor, Dr. Yen was also one of the doctors called to Dallas, back in 1963, two days after Kennedy was shot."

"He was at Kennedy's bedside, when he died? No shit!"

Ossie shook his head. "No, no, Jed. Kennedy died on the Friday, November 22nd. Dr. Yen was called in two days later, on the Sunday, November 24$^{th.}$

He was called in, by the authorities, required to treat another victim, with a gunshot wound."

Jed looked up.

His eyes widened.

Ossie smiled. "You're in good hands, Jed."

"Holy crow! I may be in good hands, like you say, but why me, Os? This *Yen* guy is a famous doctor."

"And so are you, Jed."

"I'm not a doctor." Jed was confused.

"No, Jed. You're right! You're not a doctor.

But, you are famous!"

- CHAPTER TWO -

BED SIDE MATTERS

The morning sun brightened Jed's room.

Under normal circumstances, the light would be welcoming, but, this morning, it was straining.

Jed's eyes were still sensitive. They felt dry.

Although it had not been long since Ossie's visit, the light of day made it seem like it had been hours.

Jed looked at the window. The sun was in the east, shining through.

Jed figured it was about 9:30—9:45, latest.

He closed his eyes.

He was tired.

He drifted, in and out, of shallow sleep. His mind was too full, to fall deeper.

He thought about the blow-out. He thought about Ossie. He thought about Lana and his famous 'Dr. Yen'.

He listened to the sound of Nurse Rogers walking up and down the hall, coming and going, filling water pitchers and checking tubes.

The soles of her shoes sounded like taps.

He opened his eyes.

Nurse Rogers was standing beside him holding two full pitchers of water.

He looked at her as she was examining the bag and intravenous tube.

She looked at her watch.

Jed was happy to see that she was wearing one.

He asked her what time it was.

She looked down at Jed and smiled.

"It is time that we changed that bandage." She pointed to Jed's head.

"Thanks for the water."

"You're welcome!" She looked sincere. "I know how thirsty you must be."

She walked over to the window. She closed it.

She shook her head. "It's a little cool in here."

She looked at her watch, again.

"I'll be back." She left the room.

As the sound of her tapping shoes faded into the distance, Jed's world returned inward.

He wondered about the time.

He was disappointed that Nurse Rogers skirted his question; or at least appeared to skirt it.

He attributed her response to medical rationale.

Maybe they aren't supposed to tell me. Perhaps it has something to do with my injury or the medication.

Jed looked up at the bag that was filled with the purple liquid.

He looked at the tube, the tape and the needle in his arm.

He studied the liquid, as it dropped steadily from the bag, into the tube.

It dropped in rhythm.

He looked out the window.

Clouds were rolling in.

He closed his eyes.

He thought about Ossie's statement regarding the medication.

He wondered why and how Ossie knew so much.

He thought, once again, about Doctor Yen.

Where is he and what is he doing?

Jed wanted to see him.

He needed some questions answered.

Whether or not they will be answered, is another story, of course.

Jed thought about Lana.
I wonder what Lana is doing.
He wasn't certain if she were at school or not. He also wasn't certain whether it was the weekend or a weekday.
Jed was frustrated.
He tried to get up.
As he placed his feet on the cool hospital floor, he felt nauseous.
His efforts were in vain.
The room started to spin.
He felt dizzy.
He felt like he was drunk.
He lay down, again.
He closed his eyes.
He wanted the room to stop spinning.
He asked himself what was making him feel so lousy.
What is it that is making me feel so weak?
He thought about the medication.
What had Ossie said?
What had Dr. Yen administered to him?

What really did happen at the rig?

He began to drift.
The room stopped spinning.
He was no longer dizzy.
He fell asleep.

With every drip, of the calyx, he sunk deeper and deeper and deeper.
His thoughts turned and twisted, like the oozing mud, at the rig, on the night of the blow-out.

He dreamed.

The sun, slowly, made its way across the Alberta sky.

He dreamed about being on a beach, somewhere, far away.

The sky was beautiful.

The sand was soft.

Unlike the hospital floor, the sand and the water were warm.

The person standing beside him was, like the water, warm.

She looked like Rachel but sounded like Nurse Rogers.

There was a man, in a little boat, beckoning him to come into the water.

"Come out deeper," he invited.

"Keep walking. You can do it!"

Jed walked towards the boat but wasn't getting any closer.

The water, however, was getting deeper.

It was getting deeper and cooler.

Jed looked over his shoulder at the girl standing on the sand.

She was far away.

It was difficult to see her face.

She did not look familiar.

When he turned to look ahead, at the man in the boat, he was gone.

Jed was now standing in the middle of the ocean.

He was on a sandbar.

The beach looked like it was miles away.

The water continued to rise.

The tide is shifting.

Jed looked at the water.

I must swim to shore.

Suddenly, the shore disappeared beneath the horizon. Land was nowhere in sight.

Water was everywhere. It continued to rise.

Jed's legs were covered; then his chest; his neck; finally his head.

He was standing under the water but he could still breathe.

How is this possible? How is it that I am not drowning? From what or whom am I getting my oxygen?

He tried to close his eyes.

The salt was stinging them.

His vision was blurred.

Then he felt her lips.

The girl, on the shore, was back.

She was there with him, under the water, breathing life into him.

She smelled like fresh flowers.

She felt smooth, like a dolphin.

Jed couldn't see her face.

She was too close.

He could hear her voice, though.

She sounded like Lana.

Lana?

Could it be possible?

I must be with a mermaid.

I must be dreaming.

Are you a mermaid?

No response.

Are you Lana?

Rachel?

My nurse?

No response.

She just kept breathing life into him.

As she caressed his head she kept her lips firmly pressed against his.

The water did not feel cold anymore.

The level began to drop.

Jed was still standing.

He was above the water, now.

The man in the boat was back.

He had a familiar face.

"Do you like my boat? Do you like to read, on boats? Did you like the book?"

He asked questions but didn't wait for responses. He didn't give Jed the opportunity.

The answers, though, were obvious.

The boatman was asking rhetorical questions.

"Did you learn the truth? Now you must know it."

He pointed to his head.

On his arm, there was a tattoo.

Like his face, the tattoo was familiar.

" Jacqueline loved him," he said.

"She loved him but he loved another. I helped people ease their pains. I helped Caroline, like she is helping you."

He pointed to the girl who was standing beside Jed, caressing his head.

"I am the *cabeza de turco*."

He leaned on the edge of the boat.

"I was shot but I lived."

He paused.

Jed looked at his face.

Lee?

"I bled." The boatman smiled.

"My doctor stopped my bleeding."

He repeated the statement, changing only one word.

"Your doctor stopped my bleeding."

He smiled

"I lived.

I lived on my boat."
He pointed to his sail.
"Come on to my boat.
I will bring you ashore."
He stretched out his arm and offered Jed a hand.
Jed looked up at the canvas.
There was a picture on the sail.
It looked familiar.
It was a painting of a man hiding behind a rock.
The rock was protecting him from a big wave.
It was attempting to crash down, on him.

Jed felt the girl's lips on the back of his neck.
Her lips felt nice.
He could feel her breath.
She had the breath of life.
She looked like Rachel but she sounded like Lana.
"Get up.
Get up on to that boat." She pointed.
"He will bring you home. He will bring you back. Get up!" She pushed Jed towards the boat.
"Get up!" she repeated. This time she pleaded.

"Wake up, Jed" she pleaded, again.
"Wake up Jed. It's me, Lana. I am here with, Dr. Yen, Jed. He says you can wake up now.
It's ok, Jed. Wake up.
Get up."

Jed opened his eyes.
He saw a familiar face.
"You're here." He smiled. "How are you doing?" His voice sounded raspy. His eyes were heavy.
He looked at the man who was standing beside Lana.
"Hello Dr. Yen. Nice to see you again."

Dr. Yen responded with a warm greeting and asked Jed how he was feeling.

"I was dreaming, I think. I think I might have been dreaming about you, Lana." Jed smiled at her.

"You were one of a few people, in my dream. There were others." Jed nodded.

Lana was smiling but Jed could see that her eyes possessed a look of concern. He looked over at Dr. Yen who was examining the intravenous tube and studying the drip, from the purple liquid.

Dr. Yen sat down on the edge of the bed.

"I am happy that you are awake, now, Mister Jed." He touched Jed's knee.

Like Lana, Dr. Yen was smiling but unlike Lana, his eyes possessed a look of satisfaction. "Now, I should get to know the healthier Mister Jed. Let me have a closer look."

He leaned over and with the instrument that looked like a miniature pool cue, he examined Jed's eyes. He nodded as he made a sound of approval.

"You are doing much better, Mister Jed. You are healing slowly but surely. There is no doubt about that." He smiled at Jed.

Jed thanked him for his encouragement and then looked over at Lana. She was standing by the window.

"Can I get up now?"

Jed struggled. He tried to lift himself, higher, in his bed.

"I tried earlier today, but, then, I felt dizzy. I even felt sick. After my short and unsuccessful attempt, I guess I fell into my deep sleep. But I dreamed, though."

Lana approached the bed.

Dr. Yen stood up and placed his miniature pool cue into the upper left-hand pocket of his lab coat.

"Jed, you have been asleep for two days." He looked serious.

"You have been in a coma." His spoke candidly.

"We have been waiting for you to wake up. When you tried to get out of bed, you must have tugged at this." Dr. Yen held up the intravenous tube to show Jed. "It is little wonder that you felt sick and dizzy. I am also not surprised that you went into a coma." He stood beside Jed's bed. He pointed at him.

"Now, to answer your question, Mister Jed—No! You cannot get up now. Not today, anyway. I do not recommend it."

"Dr. Yen has told me that you've got to stay hooked up to the calyx for a few more days, Jed." Lana took Jed's hand, gently, into hers.

"It will help to heal your head," she encouraged.

Jed frowned. "What exactly is wrong with my head?"

Neither Lana nor Dr. Yen responded.

Jed spoke again. "Two days, Lana? Are you sure?"

Jed looked at Dr. Yen.

"Is that right Doc? Two days? Impossible!

I just spoke with Ossie and Clem a little while ago." He paused. "And Nurse Rogers was in and out, checking on stuff."

Jed looked at his arm.

It was bruised and swollen.

He looked up at the tube and the grape colored liquid that was flowing through it.

Its color reminded him of coral he had seen, years ago, on the bottom, of the Caribbean Sea.

He looked up at Lana.

"What day is it Lana?"

"It's Friday, Jed. Your favorite!"

Doctor Yen walked over to the window.

He looked outside.

"It looks like it's going to be a nice weekend." He looked back at Lana and then at Jed.

He sighed.

His sigh was heavy.

"Mister Jed, it is best that you remain in bed until you are stronger and ready to be on your feet."

Jed frowned. "How long will that be Doctor? I'm getting restless in here."

He looked around the room. "I need to be up and about." He pointed to the window.

"I need to be outside. I need fresh air." He emphasized the word need.

Dr. Yen adjusted his glasses.

"In time, Mister Jed. In time."

"How much longer Doc?" Jed was frustrated.

Doctor Yen tugged at his whiskers. He shrugged his shoulders. He looked at his watch.

"I have to go. I have to make my rounds."

He bid farewell to Jed. He did the same to Lana.

He headed for the doorway.

Before he reached it, he turned and looked back at Jed.

"You'll be in this room until Sunday. Then I will be moving you to *The Center.*

I will have Nurse Rogers check in on you later."

He left.

Jed looked at Lana.

"Did he say the center? What do you think he meant by that?"

Lana smiled. "You'll see."

She sat down on the bed, close to Jed. She rubbed his hand.

"I think he is a good doctor, Jed. He has shared a lot about your condition and the treatment he is providing."

Jed closed his eyes.

"Keep talking. I'm listening. I just want to rest my eyes for a minute."

Lana put her hand on Jed's forehead.

"These bandages must be so hot and so uncomfortable."

She touched Jed's lips.

She ran her fingers along his cheekbone and down the bridge of his nose.

"You'll be okay, Jed."

His eyes remained closed. He nodded.

"You have to be okay, Jed."

His eyes remained closed.

"You must be tired.

I'll let you sleep."

She kissed his hand.

- CHAPTER THREE -

GOOD DRUGS IN DALLAS

Ossie left Edmonton.

He went to Cold Lake to visit the rig. His departure went unnoticed.

It went unnoticed by everyone; by everyone—except Clem.

On Sunday, as expected, Jed was taken off the Calyx and moved from his room in C Block, downstairs to *The Center*.

Clem was assigned to Jed for phase two, of his recuperation.

In time, he and Caly would prove to be the healing force behind Jed's return to wellness.

Through their talks and 'cat walks' Jed would learn a lot, about Clem.

He would also learn a lot about Dr. Yen.

Dr. Yen was a good doctor.

Lana was right!

Clem was with the best.

As Clem would say, "Dr. Yen, he be different man but he be cool."

Jed would laugh at that. He agreed that he was in good hands. Dr. Yen's Calyx *wonder drug* had worked its magic – once again.

Although he was a little more serious than Clem, Dr. Yen was, in Jed's opinion, the kind of innovator and risk taker that the medical world needed.

Clem agreed.

His idiosyncrasies didn't bother Jed.

On the contrary, Jed kind of liked them: the way he would, at times, avoid your question only to answer it, when you least expected.

Or, the way he would tug at his whiskers before he told you something you didn't want to hear.

Jed trusted his wise old Asian doctor; the doctor with the 'history changing' past.

Jed also trusted Clem, his new doctor; the 'rasta medicine man' with the promising future.

Clem told Jed that he was lucky to be one of Dr. Yen's protégés.

"Dr. Yen, he be like a father to me. Ya man. Yen be cool, man."

Clem ran his fingers through his dread locks. "Yen be cool."

Jed enjoyed listening to the way Clem spoke. He was entertained by both *what* he said and *how* he said it.

He shared some of his life experiences, with Jed.

He spoke about how he met Dr. Yen and about his life in Jamaica and Juventud.

Jed appreciated that. He wanted to know more about the islands.

He reciprocated with his own stories about growing up in Alberta and vacationing, on Cape Breton.

Clem appreciated that. He wanted to know more about Canada.

It was late Monday night, when Clem and Jed were sitting around *the island,* in the middle of *The Center's* kitchen, that Dr. Yen asked if he could join them.

Clem and Jed replied affirmatively. "Of course!"

Dr. Yen asked Jed some questions about the oil patch and his role as a 'veteran' driller.

Jed responded as best he could.

He was surprised that Dr. Yen was so interested.

Clem was his usual happy self. He smiled and listened.

It must have been a good hour of talking and sharing when Jed asked Dr. Yen a question about his profession and his role as an 'experimental' doctor.

At first, Jed thought that the word *experimental* offended Dr. Yen.

It didn't. *Thank goodness.*

Dr. Yen said that he had never been described as 'experimental'; "Other adjectives have been used, Mister Jed—but never one so honorable."

Clem and Jed laughed at the word honorable.

Dr. Yen did, too. Jed noticed, again, the whiteness of his teeth.

Jed asked if he could think of a time when he wished he had chosen another profession.

Dr. Yen responded. "That is a good question!"

He proceeded to speak about his early years and some of the discrimination he had encountered, being Asian, in a predominantly white society.

"It was tough enough being in the minority and even tougher being in the minority in my profession."

Jed asked what kind of an impact that had on his practice.

"Not a lot," he replied,

"But there was some." He paused. "One time, in particular," he reflected.

"It was in the fall, of 1963. I had a small office, in Dallas, Texas. A couple of days after President Kennedy was assassinated, I was one of the doctors assigned to save the life of the man who was shot by Jack Ruby."

Jed looked at Dr. Yen.

Theirs eyes locked.

Dr. Yen sat down.

"I believe that I would have been given the opportunity

to save the president's life but my Vietnamese culture and my new Calyx drug were both foreign commodities to the U.S. authorities."

Jed nodded. "I understand."

Dr. Yen continued.

"I also think that if a white American had failed in saving the president's life, it would not have been looked upon so disastrously than if an Asian had failed; especially, in light of the fact that the U.S. was on the brink of war, with Vietnam.

I am sure you can understand that, as well." He stood up.

Jed nodded.

"That was one time that my *experimental* mind, as you call it, Mister Jed, and my race, were two strikes against me. I didn't strike out, though. Basically, the pitcher walked me to first base."

He smiled.

Jed smiled. "Did you make it to home plate?"

"I did end up making it to home plate, Mister Jed. However," he raised his index finger. "If there ever were a time, that I would have preferred to have been in another profession, it was on that hot November day, in Dallas, Texas, in 1963."

He paused.

Jed was curious what that might have been. He asked.

Dr. Yen was happy to respond. "A member of the C.I.A." He looked at Jed. "Or the F.B.I." He rubbed his forehead. "Then, I might have known what was really going on."

He shook his head. "All those shootings and all the stories and all the secrets – who knew what to believe?" He looked at Clem "But then again, as fate would have it—here we are!" He smiled.

"Some good does come out of some bad." He walked

to the 'island' counter and leaned against it. "Would you agree, Clem?"

Clem nodded. "Ya man. Some good, man. Dat be Ossie's dad, man. Some good Yen drug work wonder on dat guy, man."

Jed looked at Dr. Yen.

Clem stood up. "Good drugs in Dallas!"

He stretched. "I tink it's time de driller man met de cat."

He left the room and headed down the hall.

He was gone about a minute. Jed and Dr. Yen sat in contemplative silence. It wasn't an uncomfortable silence.

They were both thinking about the same thing and the same person: The calyx and Lee!

Jed couldn't believe his eyes.

"What is that?"

"It is not what, man; it is who!

Irae! Check it out! This here is Caly." Clem laughed.

He was as proud as a parent, showing off a new baby.

"She is going to help us, my man! She is going to help us to help **you**."

"Wo!" Jed was taken aback.

He was cautious.

"Is she friendly?"

He wanted to greet the lynx, but he didn't know how.

Caly looked at Jed.

Jed looked at Caly.

He backed up, slowly—very slowly – and very cautiously.

Clem laughed.

Dr. Yen laughed.

Clem removed the leash and collar from Caly's neck.

She crawled across the floor, towards Jed.

She moved slowly, with confidence and certainty.

Jed moved back, until he hit the counter. He ran out of backing room.

Dr. Yen and Clem just watched. They didn't appear to be concerned.

Jed could feel the beating of his heart.

The palms of his hands began to moisten.

Caly sensed his fear.

She stopped.

She rolled over, on her back.

She lay in the middle, of the kitchen floor, awaiting a tummy rub.

Jed breathed a sigh, of relief.

"Whew! She's tame."

"She is tame," agreed Dr. Yen.

Clem laughed. "Did ya tink dat I'd take her off dem leash if she was wicked, man?"

"Good question!" Jed was less fearful, now, but still, a little guarded.

Clem stroked Caly's ears and rubbed her tummy.

"She is a five year old Canadian lynx, Mista Jed."

Dr. Yen knelt down beside her. He, too, scratched Caly's ears.

Caly appeared to be enjoying the attention.

She began to purr.

The purring grew louder. The more Clem and Yen scratched, the louder Caly purred.

Jed moved in. Dr. Yen told him that it was okay. "Keep coming. She is like our partner, Mister Jed. I guess you could say that she is like your third doctor." Dr. Yen smiled.

Jed noticed his teeth, again.

Jed knelt down and, discreetly, joined in on the tummy rubbing and ear scratching.

Caly lifted her head. She looked at Jed.

Jed commented on how intelligent she looked.

"She has wise eyes."

Dr. Yen stood up. He walked over to the sink and turned on the tap.

"I'll let this run. She likes her water nice and cold. I bet she's thirsty.

I know I am. Mister Jed, will you give Caly some water?"

"Caly? Is that her name?"

Dr. Yen nodded. "Absolutely, like the calyx medicine."

"Great name! I'd be happy to give her some water. Does she have her own dish or do I get one from the...?"

Dr. Yen interrupted. "If you walk down to the end of the hall you will see **your** room, on the left and in its corner, by the back hatch, you will see **her** bowl."

Jed tilted his head.

He frowned.

Clem laughed. "Yes man. You two gonna be tight," he said. "You gonna get to know each other, real well."

Jed turned towards the hall and began his search for Caly's bowl.

He walked slowly.

"That's nice to see." Dr. Yen smiled. "He is steady, on his feet."

He told Clem that he thought Jed was doing well.

"Yes, man! And getting better all the time."

Caly stood up.

She cleaned herself.

She licked her tummy, the front of her chest and each side of her neck.

Jed returned with the bowl.

"That's my room?"

"And hers." Dr. Yen pointed at Caly.

"Wow! Nice room. Looks comfortable."

"We want you to be comfortable, Mister Jed." Dr. Yen took the bowl from Jed and returned to the sink. He filled it with the running water.

Clem said that Caly was going to enjoy that drink and especially because it was being served by her new patient.

Jed laughed at that. "Her new patient, eh!"

Clem laughed at Jed's 'eh' expression. "A Canadian boy living with a Canadian Lynx!"

"That's right, Clem. Me and Caly—We're Canucks!" Jed was feeling more relaxed, now.

Clem and Dr. Yen enjoyed Jed's humor.

Dr. Yen handed Caly's bowl to Jed. In turn, Jed placed the bowl on the floor, near Caly.

Before she drank, Caly rubbed up against Jed's leg and purred.

"She's almost human, eh!"

Clem nodded. "Yes man, Caly be cool, man."

Dr. Yen excused himself and recommended that Clem do the same.

"Let us leave these two alone. It is time that they got to know each other. After all, Mister Jed," Dr. Yen paused. He placed his hands on his hips.

"You will be spending at least two weeks here, in The Center, with Caly. She has special healing powers." Dr. Yen smiled.

"Let's go Clem."

Clem walked over to Jed. He gave him two thumbs up.

"Catch ya later, man."

"Thanks Clem and you too, Dr Yen."

They left.

Jed looked down at Caly.

She was still drinking her water.

"I'm thirsty, too, Caly."

Jed went to the sink.

He opened the cupboard to get himself a glass.

He turned on the tap.

The water was still cold.

He poured himself a tall glass.

- CHAPTER FOUR -

THE CANADIAN LYNX

Jed's second day, in The Caly Rehabilitation Center, was busy.
Nurse Rogers, however, helped establish order.
She familiarized Jed with his new surroundings and what would, for the next two weeks, be his lifestyle.
Although he was still under the same hospital roof, he was now living under a different ceiling.
He would also be living under a different set of rules, to which he was accustomed.
One consolation, though, was that he would not be bed ridden.
Jed's routine would include such things as strict diet, rigid exercise and patience.
Caly would help him with the latter.
Dr. Yen, Clem and Nurse Rogers all knew of Jed's passion for the outdoors and his anxiety to be a part of them. He was going to have to wait, for the *real thing*, but he would have access to some fresh air and *limited* open space.

When looking at himself, in the mirror, Jed thought that his face looked pale and that his eyes looked tired and bloodshot.
His hair was beginning to grow back, especially, around his scar, where it had been closely shaved.
Nurse Rogers recommended that he drink a lot of fluids.

Jed had no problem with that. He was always thirsty.

She told him to use the treadmill that was located, in the room, across from his. She also recommended that he start building up his muscles, by lifting weights.

"Light weights and lots of reps," she advised.

Jed told her that he understood. He didn't mind lifting weights.

"There's a set of free weights in the treadmill room."

Jed knew. Clem had pointed them out to him, earlier that day. He had even tried lifting some. They felt heavy—even the ten-pound dumb bells.

Nurse Rogers was a kind lady – strict but kind. She was not tall but she carried herself like she was. She had good posture and moved with an air of authority and confidence.

Even Dr. Yen and Clem were on their best behavior, when she was in their presence.

Caly, on the other hand, never changed.

It wasn't taking long, for her and Jed to be comfortable, with one another.

She followed him everywhere. She wouldn't let Jed out of her sight. Whenever or wherever he sat down, she would plunk herself at his feet. She would purr when he was relaxed and pace when he was restless. They were, in many ways, very similar.

"You're two peas in a pod." Nurse Rogers checked Jed's temperature. "You both possess a wild side and," she shook the thermometer, "at the same time, you're both easy to train—and tame." She looked at Caly.

Jed's temperature was normal.

He knew that if he abided by Nurse Rogers' rules and her recommended tight schedule, he would have a speedy recovery. He wanted that very much. He wanted to get back to good health and good living.

"Get some rest, now, Jed and in an hour I want you to go for a work out. Then a good meal will be in order."

"What's on the menu for tonight?" Jed was reluctant to ask.

"Liver and onions." She left Jed's room and headed for the nurse's station. He listened to the sound of her footsteps as she marched down the dimly lit hall.

"Liver and onions? Yuch! Do you like liver and onions, Caly?"

Caly shook her head.

"Me neither." Jed made a face.

He yawned. "I'm going to crash out for a while."

He went into his bedroom.

Caly followed close behind.

- CHAPTER FIVE -

THE PREFONTAL CORTEX

The Caly Rehabilitation Center was a large complex that covered the entire basement of The Edmonton General. It was more like a dormitory than anything else. It was equipped with medical paraphernalia, first-aid supplies and tubes filled with the purple calyx.

The Center housed five 'two-bedroom' apartments.

Each suite was furnished with tables and chairs, bathroom and kitchen facilities as well as the necessary bedroom comforts. Each featured a theme room, which, in most cases was the master bedroom. The themes were intentionally designed, by Dr. Yen, to expedite the healing process.

Jed's suite was embellished with a nature motif splashed with murals and paintings of the Canadian wilderness. Other suites included aquariums, filled with tropical fish, spaces stations, with space-aged furniture and some even had 'Star Trek' murals.

Jed was impressed with Dr. Yen's creative genius. Clem told him that he had some input, as well. Jed told him that he was creative, too.

One room, the Asian room, was filled with some of Dr. Yen's own personal possessions.

That is where he lived.

All suites led to the fitness facility, the swimming pool and the sauna.

Jed's suite 'The Outdoorsman' was the only one that had an outside patio.

That, of course, was convenient, for Caly.

The patio was a large fenced-in area that could be accessed from two locations: Jed's master bedroom and the fitness center. It was originally intended to be a yard or play area for Caly but previous patients found its design and décor to be both therapeutic and appealing. Consequently, Dr. Yen stated that people—and not just animals—could benefit from its use. All members of The Center were encouraged to visit the patio, at any time.

Dr. Yen and Clem spent their evening going over some notes and sharing their optimism and opinions, about Jed's prognosis: he was moving, in the right direction.

"One week, I estimate, and he will be ready to return to the rig and to his life on the *outside*."

Clem did a double take when Dr. Yen referred to Jed's life, away from The Center, as that of the *outside*.

"Ya man, cool! Irae man! But Jed ain't in prison here, Doc."

"No! You are correct in saying that, Clem, however, Jed is, in his own way, imprisoned – just as I am—and always will be. "

He paused. He looked at his hands.

"And just as Caly is."

He paused again.

He walked over to the fridge and opened its door.

From the bottom shelf, he pulled out a bottle of Red Stripe.

Then, he opened the counter drawer and rummaged through some cutlery. He found a bottle opener.

He opened the Red Stripe.

He held it out in front of Clem.

Clem awaited Dr. Yen's next move and comment.

"And just as you are, my Rasta doctor. Cheers!"

Clem just stared.

Dr. Yen took a sip.

He swallowed.

He wiped his lips.

He let out a refreshing sigh.

He spoke again.

"And—just as you are."

He passed the bottle over to Clem.

Clem thanked Dr. Yen. He took a sip and then handed it back.

"I hear ya talkin', man. I hear ya talkin'."

"In time, Mister Jed will know. Until then, we must help him continue to heal."

"Caly gonna help too, man."

"Absolutely, Caly is going to help. However, Mister Jed will have his moments; you know what I mean?"

"I hear ya. I have mine." Clem looked at Dr. Yen.

Dr. Yen smiled. "As do I.

Speaking of which, can I get you a beer?" Dr. Yen held up his. "After all, these are your favorite."

Clem shook his head." No tanks, man. I be headin' out, now. Clem's gots himself a date, tonight."

Dr. Yen raised his eyebrows. "Oh, with anyone, I know?"

Clem walked over to Dr. Yen's sink. He turned on the tap and let the cold water run for a few seconds. He tested it with his fingers and then helped himself to a glass from the cupboard. He was obviously familiar with Dr. Yen's apartment and especially with the accessories, in the kitchen.

He poured himself a tall glass.

He drank.

He wiped his lips and then drank again.

"Yes, man! You know the lady man. She be Nurse Rogers, man. She be off at nine and I be meeting her at

Mista Jed's room. Then we go for some Japanese cuisine, man. Very cool! Nurse Rogers—ya man."

Dr. Yen agreed. "And she is a good nurse, too."

Clem took another drink of his water.

"Jed goin' to love this stuff, Doc." He rinsed his glass and placed it on the counter, upside down, beside the sink.

"The dishwasher, Rasta man."

Clem tilted his head.

He frowned.

He looked back at the inverted glass, by the sink.

"Yes, man. The dishwasher."

He opened the dishwasher and placed the glass on its appropriate shelf.

He looked back at Dr. Yen.

Then, he looked at his watch.

He thanked him and then headed for the door.

"I get ready for my date, now. Then I check in on Mista Jed."

Dr. Yen stood up and followed him.

"He'll be fine, Clem. You go and enjoy your date. I'll make certain that Nurse Williams continues to monitor him throughout the night."

"I make a quick visit anyway. Jed be cool, doc. Jed be cool!"

Clem smiled and nodded.

As he reached for the door handle, Dr. Yen placed his hand on Clem's arm.

"You're right, Clem, Jed **is** going to love his liquids."

Clem looked at Dr. Yen.

Dr. Yen paused.

"He is going to **need** them too."

Clem nodded again.

Then he turned the handle.

Seconds later, he was turning the handle of the door, leading to Jed's suite.

For obvious reasons, the doors, on level B1, in The Caly Rehabilitation Center, were always left unlocked. Patients' privacy was greatly respected and duly practiced, however, doctors and nurses were able to gain access to the suites, at any time, in the event of emergency.

Clem politely knocked, as he opened Jed's door.

After letting himself in, he quietly shut the door.

The first thing he noticed was the dim lighting in the front hall.

He figured that Nurse Rogers had deliberately set it that way, knowing how soothing the soft lights would be.

As he made his way down the hall, Clem could feel a slight breeze and smell the scent of crisp fresh air.

When he approached Jed's bedroom, he could hear the sounds of music, lightly emanating, from the distance.

Upon entering Jed's room, he paused for a moment to pan the walls and murals of the Canadian wilderness. Clem was comforted as he mused over Jed's fondness of nature.

Caly saw Clem first.

She startled him.

With a welcoming purr, she rubbed herself up against his leg.

"What ya be doin my slinky feline? You scare Clem, man."

Clem looked around Jed's room. "Where Mista Jed be at?"

The patio door was open.

Clem called out. "Are you outside Mista Jed?"

Clem followed Caly out the door.

The words of The Traveling Wilburys' *"Handle Me*

with Care" harmonized, from the ghetto blaster, strategically positioned at the foot of a patio bench.

Jed was lying on the bench, with both his arms folded behind his head.

Although it was a relatively clear night the encroaching darkness made it difficult for Clem to detect whether or not Jed's eyes were opened. His head, however, was tilted towards the sky giving Clem the impression that Jed was stargazing.

"Dat's a good tune, eh Mista Jed!" Clem was near the bench.

"George Harrison always sound good, man."

Jed turned his head towards Clem.

He reached down and lowered the volume of the ghetto blaster.

He remained on the bench. He leaned up on an elbow.

Caly circled once and then dropped herself by the bench.

"Were you sleepin' man—or just checkin' out dem bright star?"

"A little bit of both, I think." Jed pointed to the ghetto blaster.

"Mostly groovin' to the tunes, though. I might have dozed off a little bit earlier."

"Ya man." Clem looked up at the sky.

He looked around the patio. He rubbed his arms and then quickly folded them, revealing his discomfort with the early evening chill.

"Are you happy with this set up, Mista Jed?" Clem nodded and smiled, hoping that Jed would do the same.

He looked around the patio. "We call this place 'De Catwalk'."

Jed lifted himself into a sitting position and, like Clem, surveyed the patio's surroundings.

"The Catwalk? That's a good name for it. It likely provides Caly with just about everything she needs."

"Ya man! Caly like dat tree and dem rocks, man. Irae Caly." Clem sat down on the bench beside Jed. He leaned over and began scratching Caly behind her ears. She rolled onto her back and lifted her front paws. She wanted a tummy rub.

Jed laughed. "She's no fool."

He got up and walked towards the patio door.

He looked at the fence and the outside wall of The Caly Rehabilitation Center.

Then, he did an about face.

"My new home is comfortable but not comforting. I sure am glad that I don't have to stay here long."

Clem stopped scratching.

He leaned back.

He tilted his head.

Jed walked over to one of Caly's big rocks.

He leaned against it.

He looked up at the sky.

He looked back at Clem.

"Don't get me wrong, Clem, I appreciate what you and Dr. Yen have done here." He extended an arm, as if he were presenting The Catwalk. "And how much you both have done to help me get back on my feet and rejuvenate my strength."

He paused.

"But," Jed shook his head.

"Something ain't feeling right, though, Clem."

Clem stood up.

He walked over and stood beside Jed.

Caly followed and then, with ease, sprang onto the rock, on which Jed and Clem were leaning.

Clem put his arm around Jed.

"I be ready to talk now, Mista Jed."

Jed looked at Clem.

"Ya man, and you be ready to listen, man."

Clem walked towards the door. He gestured for Jed to join him inside.

Caly remained on her rock. She appeared to be studying Jed, as he peeked over his shoulder.

Once inside, Clem explained to Jed that he didn't have a lot of time but that he wanted to discuss a few things before he had to leave to meet Nurse Rogers.

Jed said that he thought that it was cool that Clem was taking Nurse Rogers out for dinner.

Clem agreed. "Ya man, she be a good lady, man. We be lucky to know her."

Jed nodded. "That's for sure! She is kinda strict with me, though." Jed smiled.

Clem laughed.

"Wit me too, man.

Ya man! Wit me too."

Clem sat down on one of the kitchen stools and leaned an elbow on the island's counter.

Jed joined him on the other side.

"It's nice and warm in here, eh?"

Clem nodded. "Ya man. It not be summer out der yet."

Jed looked around the room.

"I can only appreciate these paintings, for so long, Clem." He pointed at an A.Y. Jackson that was hanging on the wall, above the fridge.

He looked back at Clem.

"Do you know what I mean?"

"Ya man, I like de real ting too, man. You and I be outdoors guys."

Clem leaned over as if he were getting ready to tell Jed a secret.

"Dat's another reason why Clem needs to talk, Mista Jed."
He looked into Jed's eyes.
"Irae man?"
Jed nodded.

Clem stood up.
Jed watched him as he made his way around the island to the kitchen sink.
"Do you want some ting to drink, man?"
Clem took a couple of glasses from the cupboard, above the stove.
He turned on the cold-water tap.

"Good idea." Jed's eyes brightened.

Clem handed him a full glass of water.
Jed thanked him.

"I know you gots to get back on your feet and I sure know dat you can do dat, man, but everyting got to be cool, man, wit you head, man, before you get to see dat big Alberta sky and dem bright yellow sun."
Clem paused.
"And not from within de fence walls of dat Catwalk, man." He pointed.
Jed looked back at the door, leading to the patio.
Clem took a sip of his water.

"Yes man!" He wiped his lips.
He smiled.
His teeth were pearly white.
Clem shook his head.

"No problem."
He repeated.
"No problem."

Jed chuckled at the way Clem spoke.
"I like your accent, Clem. It reminds me of the islands."

"Ya man, de islands—like in dem good ol' days." He looked at Jed.
Jed looked at Clem.
Clem continued.
"Dat is what I'm going to do for you, man. Clem is going to bring you back.

I'm gonna bring your head back, Mista Jed; back to dem place where you feel cool runnin' – irae—all de time. Ya man!"
He returned to the stool. "Now ain't dat irae, man?"
"Sounds great, Clem. I want to get myself back, too.

So how are you going to bring my head back?" Jed asked, as he sunk his teeth into a juicy apple, that he got from a fruit bowl, in the middle of the island.
"You be takin' three calyx tablets a day, now Jed.
No more intravenous.
Yes man!"
Clem sipped his water.
Jed did the same with his.
Clem nodded. "A clean and cool head. Yes man!"
He wiped his lips.
He continued.
"You see Jed, the calyx is some heavy stuff and you gots to be real sick to be takin' it."
Clem looked into Jed's eyes.
He raised his glass.
"Side effects, too, man."
He took a sip.

"Your head was banged up some bad stuff, Mista Jed, man. Some bad." He shook his head.

"Dr. Yen, he tink dat you be dealin' with some big time headaches if you no be takin' dem calyx, man."

Clem pointed at Jed's head. "Ya man! I tink dat you gots to be takin' dat *glial* for some days, now, man. Ya man. Dem soon come."

"Taking what?"

Jed frowned. He was confused.

Clem leaned forward.

Just before he had the opportunity to respond to Jed's question, Caly appeared in the kitchen doorway.

She caught Jed by surprise.

Jed told Clem that he thought she looked concerned.

"She is concern, man." Clem said that was only natural. "She care about you, man. She know too that you gots to be takin' dat glial, man."

"Oh ya? What is that stuff?"

Clem stood up and walked to the sink.

" You see, Mista Jed, the haemostatic calyx is a substitute for dem glial cells that be in your brain, man.

After you accident, your head be all messed up and dem neural network be totally outta sync, man.

So, Doctor Yen help put your synapses, or *spaces* in dat head, back together. Ya man!"

Clem pointed at Jed's head. Then, he turned on the tap.

"More water, man?"

"Please." Jed handed him his glass.

"You sound pretty scientific, Clem."

Jed perched himself higher in the stool.

"I hope I do, Mista Jed. Ya man, I hope I sounds like I knows what I be sayin', man."

He smiled.

"You see, me and the doctor are what you would be callin' *neuroscientists*.

Ya man, we are dem scientists, man. Dem scientists for de head, man!"

Clem tugged at his dread locks and tucked them behind his ears.

"Scientists for the head?" Jed scratched the back of his head.

Clem said that Jed looked concerned.

"What is the drug doing to me, Clem, besides healing my wounds?"

"Good question, Mista Jed! Ya man, good tinkin'!"

He paused.

"Well, it not be messing you up, man, so you can keep a cool head, Mista Jed.

No problem, man. No *big* problem, man!"

"And exactly what do you mean, Clem, by no ***big*** problem?" Jed continued to scratch his head.

"Well, it be like dis, man." Clem returned to his stool.

"De calyx fixes up dem brain, when it can't do it by hisself, man.

The brain has dem axons, which be like connectors, from dem dendrites to dem cells.

Dem brain is made up of neurons, called dat neural network, man."

"Even though you are losing me a bit, Clem, keep going.

I want to learn more about what's happening, inside my head."

Jed stopped scratching.

He reached out for Caly.

She moved in closer and slouched, by his feet.

"Irae man.

She is so irae man.

I will carry on.

The brain is an amazing ting, with lots of stuff in it, called myelin. The myelin is a fatty substance, which coats dem axons of dem neurons.

That coating is crucial, man, because it act like insulation and allow dem messages to travel quickly, without no failure in dat transmission.

It's like a link, to your memory, man."

"Like a link or a lynx?"

Jed smiled and jerked his head in Caly's direction.

"Very cool, man."

Clem smiled.

"Very cool.

When de brain be hit like yours, de calyx help all dem stuff work like dey supposed to. But when de head be better, man, you got to cool it wit dem drug, because then it start workin' in a different way, making you tired, all de time.

One of dem main areas, man, to be myelated, is in de prefrontal cortex, behind dem forehead."

Clem reached over and pressed his hand, against Jed's forehead.

"This is where decision-making, planning and higher order tinking take place.

Dat area, my man, is also associated with dat short-term memory.

I be honest wit you, man. You x-rays indicate all dat is comin' cool, wit your prefrontal cortex.

The calyx fix you, man, like it supposed to.

And so, Mista Jed, Clem be tinking dat der be some other problem, troublin' you Mista Jed, man.

Maybe not a physical one, man.

No man, Clem be tinking, that you got some other ting, you be dealing with.

Talk to me man.

Tell me something, now.

You gots to tell me, man, where you be at.

You can tell Clem, man. I'm like your new doctor, now."

Jed put down his half-eaten apple and looked into Clem's trusting eyes.

He thought that his eyes looked as brown as Caly's.

As Jed studied Clem, Caly studied Jed.

Jed took a sip of his water.

He licked his lips.

"Clem, I will talk to you."

Jed paused.

"It is now my turn to talk and for you to listen.

I am not a neuroscientist, Clem, but I think I can enlighten you with something as you, this evening, have done for me.

I will put my trust in you, Clem, my new and observant doctor."

Clem smiled.

Jed leaned over the island. This time, it was he who looked like he was the one who was going to be telling secrets.

"I will tell you "someting", man."

Clem laughed at Jed's attempt to speak with a Jamaican accent.

Jed laughed, too.

Caly stood up and then stretched like she was ready to go somewhere. Then she slouched, again. This time, she dropped herself, at Clem's feet.

- CHAPTER SIX -

PURR

When Nurse Rogers arrived, Clem asked for a few minutes. He and Jed were still working things out.

Nurse Rogers understood.

She busied herself, in the living room, with a crossword puzzle. She browsed through a sports magazine and a 'People' magazine.

In the kitchen, Jed shared his thoughts.

He talked about how he pretended to have memory loss, when he came out of his coma. He explained that he had been wrestling with things. He didn't know who to trust and what to believe. He told Clem that he still had his doubts. Clem understood.

Jed said that he didn't think the accident should have occurred.

Clem responded, "Dat's why dey call dem tings accidents, man." He cautioned Jed not to be too suspicious. He told him that Ossie could be trusted. "He's a good man. I knows dat guy, for a long time, man. He be cool."

Jed knew that Ossie had gone to the rig to do a thorough investigation. He was grateful, for that. He told Clem that he agreed that Ossie was trustworthy. "I trust him, fully, Clem. It's just that, at the time." Jed shook his head. "I don't know."

Clem stood up. He went to the sink for some water. He looked concerned. He told Jed that feigning memory loss could backfire, especially since Jed was on the calyx. "We got to know how you head be, man. Wit no mind games."

Jed promised that he was 'true blue', now. He wouldn't be faking anything, anymore. He only did it, temporarily, when he was worried about stuff.

As for being wary about people, Clem told Jed not to be.

He didn't think that somebody would deliberately set the explosion.

Jed respected Clem's thinking, but insisted that he was caught off guard, when he woke up in a hospital bed, with tubes stuck in his arms.

"Something," as Jed put it, "Just wasn't sitting right."

Jed explained that there were just too many coincidences.

"Number one:" he stated, "Some of the people, who have or have had connections to Lee, just happened to be in Edmonton, at the time, of the blow-out, or shortly thereafter."

Clem frowned. "Who dat be, man?"

Jed pointed at him. "Well, you, for one, Clem." Then he mentioned Ossie and Dr. Yen.

Clem shook his head. "But you didn't know, man, at dat time, dat me and de good doctor be connected to Lee, man." He smiled. He drank some water.

Jed agreed. "True."

"You be paranoid, my man, Mista Jed."

Jed shrugged. "Perhaps."

Clem urged Jed to 'stay cool'. "I set dem record straight, man."

He reminded Jed that, at the time, of the blow-out, he and Dr. Yen had been in Edmonton for two years.

"Ya man! We be workin' here, man, like we be doin' for two years, man. Me and the good doctor been here since we come down from Fort McMurray. It don't matter dat we be connected to Mista Lee, man."

Jed frowned. He tilted his head, in reflective thought.

"Clem? If I ask you a question, will you answer me, honestly?"

Clem looked serious. Jed was not accustomed to that look. Clem was usually given to smiling and laughing, when in the company of others.

He finished his water. He sat down beside Jed. "Clem never lie, man. Clem be honest!"

Jed nodded. "I thought so. That's why I'm going to ask you if you and Dr. Yen were specifically assigned to me, after I was brought in, after the explosion?"

Clem swallowed. He dragged his fingers through his locks. He stood up He leaned against the island. He looked at Jed.

"Yes, man, we be assigned."

Jed nodded.

Clem continued. "Dr. Yen got de call from Mista Lee, man." He breathed a sigh of honest relief. "We be tellin' you, Mista Jed, man, soon come, but we tink we wait, irae?"

Jed thanked Clem for his honesty. He told him that he felt better, now, after talking. Clem said that he was happy, now, that Jed was feeling 'irae'.

Jed asked if he could ask one more question.

Clem nodded. "One more, man, den I gots to go." He gestured to the living room where Nurse Rogers was, patiently, waiting.

"Last one, Clem—for real." Jed paused. He stood up and walked over to the island.

He looked at Clem. "Who notified Lee, about the blow-out, before he called Dr. Yen?"

Clem smiled. "Dat be easy, man." He opened the dishwasher and placed his glass on the appropriate ring. "Slim Jim ol' lady, man. She be cousin to Lee ol' lady, man. She call Marina. Marina tell Lee. Lee tell Yen. Dat be how all dem ting be happenin'. Irae, man?"

"Wow!" Jed was surprised. "That's incredible!"

"What?" Clem closed the dishwasher.

"We're all connected." Jed shook his head. He sat down, again.

"No, man." Clem put a hand on Jed's shoulder. "We all be linked, man." He looked down at Caly who was faithfully, sitting by Jed's side. "We all be lynx, man." He smiled. He looked at his watch. "Gots to go, man." He left the kitchen.

Jed followed.

Caly followed Jed.

"Clem?"

Jed was curious.

"Yes man."

"You don't happen to know what happened to my watch, do you?" He emphasized 'my'.

Clem turned. He looked at Jed. "More question, man?"

Jed shrugged. "Different topic." He smiled.

"You watch, man?"

Jed nodded. "Yes! Ever since the blow-out my watch has not resurfaced."

"Maybe it fell off when dey load you on dem stretcher, man." Clem shrugged.

"I came in on a stretcher?" Jed was surprised.

"Yes man." Clem laughed. "You be on dem stretcher but no watch be stretchin' on dem arm."

Jed smirked. "Funny guy."

Clem reached out for Jed's arm and placed his hand around his wrist. "You don't need no watch, man. Dat wrist look good witout one."

They entered the living room.

Nurse Rogers looked up. She was sitting on the couch, with the newspaper sprawled out before her, on the coffee table.

"Hello gentlemen!" She smiled. She was all dressed up. Jed thought that she looked pretty.

"I be ready now, my lady." Clem smiled. He extended a hand.

"Thanks!" She looked at Jed. "How are you doing?" Her concern was genuine.

"I'm feeling a lot better, thanks." Jed nodded.

She looked at his head.

She looked into his eyes.

She didn't say anything.

She turned to Clem. "We're okay to head out, now? Jed will be fine.

Nurse Williams has prepared some stew." She looked at Jed. "Better than last night's liver and onions, eh?"

Jed said that they weren't all that bad. "You can heat up the stew, whenever you're hungry. But, don't eat too late, though." She paused. She looked at Clem.

"His fridge still has plenty of fluids, in it, I presume?"

Clem nodded. He pointed towards the kitchen.

"And dem tap gots lots of cool water, man."

Jed smiled.

"I'll be fine. Go have supper."

Nurse Rogers and Clem bid Jed, goodnight. They told him that if he needed anything that Nurse Williams was on call.

She pointed at the pager, by the couch.

"There are call buttons in every room."

"I'll be fine." Jed wished them both a delicious dinner and then closed the door behind them.

"Come on, Caly." Jed led the way, back to the kitchen.

"Do you want something to drink?"

He picked up her bowl and went to the sink.

She followed.

"And so Caly, what do you make of all this?"

Caly looked up at Jed as if she understood exactly what he was asking.

He filled her dish with cold water.

The water felt good as it splashed on Jed's hands and arms.

Jed then placed the dish on the floor beside Caly's food bowl.

"There ya go. Enjoy!"

Caly was thirsty.

She drank quickly and noisily.

When she finished, she walked over to Jed and rubbed up against his leg.

Her fur felt nice.

Jed went into the bathroom.

He looked at himself in the mirror.

His hair was growing back.

It was covering his scar

The stitches were dissolving.

He was no longer suffering from migraines or heavy fatigue.

He was more alert.

He was determined to return to perfect health, as quickly as possible.

He was anxious to get back to the rig and back to nature.

He left the bathroom and headed for his room.

He picked up the remote control for the ghetto blaster and scanned for something upbeat.

Caly stayed close by his side.

"So what kind of music do you like, Caly?"

She slumped onto the floor.

"The Stray Cats?

Cat Stevens?"

She looked up at him.

She licked her chops.

Jed patted the top of her head and scratched behind her ears.

She liked that.

The purring was soothing—for both of them.

PART 4

THE MEMOIRS OF
C. LEE BOUVIER

- CHAPTER ONE -

CAMELOT

After settling into the comfort of the COPS tug, Jed sipped at some black coffee. He opened the book to page one. He was a little nervous. That was out of character, for him. Under normal circumstances, fear would not be a factor.

Now, it was.

Knowing too much is not good, he told himself to pretend he knew nothing.

He reread the greeting from Caroline Bouvier and pondered her words: *To Lee! Thought you might appreciate these. Thanks for your pains. Caroline, 1964.*

The coffee tasted strong. It also tasted thick. Actually, it tasted lousy.

Jed wanted to remain alert. He drank it, anyway.

He felt that it was crucial for him to read carefully and slowly. He didn't want to miss a thing.

He was in the mood to read.

He was in the mood to learn.

He knew that he needed quiet and alone time, since the moment he had set his eyes on Caroline's book. The interesting thing, though, was that he didn't feel totally alone.

It was as though Caroline was right there beside him, on the tug, telling her story.

Jed held her book, in his hands, like it was sacred. He knew that the book was precious. It would serve to reinforce all that he was feeling; all that he was thinking; and all that he was hearing: feelings from Ossie – thoughts from within—words from Lee.

Jed took another sip of the coffee.

He turned the page to Chapter One.

Caroline's words possessed a tone that invited him into her world. The narrative voice was honest, sincere and welcoming.

Jed inferred a sense of loneliness and frustration. He couldn't help but think that she was writing the words for Lee, and to Lee, and not simply for herself and about herself.

Jed read:

"Marilyn was a doll. He would pull and he would push like she was a thing and not a person. When Jack first introduced her to me, he did so in a manner as one might do when introducing a new hair product or brand of toothpaste. Marilyn would just smile and nod her head at everything Jack said and at everything Jack did. When he touched her, she moved in closer—but the closer she moved the more distant she became. He showed off his 'Barbie' and she allowed him to do it. She was a doll. She was his doll. I often wondered how Jacqueline felt."

Jed stopped reading. He took another sip. He closed the book and rubbed his eyes. They were stinging, a little. He wanted to read some more. He got up to replenish his coffee. He went out onto the upper deck and followed the sun as it sank into the Caribbean. The lights of Juventud were, slowly, coming alive. He could hear the sounds of the Spanish rhythms, flowing, across the water, emanating from nearby boats. He wondered what the patrons might be doing down at the Que Pasa, in Havana.

He thought about Lana.

He thought about Rachel.

He thought about Caroline.

He thought about Jacqueline.

The coffee tasted stronger, now.
Jed went back inside.

Chapter two was different.
In the second chapter, Caroline's tone was more jovial. She poked fun at herself and she even took a few jabs at her sister.

In Chapter two, she wrote about her myriad of experiences in New England. She wrote about her teenage sweethearts, her screen idols, and her successes and failures at middle school and high school. She wrote about her first job working in the Greenwood Plaza as a bus girl and how she gradually advanced to the position of front desk receptionist. She described her short but memorable career as a translator, translating *New England* English into Parisian French. She raved over the guests and painted a vivid picture of their children – most adorable but extremely spoiled. Jed was not surprised to read about that.

It wasn't until the latter part of chapter two, when she alluded to the myriad of experiences working in the Texas Book Depository, that Jed intensified his reading and his inferential eye. He panned the words like a submarine periscope checking the horizon for icebergs and enemy ships. The sentences unfolded before him and, like biblical readings, leaping off the pages informing, entertaining and, most importantly, enlightening. He read:

· *"My knowledge of Russia was based solely on that which I got from American history books and television. I even remember praying for the Russians, specifically, to the Virgin Mary, requesting that they be freed from their bondage and saved from eternal damnation. I knew as much about Russia as I did about Cuba. Both places, in my indoctrinations, were reported as satanically doomed. It wasn't until I met one of my fellow employees that my feelings about Russia and Cuba changed. He shared with me passionate stories about his Russian wife and his Cuban friends."*

Jed put down the book.
He looked at his watch.
He had been reading for over an hour.
He returned to the tug's parapet and leaned over. He looked down at the water. It seemed darker, now, than it was when he first arrived. Like the sky, it was not as bright—not as green—and not as welcoming. He thought that a cigar would go well to enhance the mood.

Jed was not a heavy smoker, however, there were occasions when he would treat himself to a cigarette or a cigar. Unfortunately, on this occasion, he didn't have any smokes.

He returned to Ossie's 'captain's chair' and turned the pages of **Caroline's Memoirs** to Chapter Three.

In this chapter, he learned about her love for writing. He learned that she found it therapeutic. He also learned that, for her, writing was an escape—a friend—and a confidante.

Jed was honored to read her words.
He felt like he was getting to know her.
Her tone evoked a sense of warmth. It provided Jed with a feeling of trust and comradeship.

Jacqueline had a very special sister. It's little wonder that she and Jack named their first daughter after her.

Jed continued reading.

"I always knew that they were more involved than they should have been. Right from the start, whenever Jacqueline spoke about Sammy and his family, she did so in a

manner that was both protective and defensive. She would shrug it off to 'their world', and called it a world of money, politics, and entertainment. She would defend Jack when he was away celebrating with Peter Lawford and Frank Sinatra. The 'family', as she called it, was closely knit. We were 'hand in hand' she would say and besides, Jack loved them all...and they loved Jack. After all, along with Joe, they helped pave the road for his presidency.

Jed paused for a moment.

He looked out the porthole. The Caribbean sky was turning black.

He looked down at the opened page.

He continued to read.

I loved her for her compassion. I loved her for her understanding. I loved her for her loyalty. I especially loved her for the way she loved her children.

But I hated her too.

I hated her naivety and her innocence. How could such an intelligent and beautiful person be so gullible? How could my sister be so fooled? I guess that's what they call being a devoted wife trapped in the world of politics.

Wait a minute... maybe she wasn't being fooled. Maybe it was I, all along, who was the naive one.

She did, after all, marry Aristotle.

Jed stopped reading.

He looked at his watch. 7:13.

He placed the book on the 'pull-out' table beside the 'captain's chair'.

He rubbed his eyes.

He picked up the book.

This time, his intention was not to read it.

He turned to page 63—the page on which lay the picture of Caroline and Lee. It was the picture of the two of them in front of (what appeared to be) a barn or a large storage shed.

Jed recalled the first time he set eyes on that picture.

Its original was housed in a little frame, on a shelf in Lee's study.

He examined it. His examination was close and thorough.

He thought that it might be set somewhere in the mid west of the U.S.

Of the barn or shed, however, he was not as certain.

It could be one of many storage sheds that can be seen along the roads of Cuba and Juventud.

If that is the case, the setting might not be in the U.S.

He read the inscription.

To Lee, Love, always, your friend, Caroline.

Jed closed his eyes.

The caffeine was losing the 'sleep' battle.

He leaned back in the 'captain's chair'.

He nestled his head, into the leather folds.

He swiveled.

He rested his feet on the 'pull-out' table.

He began to drift.

The water, the sky and his mind were all dark, deep and distant.

He dreamed.

He dreamed of a writer – an insightful writer.
However, her words could not be published.
What a shame!
The truth could not be told.

He dreamed about a prince and a princess; their marriage was a fairytale, beautiful and romantic—a fairytale.

He dreamed about a family – its members would kill in the name of politics.

He dreamed about an intellectual who became a scapegoat, a patsy, and a cabeza de turco.

He dreamed about Rachel and her sister.
Rachel was warm and she smelled nice.
Her sister was invisible.
Rachel was a smooth swimmer; she was tender and seductive.
She was slippery!
Her eyes were dark and enticing.
Her sister, on the other hand, had no face.

In his dream, Jed told himself to remember what he was dreaming. He wanted to wake up immediately and write it down. Fortunately, that would not be necessary. It was already written.

In a sense, his dream was already recorded!

Upon awakening, he would simply have to open a book entitled ***The Memoirs of C. Lee Bouvier.***

- CHAPTER 2 -

THE CHIEF

Jed opened an eye.

He looked down at his wrist.

The night light of his *Aqua Indi* illuminated the time: 5:01.

He looked around the tug.

He was disoriented.

He looked outside.

It was dark.

He opened his other eye.

He looked down at his watch again and then rubbed both eyes.

He leaned forward.

His neck felt cramped.

He was hungry.

His mouth felt dry.

He was cold.

Juventud's early morning was humid, damp and thick.

It reminded Jed of his mornings, on the rig.

After he stretched, he pushed himself from Ossie's captain's chair and dragged himself into the kitchenette.

He rubbed his stomach. He could hear and feel it growling. It didn't hurt, though, but Jed knew that he needed to eat, really soon.

He hoped that Ossie had left some food in the pantry.

He opened the latch of the 'canned goods' door and

smiled at the sight of a label marked **chopped pineapples.**

Ossie, and his pineapples. Jed chuckled.

And now, if I could only find the ingredients to make a pizza.

After struggling to find a salt-crusted can opener, from the cracked wooden drawer, Jed opened the crusty lid.

He gobbled down some pineapples—two cubes at a time.

He continued eating as he walked out onto the deck.

He looked down at the water. It was splashing gently against the side of the tug. It still looked dark.

He looked up at the sky.

Jed could see that it was getting a little brighter; especially in the east.

He shivered. He scooped up the remaining pineapple pieces from the bottom of the can and then went back inside.

He returned to the pantry and searched, once again, for something to eat.

Concealed and, what appeared to be intentionally well hidden behind a jar of peanut butter, was a box of animal crackers.

That'll do.

He had to work hard to loosen the lid, off the peanut butter jar. All that tong tightening, on the rigs, finally came in handy.

He dipped the first cracker into the jar. It was an elephant.

Although the elephant was a little stale, the peanut butter masked its taste.

Jed reached into the box for another cracker.

He pulled out a monkey.

Following that was a giraffe, another monkey, and then a pig.

Jed spoke to the little pig cookie. "A pig for a rig pig!"

Then he popped it into his mouth. "That's the end of that."

Jed returned to the captain's room.

He looked at Ossie's chair and then at the book sitting on the side table.

He looked out the window through the tiny porthole.

The sky was almost completely bright.

He still felt tired.

He also felt a little restless.

He walked towards the book and then stopped. He turned towards the four little steps that led up to the deck. He walked towards them.

"I've got to get off this tug for a while and go for a walk. I should get some fresh air and exercise."

Jed was not uncomfortable talking to himself.

He climbed the steps leading to the upper deck. With each step he thought more about Caroline's writing. He said her name to himself and then repeated her middle name as he arrived on deck. He walked towards the gangplank. *The name Lee? It's hers, it's his, and it's even the name of that famous American general. Just too many connections.*

"Just too many loose ends," he said aloud. "A story that might have fooled us all—Well, mostly all of us."

He walked towards the market place.

He recalled a line from a movie entitled ***One Flew Over the Cuckoo's Nest***.

It was a line from the scene where R.P. MacMurphy, whose character, played by Jack Nicholson, says to the Chief, "You fooled 'em Chief; you fooled 'em all."

He recalled when MacMurphy offered the Chief a piece of Juicy Fruit gum—and the Chief, who was supposedly deaf and dumb, at the time, gratefully accepted with a "thank you!"

What a scene! Jed chuckled to himself.

What a sting! He laughed out loud.

"I could use a piece of Juicy Fruit gum myself, right now." He spoke out loud.

Jed wondered whether or not they sold gum at the market.

He continued heading east.

The sun was considerably brighter, now, than it had been when he first woke up.

He squinted as he looked ahead.

He wished that he had remembered his sunglasses.

He told himself that he must get some new ones, along with some chewing gum, while sauntering through the 'Juventud Docks Market' – '*El Muelles Juventud*'.

He thought about Rachel.

He stopped walking.

He looked back at the tug.

It was quite a distance away. Nevertheless, it still looked safe and inviting.

He paused.

He looked out at the water.

He looked back at the tug.

Thank you Caroline. He nodded.

He looked southerly, in the direction of Lee's home—way up in the hills of Juventud.

He paused.

He took a deep breath.

Thank you Lee!

He turned back in the direction of the market.

He continued walking.

First stop: shades!

- CHAPTER 3 -

THE SETTING SON

There was a slight breeze blowing off the Caribbean.

Jed could smell, taste and feel the salt as it refreshed his nostrils and sparkled his arms.

He stopped walking.

He looked out at the water.

It looked tempting—he thought about taking a plunge.

He had vowed, the last time he was on rig tower, that on his next 'long change', he would do some reading and swimming.

He wanted to be faithful, to his vows.

To the latter, his intention was to repeat a visit to the beach; this time, unfortunately, he would be on a solo mission – without Rachel and her underwater 'breaths of life'.

The Juventud Market or '*El Muelles Juventud*' was similar to the market in Guane, on Cuba.

The *El Muelles*, however, was smaller; nevertheless, it featured shopping and trading for both locals and tourists. At this time of year, the shops were busier with the local fishermen and Cuban sailors. It was not a busy time for tourists.

For half a second, Jed felt a little lonesome.

It wasn't a homesick feeling nor was it a feeling of missing anyone.

It lasted for only a brief moment.
Jed shrugged it off.
He looked back at the tug.
It was now at least a kilometer away.

The boardwalk was starting to come alive.
Merchants were busy setting up and shoppers looked like they were getting ready to browse and purchase.

People looked at Jed.
Many of them smiled, at him.
Some said 'Buenos Dias'- others simply nodded.

Juventud is a friendly place, Jed thought.
All of Cuba is, I guess.
With his new, sporty, shades, that he purchased from the 'trinket man', he made his way through the counters and tabletops. He stopped at the fruit vendor's.

He bought two oranges, from the dark-haired plump lady.

The oranges didn't look very fresh but Jed had a craving and he hadn't come across any chewing gum yet—and besides, that was all she had in her basket.

Jed headed further down the market.

He stopped by the stand where a bald-headed black man was selling watches and necklaces.

A little red and yellow pocket watch caught his eye.

It was on sale for five American dollars.

Jed didn't bother to barter. *Five dollars*, he figured, *is a pretty good price.*

Jed thought that it was a great souvenir.

It would always remind him of the unique *time* he had on 'Treasure Island'.

He looped it through his belt and carefully slid it into his pocket. Then he walked to the edge of the boardwalk.

He leaned against a rope post and looked down at the water. He followed each wave as it rolled in and then rolled out again.

He sat down.

Time and timing were important commodities for Jed.

Timing was crucial because when on tower, a split second error could result in an ankle twist, a limb jam or a broken finger ... or worse!

Similarly, time, like timing, was important to him, as well.

Both 'time on' and 'time off' provided Jed with a sense of control, assurance and direction.

Jed would often watch time as it slowly moved across the West Indian sky.

He would perch himself on the derrick, and follow the majestic sun, as it sank into the Caribbean.

He often wondered how it looked from the other side.

As it fell from view in the west, he knew that it would be rising in the east.

Night on the Atlantic; day on the Pacific!

Jed would think about his father, who was on the other side of that setting sun, flying rig helicopters, between Australia and Singapore.

Years ago, the South Pacific Drilling Industry required his service and expertise.

When Jed was only a boy of fifteen, his father leapt at the opportunity to begin a new life on the other side of the world.

He remarried an Indonesian lady, ten years his junior.

He loved to fly and he loved the Pacific.

He also loved his bride.

Jed had never met her but he had seen pictures of her that were included in letters that he and his father had exchanged at Christmas and Easter.

The setting sun would always bring Jed to think about his father.

He would ponder what he might be having with his morning toast and coffee. Would he be smothering his toast with raspberry jam and sweetening his coffee like he had always done, with six sugar cubes?

Something caught Jed's attention.

A seagull landed on a rope post, in the water, about ten feet away.

Jed whistled at it. It just looked at Jed and then quickly flew away.

Jed stood up.

He looked back at the tug.

He started walking, in its direction.

I must get back.

I should go for a swim.

As he got closer to the tug, he pulled out his new pocket watch. It was clearly marked by the Roman numeral 'number system'. It had thick spear-shaped hands.

When Jed looked, the smaller of the two hands was on the X and the larger was approaching the V. *Almost ten twenty-five*, Jed read.

His Aqua Indi, on his left wrist, however, read 10:15. *I wonder which watch is correct?*

As he walked, he bit into one of the oranges.

It was surprisingly juicy, considering its dried exterior.

He continued walking.

He polished off both oranges.

He arrived at the tug.
He walked up the gangplank.

Before his swim, he would need to get two things: a bathing suit and a book.
A very special book!

- CHAPTER FOUR -

ANGELS

The body surfing was okay.

The waves, however, were not as high or as fun as they once were on the beaches of Big Sur, in California or Port Hood, in Cape Breton.

Jed loved being in and by the water.

He loved the beach – he loved it even more when the surf was high.

He loved bodysurfing.

His first surfing experience was when he was eight-years old.

At that time, he and his cousin Rossie, were on vacation in Cape Breton, Nova Scotia. He and Rossie spent their summers together, with their grandparents swimming, surfing and building sand castles.

It was a special time for Jed.

His grandfather, R.L. MacLean, mayor of Port Hood, taught the boys, as he described it, the "real way" to surf. He would tell Jed that he and Rossie were the boards and that angels were riding on their backs.

Jed loved that image.

He got badly sunburned, that summer—the summer of his eighth year—giving angels free rides on his red back.

His cousin, Rossie, on the other hand, did not burn. His skin turned brown. Jed would ask his grandfather why his skin burned and why Rossie's turned brown. His grandfather comforted Jed by telling him that the angels liked different colored surfboards. He even went as far as to tell

Jed that the angels, on Port Hood Beach, preferred red boards to brown ones. For a moment, those words made Jed's sunburn feel less painful.

Jed felt very special when he was with his grandfather. He felt that he was his grandfather's favorite.

Jed tied his T-shirt, on his head, like an Arab. He looked like he was from Saudi Arabia. The heat of the sun soothed his body as it dried the sparkling drops of water. He pushed up some sand and propped up his sneakers, behind the small of his back. He got into a comfortable position.

The sand felt soft and warm.
He leaned on an elbow and looked down at the book.
He picked it up.
He turned the page to Chapter Seven.
He began reading:

"He told me that they were going to assassinate him but I thought that he was only kidding. I didn't believe him. I was wrong. I should have warned Jackie but she wouldn't have believed me either. I didn't believe him. She wouldn't believe me. Well, then again, maybe she would have. Perhaps she was not as naive as I have made her out to be. Jack's so called friends had ulterior motives. They wanted war. He wanted peace. Lee would then allude to the famous line from Shakespeare's <u>Mac Beth</u>*, 'fair is foul'. The president's friends, he would say, were wolves in sheep's clothing. Jack Ruby, Sammy Giancana and Joe, Jack's father, were good at socializing. Frank Sinatra and Peter Lawford threw good parties. Joseph, Ruth, Bobby and Ted were all at risk. They, too, were subject to being the wolves' breakfast: the sluggish caribou.*

The star spangled banner was beginning to rip at the seams. The ink from the Stars and Stripes was beginning to smudge and stain. The gangsters laughed and talked of peace. The beatniks laughed and searched for peace. And the president continued to attend parties and flirt with glitter.

Meanwhile, Lee kept warning me and telling me to remain anonymous because the wolves were getting hungry and the caribou was beginning to weaken.

The vulnerable caribou was slaughtered on a November day in Dallas, Texas.

I should have listened to him when he was talking to me and speaking the truth. It was all too incredible. Who would have ever expected it? Vietnam was inevitable. It was something that was going to occur no matter what. The time was ripe. The U.S.A. needed unity and the wolves were hungry. The herd did not protect the vulnerable caribou. They let him run slowly and they let him run naked. And then the wolves attacked."

Jed looked up from the page and out at the horizon. There was a haze sitting on the ocean. It looked like it was simmering on the back burners of the world. He looked down the beach, first one way and then the other. Then he looked back to the page and to the last line of the paragraph, *"And then the wolves attacked."*

He asked himself, w*hy was the caribou left so exposed?*
Lee knew.
Who else knew?

Jed moved his sneakers so that they could serve as a pillow. He leaned back. He closed his eyes. He let the heat of the Caribbean sun soak up his thoughts. He thought about Marilyn Monroe. He thought about that famous picture of her when she was standing on the street above an air vent. She was smiling and trying to cover her exposed legs with her white dress. The eye of the camera caught her when she was, like the caribou, naked and exposed.

She died.
He died.
Maybe they were supposed to be together but not when they were living. Maybe he should have married her. But she married Arthur and he married Jackie.
Oh well ... C'est la vie!

Jed put the book down on the sand, beside his shorts. He removed the sneakers from behind his back. He lay back and stretched out. He extended his arms on both sides.

He cupped his hands and dragged the sand towards his body and then pushed it away again. With his outstretched arms and legs he made a sand angel that was similar to the ones he used to make, years ago, in the snow, in his front yard, in Brooks, Alberta.

- CHAPTER FIVE -

THE CLEANSING

On his way back to the tug, Jed bought a couple of 'bottled waters' from a young lady, on the pier, who was selling them, from, what looked like, her own 'home' cooler.

When Jed got back to the tug, he opened one of the waters and treated himself to a nice long swig. The water could have been colder.

I guess her cooler was old.

He was thirsty!

For bottled water, though, it tasted pretty good.

Caroline's book was sitting on the kitchenette counter. Jed looked at it.

He couldn't resist.

He reached for it.

He opened it to ensure that the book-marked page was, in fact, the one to which he wanted to refer. He reread a few lines that had caught his eye, earlier, that day, when he was on the 'Boardwalk Beach'. He removed his watch receipt that doubled as a bookmark.

He read:

Who was his informant? How did he know? Who told him? Why did Jack become another Lincoln? Was it a co-incidence or did he really know that Jack was going to be shot, like Lincoln, by somebody who was closer than he/she should have been?

He often spoke about Jack Ruby. I wonder if he were there. He hinted that Sammy might be, too. Who else?

*I once read a book entitled **Tragic Heroes**. It claimed that most people are killed and die very close to their enemies. Very close!*

Claudius lay on the same floor as Hamlet. Mac Duff's sword lay on the ground beside Mac Beth's severed head. And on the night of April 14, 1865, John Wilkes Booth watched the same play, from a box seat behind Abraham Lincoln. Seconds before the closing scene, Booth put a bullet, through the back of the president's head.

There was a time when I shrugged this off as 'book room' dialogue and political frustration.

In hindsight, I think that it was much, much more.

Jed closed the book and carefully placed it on the counter. He went into the bathroom. He looked at himself in the rusty old mirror. He scratched at the whiskers of his rough and grizzled chin.

He took out a can of shaving cream, from his kit bag. As he spread the cream on his tanned cheeks and stubbled chin, he thought about some of the words in Caroline's book.

As the blade moved along his face, slowly removing soap and tiny hairs, Jed thought about the line from ***Tragic Heroes***: *people die very close to their enemies.*

As he rinsed the blade and tapped it on the side of the sink, he thought about Lee.

He would hold on to those thoughts, for a long time.

With them, he would be reflecting upon his own life and *near death* experience—at another time and place—thirteen years hence.

- CHAPTER SIX -

FAIR IS FOUL

Ossie arrived.

Sammy had driven him – not Rachel.

Jed was reluctant in giving the book to him, to return it, to Lee.

He had no choice.

They didn't say much, to each other.

The next morning, at 8:00 a.m. sharp, Jed and Ossie were to report, on tower.

'Long change' had come to an end.

It would be another four weeks before they would get some more 'time off'.

Jed had completed ***Caroline's Memoirs.***

He shared how much he had enjoyed the book and how many times he would read and reread the same sections.

"Its mood and tone," he complimented, "Were effective, but the content, Ossie, now, that was the best!"

Ossie said that he was glad that Jed enjoyed the book.

He didn't say much more.

Jed spoke a little about his days and nights on the tug, the beach, the boardwalk and the market.

To that, Ossie said again, that he was glad Jed enjoyed himself.

He didn't share much about his days and nights back at his parents'.

Jed chose not to pry.

Instead, he talked about how good it was for both of them to have had the time off and especially for him to have some relaxation and reading time. He was grateful. "Thanks for the tug, Os. It was great! But you know something? I don't know if I'll be coming to Juventud next days off." He paused. "I may head home, to Canada or visit the U.S., next month. There are some people and places I want to check out."

Ossie said that was okay, "Whatever." He told Jed that he was 'bagged' and that he was going to 'crash out'.

"I have a feeling that we are going to be busy, tomorrow."

"I bet we will be," Jed agreed. But, he wasn't ready to pack it in, just yet. He had more that he wanted to share.

"When I return to the rig, tomorrow, Ossie, I will be going back with a whole new outlook on life—its past and its future."

Ossie looked at Jed. "Oh ya? Like what?"

Jed was enthused. "I will look at the good in what others might see as bad." He went to the fridge, for a beer. "Want one?" Ossie shook his head.

"I will see hope in what sometimes is described as hopeless." He cracked opened the beer.

"I will find humor in sadness." He took a sip. "I will work hard when I am tired."

He put the beer bottle down, on the counter, with authority.

Ossie frowned. He started unpacking some gear from his duffle bag.

He appeared to be getting ready for bed.

Jed leaned against the counter. "You know Ossie." He took a breath. He took another sip.

" I call to mind a line from one of Shakespeare's famous plays:

Fair is foul and foul is fair." He looked at Ossie.

"I appreciate that paradox now more than ever."

Ossie didn't say anything.

He lay on his cot.

Jed told him again that he enjoyed reading his father's book.

Ossie corrected him and said that it was Caroline's book and not his father's.

"Of course," Jed smiled.

"You have learned a lot from your readings, Jed." Ossie folded his arms behind his head.

"Yes."

"You have learned more than what you would have ever believed."

"Yes." Jed nodded.

Ossie smiled.

He looked at Jed.

"Goodnight, Jed." He turned on his side, with his back to Jed.

"Goodnight, Ossie." Jed blew out the candle that was burning, in the neck of a wine bottle. It had dimly illuminated the kitchenette and the steps to the lower deck.

Jed looked around and waited until his eyes adjusted to the darkness.

Then, he headed down the steps, to his cot.

Before lying down, he sat on the edge of the bed and looked out the tiny porthole, that was a meter, above his head.

He looked at the sky.

It was dark.

He could see that there was some cloud coverage.

He thought about what Ossie had said about the rig being busy.

Then he lay down.

PART FIVE

THE CANADIAN LINKS

- CHAPTER ONE -

THE AGENT OF HEALING

Jed was in his final week of recuperation.

He was ready to leave the Caly Rehabilitation Center. For him, it had already been too long. For Dr. Yen and Clem, recuperation was never long enough.

Dr. Yen had given Jed a clean bill of health and told him that at the end of the week, he was free to go.
Jed was off the haemostatic calyx.
It would remain a part of him and his system, however, for the rest of his life.
His injuries had healed; he was sleeping and eating on a normal schedule.
Dr. Yen was confidant that the concussion was not going to have any side effects and that the myelin, in the neural network could now be released in its natural stages.
" Your cell membranes," Dr. Yen was succinct, "Are open, permitting the ions to move through their channels, without the support of chemical stimulation."
Jed hoped that was good news. It sounded favorable, in medical terminology, that is.

As for the calyx—there would be side effects.
In time, Jed would learn about them and how to live with them.

He was anxious to leave.

His anxiety, however, was not without mixed emotions.

He enjoyed the companionship of Caly, Clem and Nurse Rogers. He had come to learn from them, respect them and trust them.

He longed for other companionship, though, and not exclusively the kind that came from the medical profession. Jed also needed to talk to someone that walked on two legs and not four.

Caly was indeed very special; in some ways, more special than many two-legged walkers. Nevertheless, Jed preferred to sleep with someone with a little less fur.

He was looking forward to seeing Lana.

He hadn't seen or heard from her in quite some time.

She hadn't visited since Jed was moved into The Center. Her absence was due to Dr. Yen's strict orders, and not, as Jed feared, Lana's wishes.

He missed her.

Being a Saturday, Jed assumed that Lana was at home and not at school, where she spent three quarters of her life.

Their telephone conversations, over the past month, had been brief and infrequent.

Again—Dr. Yen's orders – Jed hoped.

He decided that he would not call her.

He thought it was best to set aside any telephone conversations, for the time being.

He was well aware of the frustration and pain of telephone relationships and long distance romances.

He had experienced enough of that during his 'off-shore' drilling days.

He would not blame Lana if she wanted to go out and do other things.

He had witnessed her impatience, before.

Waiting for him to be released from The Center was probably a 'real drag' – and too long.

Earlier that day, Clem told Jed that Ossie was still in Edmonton.

Jed hoped that perhaps he and Lana had been going out and enjoying themselves.

Perhaps they're keeping each other company. That's okay.

Jed tried to convince himself.

Ever since Jed had been moved to the Center, he had been spending most of his time with Caly.

Both Dr. Yen and Clem recommended the 'one on one time' and for Jed not to have any 'outside' *human* visitors.

"It could complicate things. It could play havoc with the therapy and might break down the healing process." Dr. Yen was adamant.

Jed trusted his judgment. He trusted Clem's, too. After all, it was the two of them who had resurrected him, from his deep and distant sleep.

Based on his improved health, Jed believed that Dr. Yen was right. Jed had cooperated. It helped having Clem as 'The Reinforcer'. Clem had been good to Jed and had constantly reassured him that Dr. Yen was the best. Clem told Jed that he was going to be in even better shape, in the days to come, than he was before his treatment.

Jed liked hearing that.

Spending time with Caly also helped.

She and Jed had shared a lot.

Both were products of Dr. Yen's 'successful experiments'.

Both were Canadian; she the lynx and he the link.

Both were lovers of the outdoors and both longed to return to the wild.

Both were agents: she – of 'healing'—and he – of 'the healed'.

"Maybe Dr. Yen will see the benefits in keeping the two of us together, Caly. You could come back with me to the rig and be able to enjoy the fresh and free outdoors."

Jed knew that Caly was domesticated enough to stay with him and yet intelligent enough to take care of herself, in nature, if the need arose.

"The natural environment might ignite your feline spirit."

Caly looked up at Jed. She gave him a look like she understood his wishes but that she was needed elsewhere – and by others. Jed knew her commitment and obligation to both Dr. Yen, Clem and the Center.

"I understand, Caly. I do."

He patted her head and scratched behind her ears.

She purred.

"Although I still think you've got the wild, in your blood, I know how much you are needed here. You've got a gift, Caly. You are able to calm the turbulent waters within the heads of accident victims like me. You are a gift!"

Jed rang for Nurse Rogers.

He asked her if she wanted to join him and Caly, on The Catwalk.

She thanked Jed and said that she would be delighted.

"I'll be right there."

- CHAPTER TWO -

THE CATWALK

Caly's 'catwalk' was a grassed-in area that could be accessed in two ways. Both were located by the south west corner of the Rehabilitation Center. One was by the fitness center near Nurse Rogers' station and the other was, of course, in Jed's room.

Caly was free to use the patio or 'catwalk', as Clem christened it, whenever she wanted. For the most part, she occupied the facility for exercise, fresh air and bathroom breaks.

By pushing on a little gate, with her paw or nose, she was able to come and go.

The hinges, on one of the gates, were a little squeaky.
Nurse Rogers said that was good.
The sound alerted her when Caly was making her moves.

In Jed's room, there were two regular sized patio doors beside the second of Caly's swinging gates.

The catwalk was fenced-in and flanked on all sides by climbing trees and big rocks.

Caly had tracked a well-worn path, from the entrance to her pond, by her constant pacing back and forth. The path evenly divided the 12 by 20 meters, of grass-covered yard.

The pond, although not large, was deep enough for Caly to bathe and play in. She was not much of a swimmer, though. The water temperature was warm. It was maintained, by Nurse Rogers, at 76 degrees Celsius. That way, it was certain not to freeze on Edmonton's frosty, winter mornings.

At first glance, the catwalk appeared to provide Caly with everything she wanted.
When Jed first saw the facility, he thought it was fine.
After being a part of it, for almost a month, Jed looked at the area a little differently, now. He viewed it as nothing more than a place that met Caly's needs, but not her desires.

The sun was bright.

Jed was happy that Nurse Rogers had loaned him a pair of sunglasses. "I'm sure glad you gave me these shades, Nurse Rogers."
"Loaned you those shades," she corrected.
Jed smiled.
She handed him a chilled 50-ml. bottle of water.
She had two bottles.
She kept one for herself.
"Cheers Jed! To your health!"
"Thanks. And to yours!"
Jed raised his bottle.

He took a swig.

His nurse did the same.

- CHAPTER THREE -

CATNIP

Two days had elapsed since Jed's fall.

Fortunately, it was not that serious.

He had been out on the catwalk, joining Caly, on one of her rocks when he got light headed and fainted.

Nurse Rogers was with him, at the time and was quick to react to break his fall.

Jed scraped his knee and elbow but did not hit his head.

"That was good," commented Dr. Yen.

He then explained to Jed that, although he was better, he should continue to take caution and not rush the return to his previous pace and lifestyle.

"That is why it is so important not to rush one's recuperation. You have been true to your program, Jed, but you are very anxious to get back to the rig and to the way things were, before your accident."

Jed hated hearing about his accident.

"Be patient, Mister Jed! The calyx is a powerful drug. Your system has come to rely on it. Now that it is not traveling through your veins, your constitution must adapt and learn to get by without it. You are trying too hard to get back to your previous lifestyle."

Jed frowned.

"Walking around a fenced-in catwalk with a cat and a nurse ain't exactly, what I would call my previous lifestyle."

Dr. Yen shook his head.

Jed apologized.

He explained that sarcasm was not really his style.

"I'm just 'bummed out' that I'm not back to one hundred percent perfect health, yet.

You are right about my impatience, Doc."

Doctor Yen touched Jed's shoulder.

"I know. It won't be long now, Mister Jed.

Keep riding the stationary bike and eat everything that Nurse Rogers prepares for you.

Keep the liquids up; lots and lots of water."

Their eyes met.

"Two more days, Jed, and then you're out of here."

Jed thought that Dr. Yen looked tired. Before he left, he told Jed that he would check in on him later.

As he walked towards the door, Jed noticed how slowly he moved.

"Are you all right, Dr. Yen?"

"I'm fine, Jed. Just a little tired, that's all."

After he left, Caly slumped down by her food dish.

She seemed bored.

She had not been as close to Jed, as she had been earlier in the week and certainly not as affectionate as she was when he first entered The Center.

It was as though she knew that Jed was getting better and that he would soon be leaving.

She did not rub up against him like she did when he was on the calyx.

With the warmer weather, she was spending more time outside, on her branches and rocks. Jed tried to join her, as often as possible.

She seemed aloof.

"You mustn't like my smell anymore, Caly.

Is that it? I don't smell like I did when I was on the calyx, right?"

Jed was beginning to understand. He recalled the words of Nurse Rogers, when he and she were out on the catwalk. At the time, just before his fall, he was confused. Now her words made perfect sense:

The calyx is like your catnip, Jed.

- CHAPTER FOUR -

FOR THE RECORD

Dr. Yen was true to his words. He returned to Jed's room, later that evening.

Jed was reading the paper when Dr. Yen knocked at his door.

"How are you doing now, Mister Jed?"

"Come in, come in, Doctor."

Jed asked him if he wanted something to eat or drink.

"I have some cheese and crackers, some juice and of course, lots and lots of ice cold water." Jed gave him a thumb up.

"Just a small glass of juice. That would be nice."

Dr. Yen sat down on the couch and picked up the paper that Jed had been reading.

"I see that Princess Diana is starting to make a go of it, on her own."

Jed replied that he had just started reading that article.

"Yes, I think she is even starting to go out on dates. Imagine that!"

"Good for her," commended Dr. Yen. "She is still young and why not? After all, who says that she has to stay cooped up in a place that results in an eating disorder."

Jed agreed.

"That's right Doc. Nobody deserves to be cooped up anywhere."

"Except murderers," Dr. Yen was emphatic.

"Cheers!" Jed raised his glass. "I'll drink to that."

Dr. Yen raised his. "Cheers, Mister Jed. Here's to you. I am going to miss you. You have been a good patient and like Caly you have served to reinforce my credence, in the haemostatic calyx."

"Thank you Dr. Yen. And you have been a good doctor."

Jed paused, for a moment, and then looked at Dr. Yen. "Dr. Yen? Can I ask you something off the record?"

"Nothing is ever off the record, Mister Jed. But go ahead and ask."

Jed took a sip of his water.
Dr. Yen took a sip of his juice.

"I don't know if there is an easy way to ask this but I am going to do my best."

Dr. Yen tilted his head.

For a moment, Jed thought that he looked a bit like Caly.

"Fire away, Mister Jed.

I will do my best to answer you, accurately and honestly."

Dr. Yen took another sip of his juice.

Jed stood up.
He finished his water.
He braced himself.
He took a breath.

"Other than I, Dr. Yen, how many people know what *really* happened, back in Dallas, in 1963?"

Dr. Yen smiled.

He took a pen from his upper pocket.

"What makes you think that you know what *really* happened?"

By his expression, Jed knew that Dr. Yen was teasing.

He wrote something down on the front page of the newspaper.

The room fell quiet.

For a little over a minute, all Jed could hear was the sound of Dr. Yen's pen on paper—and his breathing.

Jed looked down at what he was writing.

He noticed that Dr. Yen was jotting down numbers. Just to the right of Princess Diana's picture were the numbers one to eight.

Beside each number was a name.

"There you go Mister Jed."

Dr. Yen handed him the paper.

Jed recognized all eight names.

"Is that it? Only these eight people?"

Jed was surprised.

Dr. Yen smiled and held out his pen.

"You see this pen, Mister Jed?"

Jed nodded.

"And this paper?"

He pointed to the paper.

"There is not enough ink in this pen for me to write down all the numbers and names of those who know what *really* happened."

He held up the newspaper.

"Even if I had more ink, you would need another dozen of these for me to write."

He returned the pen to his pocket.

He threw down the paper.

"These names," he tapped on the paper, "Are the ones you know.

These names are the only ones you know.

As for the others," he paused.

He looked up at the ceiling. He jerked his head.

"As for them, God only knows." He laughed.

"Well, God and a few others."

He winked.

He stood up. He appeared to be getting ready to go.

"Thanks for the juice, Mister Jed."

"My pleasure. Thanks for coming to see me. And thank you for answering my question."

"You're welcome, Mister Jed."

He reached out to shake Jed's hand.

"You are looking well, Mister Jed.

And you are feeling okay?"

"I'm fine, Doc. I think I'm ready to leave."

"Two more days, Mister Jed."

He looked around the room.

"Where's Caly?"

"Oh, she is likely out on her perch. She has been a little distant with me, lately. She is spending more and more time outside, on her catwalk."

"I'm not surprised. She has done her job. Now she wants to spend a little time on herself.

She is entitled to that." He paused. He looked at Jed.

"Wouldn't you agree, Mister Jed? After all, she is a lynx."

"Absolutely, Dr. Yen. You're right. That is what she is.

She's been great, by the way. I am going to miss her.

At one time, I was going to ask you if I could take her with me, when I returned to the rig.

I have since changed my mind.

I know how much she is needed here." He looked around the suite.

Dr. Yen looked at Jed and then looked down at the floor.

"What?" asked Jed.

He could see that something was on Dr. Yen's mind.

"What is it Doc?"

"Mister Jed? Have you ever considered any other kind of work, other than the oil rigs?"

Jed frowned.

"Not really. I love the rigs! That's all I know. Why?"

"Well, I must tell you, Mister Jed, that the haemostatic calyx does have its side effects and I want you to be aware of that."

Jed looked concerned. "I know the side effects, Doc. You told me, a couple of weeks ago when I was in the hospital: Discomfort and visual fatigue. Right?"

"Well, yes." Dr. Yen removed his glasses from his eyes and started to clean them, with a red handkerchief.

"That is correct when one is on the calyx, Mister Jed. But it is quite a different story, after one ceases to take it.

The long-term effects are fascinating.

That was the purpose of my visiting you tonight, but you side-tracked me with your question, about Dallas."

Jed swallowed.

"When you say fascinating, doctor, just exactly what is it that you mean?"

Dr. Yen turned and pointed back at the living room.

"Let's go and sit down, Mister Jed. I will give you some examples."

Dr. Yen asked if he felt any differently than he did before his accident.

Jed replied, "Not really."

He paused. He thought.

"Well, now that you mention it, in a way I do feel a little bit differently."

Dr. Yen nodded his head. "Yes, Mister Jed. Of course you do."

Dr. Yen took his pen from his pocket.

"Allow me to try a simple test with you, Mister Jed, that should serve to make things a little bit clearer."

He wrote some words down on the same newspaper on which he wrote the eight names and numbers. This time, he wrote on a different page.

When he finished, he said to Jed,

"Mister Jed. I have just written down 25 different medical terms. None with which you should be familiar. I will read them out to you and then I will ask you to repeat them to me in the same order, term by term."

Jed laughed.

"Ya right. As if."

Dr. Yen ignored Jed's cynicism.

He began reading.

He read at a steady pace.

Some of the terms, Jed thought he had heard before but, in most cases, he did not know their meanings.

When Dr. Yen got to number 25, he looked up at Jed and said that it was now his turn.

Jed laughed. "Do I get to use the paper like you did, Doc?"

Doctor Yen smiled. He gestured with his hand for Jed to begin.

"Remember Mister Jed, word for word and in the exact order that I read to you."

"Whatever you say, Doc."

Jed began. He paced back and forth with every word.

"*Glucose, cerebral, metabolism, organelle, mitochondria, glycolysis, neurological, hemorrhage, hippocam-*

pus, cortex, pituitary, thalamus, medulla, limbic, myelin, axon."

Jed stopped and looked at Dr. Yen.
"How am I doing so far, Doc?"
Doctor Yen did not answer Jed's question.
He simply smiled and told Jed to continue.

"Here are the final nine, Doc."
Now Jed was smiling.
"This is fun." He stopped pacing. He stood directly in front of Dr. Yen.
"Amino, glutamate, monoamines, epinephrine, melatonin, dopamine, peptides, endorphin and last but not least, *acetylcholine."*
He stopped.
Jed was still looking at Dr. Yen.
"Wow! That's incredible.
I don't even know what half those words mean."
"Yes, Mister Jed, it is incredible."
Dr. Yen stood up.
"And that's not all.
Not only do you have a photographic memory, Mister Jed, your level of E.S.P. has escalated, as well."
"What do you mean, Doc?" This time Jed sat down.
Dr. Yen paced.
Jed laughed. "This is different. Should I be giving you a memory test, now Doctor?"
Dr. Yen shook his head. "That is not necessary."
He stopped pacing. He looked directly at Jed.
"In the last few days, Mister Jed, did you, at any time, think that you knew what Caly was thinking?"
Jed frowned. "I didn't think that animals could think."
"Most can't. But remember, just as you are experiencing the side effects of the calyx, so is she. Like for you, Mister Jed, the calyx was used to heal her concussion and internal bleeding.

Furthermore." He sat down on the couch beside Jed.

"It is quite possible that her level of E.S.P. has escalated, too."

Jed shook his head. "Wow! This is something else, Doc.

Are there any more surprises that you have in store for me?

I mean," Jed shook his head, "This is unbelievable."

"Yes it is, Mister Jed. It is, as you say, *unbelievable*."

Doctor Yen stood up.

"Like many things in this life, Mister Jed."

He gently touched Jed's arm.

"Like what really happened that day, back in 1963, in Dallas, Texas."

Their eyes met.

"Now you know why I did not recommend any visitors, while you were recuperating here, at the Center.

Your life has changed Mister Jed. When you leave here, on Thursday, you will see the world in a completely different way.

You will look at people differently.

You will come to know things that you wish you hadn't."

Jed rubbed his eyes.

He looked at his hands.

"That explains why you asked me if I had ever considered another line of work."

Dr. Yen nodded.

Jed did not say anything.

He simply shook his head and repeated the words: wow and unbelievable.

Dr. Yen stood up and said that this time he really was going to leave.

"Don't get up Mister Jed. I can show myself to the door. I know the way out.

I will bid you goodnight, Mister Jed, and I will see you in the morning.

Your second last morning, here."

He walked down the hall.
Jed listened to his footsteps.

"Get some sleep, Mister Jed."
"I will. Good night Doc."

Jed remained sitting, on the couch.
He thought about many things.
His mind was racing.

He got up.

He went into his bedroom and then headed for the patio.

He looked out onto the catwalk.

He called for Caly.

- CHAPTER FIVE -

TELEPATHY

When Jed, finally, woke up, he was pleasantly surprised to find Caly at the foot of his bed.

Their visit on the catwalk had been a good one.
He had spent time petting her and talking to her.
She was reluctant, at first, to be affectionate.
Then, she came down from her perch.
Jed was determined to put her at ease.
He shared what he had learned from Dr. Yen.
He told her that he understood how difficult it must be for her to be so close to her patients and then, "Just like that, they leave. You spend uninterrupted quality time," he told her, "And then the void."
He said that she was not alone in her loneliness.
"I know somebody who could relate to you." Jed thought about Lana.
"After you help heal another's heart and head, you're alone again—until the next time."

Caly understood. She licked her chops.
Jed could tell. He could feel it. She was going to be okay. So was he.
It had been a productive visit.
Caly leapt up, on his bed, when she noticed that his eyes were opened.
Jed thought that she felt lighter than usual.
Her coat was not as full.

Her fur was not as thick.

"Well, Caly, tomorrow I begin a whole new life.
I think I'm ready to take on the world.
I hope I am, anyway.
My wounds are healed.
I think my wounds are healed."

Caly purred.
She licked her front paws.
"After my workout and shower, let's spend some time on the catwalk. We should spend as much time together today, as possible.

Maybe Dr. Yen will be able to join us." Caly perked up her ears, at the sound of his name. "He should be making his rounds.

He told me that he would be here, sometime, this morning."

Jed looked at his bare wrist.
"I've got to get myself a watch. I used to have two.
This, not having even one, is crazy."

He got up and headed for the fitness room. He made a pit stop, at the washroom.

Caly jumped down from the bed and stretched.
She let out a yawning growl.

Then, she headed for the catwalk.

- CHAPTER SIX -

THE YOUNG DOCTOR

When Dr. Yen arrived, he was accompanied by three other people.

Jed recognized Clem and Nurse Rogers, but the tall gentleman, whose hair and beard were as gray as the rock, on which Caly was perched, was not familiar.

"Hello, Dr. Yen!

Caly and I were just wondering when you were going to get here."

"Hello, Mister Jed. Hello, Caly!"

Caly stood up and stretched. Then she slumped down, again.

"It is nice to see you looking so well, Mister Jed. I have brought Nurse Rogers, Clem and Dr. Young with me. We all wanted to pay you a visit."

Jed thanked them.

"Dr. Young, here," Dr Yen introduced him to Jed, " Is the doctor who treated your rig companions: Jim, Al and Stewart."

"Hello, Jed," greeted Dr. Young, "It is a pleasure to finally meet you."

"Likewise, Dr. Young."

Jed was curious. "So how are Slim Jim, Stewie and Big Al doing, anyway?

Are they still in the hospital?"

"Jim and Stewart were released last week.
Al stayed with us only the one night."

Dr. Young looked over at Caly and then turned to Jed.

He scratched his beard. "Al's injury, unlike yours, was minor." He paused.

"I believe they're all back on the rig and probably getting ready to resume the drilling. Isn't that right, Clem?"

Clem walked over and leaned on Caly's rock.

"I tink so, man. Ya man I tink dat be dem way dose tings are shapin' up."

"That's good news." Jed nodded. He stood by Clem.

"Big Al wouldn't want to stay in a hospital more than one night, anyway." Jed smiled.

"He's more restless than I am."

He looked at Dr. Yen. He was crouched down, leaning on one knee. He appeared to be examining a grassy section of the catwalk.

Nurse Rogers placed her hands on her hips.

"We know about your restlessness, all right." She smiled. She shook a finger.

Clem laughed. "Ya man, cool. You be restless man."

Nurse Rogers rolled her eyes in her usual manner. Then, she asked Jed how Caly was feeling, now that she knew that he was getting ready to leave.

Jed looked up at Caly.

She yawned.

She began cleaning her front paws.

"We're doing okay," Jed nodded. He reached up and patted her head.

"She's fine. I'm fine, too." He smiled. "We'll make it."

Nurse Rogers agreed. "Yes, Jed. You'll both be fine." She approached Jed and gave him a reassuring hug.

"Thanks." Jed returned the hug.

Dr. Young moved closer to the rock. He said that Caly was very special.

Jed thought that his teeth were as white Dr. Yen's.

"All you doctors have such white teeth. Is it a bleach thing or do your dentist friends exchange favors for samples of the Calyx?"

Dr. Yen stood up.

He looked at Jed.

He didn't laugh at Jed's jab.

For a moment, there was an uncomfortable silence. Everybody looked at each other.

Dr. Young broke the silence.

"Perhaps, it is time that we all went inside."

Clem made the first move. "Jed, my man. You be leavin' us soon, man." He put his arm around Jed's shoulder.

"Let's go. We be doin' some chattin' in dem Center." He pointed towards Jed's suite. He motioned for him to follow.

He invited Caly.

She immediately leapt from her rock.

She ran towards The Center.

The others followed.

Their gait was not as quick as hers.

Jed found the whole ordeal to be rather formal – somewhat surreal.

"Heh!" Jed stopped.
"What's happening?
Everybody seems so tense?"

No response.

Jed laughed.

No reaction.

As they made their way into the suite, the mood, immediately swung from tense to intense.

Everyone looked like they were in deep thought – even Clem.

That got Jed thinking.

As they gathered in the living room, Dr. Yen asked Jed to take a seat.

Jed shook his head. "I'd rather stand, thanks, just the same. One is smarter when he is standing.

By the look of things, something tells me that I am going to need my wits.

No. I'll stand."

- CHAPTER SEVEN -

THE DEPARTURE

Nurse Rogers sat down.

"I'll take a seat. My feet are killing me."

She loosened the laces of her shiny white shoes.

Everyone watched and waited until she settled into the comfort of Jed's couch.

"There! That's better." She let out a sigh of relief.

Then, she sat upright and folded her hands, on her lap.

Her demeanor beheld that of a person waiting for an announcement or attending a prayer service.

Dr. Young sat down, in a chair that was adjacent to the couch.

Dr. Yen sat, on the couch, beside Nurse Rogers.

Like Jed, Clem remained standing.

Jed leaned against the half wall that separated the living room, from the kitchen.

Caly dropped herself at his feet.

Jed looked around, waiting for somebody to say something.

Nurse Rogers spoke again.

She asked Clem if he would be so kind as to bring everyone a glass of water.

"I'm sure that there's a jug in the fridge." She gave Jed a look.

"And the glasses are on the shelf, above the sink." Jed pointed.

"I know where dey be at, man. I know dis place, man, you know.

And the good nurse knows I knows it."

Jed smiled. "Of course."

As Clem opened the fridge, he turned and winked at Nurse Rogers.

Jed watched for her reaction.

With the same expression, that she sported, on the catwalk, she affectionately, rolled her eyes.

Clem started filling some glasses.

Once again, Jed looked around the room.

This time everyone looked like they were awaiting the arrival of a courtroom judge.

Jed folded his arms.

He looked at Dr. Yen.

"So what's the verdict?"

Clem arrived with a tray of glasses, filled to the brim, with ice-cold water.

He placed the tray down on the coffee table, in front of Nurse Rogers and Dr. Yen.

He was careful not to spill a drop.

"Der now. Help yourselves!"

Dr. Yen cleared his throat. He thanked Clem for the water and asked Dr. Young if he would like to begin.

Dr. Young nodded.

"Thank you, Dr. Yen. And thanks for the water, Clem."

He leaned over and helped himself to one of the glasses.

Clem responded. "Irae man. No problem!" He took a glass from the tray and then sat down, cross-legged, on the floor beside Caly.

Again, he was careful not to spill a drop.

Dr. Yen looked up at Jed. "Water?"

Jed nodded.

He approached the table.

He lifted one of the glasses, from the tray and then returned to his spot, by the half wall.

He raised his glass to the room.

He took a sip.

Dr. Young leaned back.

Dr. Yen and Nurse Rogers sipped at their water, simultaneously.

Clem was thirsty. He drank his like he was drinking a Red Stripe, on a beach, in Jamaica.

Caly licked her lips.

Dr. Young took a sip of his water. He placed the glass gently on the floor, beside him.

He spoke again.

"Jed, as you are aware," he cleared his throat, "You now possess certain strengths that you did not have before your treatment."

Jed nodded. "I know."

He looked over at Dr. Yen.

Dr. Yen did not return his look. Instead, his eyes remained locked on Dr. Young.

Nurse Rogers, on the contrary, smiled at Jed.

Her look was comforting. Jed still felt that there was too much tension, in the room, though.

Clem stroked Caly's ear.

Dr. Young continued.

"You are also probably aware that our methods, although highly unorthodox, are very effective."

He pointed to Caly and then asked Jed what time he thought it was.

Jed frowned.

He looked down at his bare wrist.

He looked back at Dr. Young. He shook his head.

Dr. Young motioned for Jed to go ahead and tell everyone what time he thought it was.

"Well!" Jed shrugged his shoulders.

He looked over at the patio doors and saw the light of day shining on them and on the floor in front of them.

He looked back at Dr. Young.

Nobody spoke.

Everyone remained seated, awaiting Jed's 'time announcement'.

Jed took another sip of his water.

He stood up straight.

"If my memory serves me correctly, when we were out on the catwalk, I looked up at the sky and noticed that the sun was sitting at the eleven o'clock position.

I would hazard a guess and say that it was now about 11:15."

Dr. Young shook his head. "Don't guess, Jed. Think!

I am telling you to think, Jed.

It's that simple."

Jed walked around the half wall and placed his glass on its shelf.

He then leaned against the wall, rested his elbows on the top and looked at the room and the people in it.

He chuckled. "I feel as though I'm at the pulpit ready to deliver my homily."

Dr. Yen looked at Dr. Young. Clem looked at Jed and Nurse Rogers looked over at Clem. Caly left her spot and sauntered into the kitchen towards her water dish. Jed listened to Caly's lapping.

He lifted his glass from the counter.

Then he raised it to the other side of the half wall.

"Cheers!"

He took a sip.

He wiped his lips. He placed his glass back down on the wall's shelf.

"Which one of you is wearing a watch?"

No response.

"How will I know if I am correct or not, when I tell you the time?"

No response.

"Not one of you is wearing a watch?"
Jed shook his head. "I can't believe it.
What's the big deal with this time thing?"
Dr. Young wanted to clear the air. "We don't need to wear watches, Jed." He exposed a bare wrist.
He stood up. He repeated. "We don't need to wear watches."
Dr. Young looked at Nurse Rogers. "I mean, we can if we want—but we don't **need** them. Sometimes we wear watches purely for cosmetic purposes. Isn't that right Nurse Rogers?"
She agreed. "That's right, Dr. Young." She looked at Jed.
Dr. Young reached down and lifted his water, from the floor beside his chair.
"And so, Jed. What time is it?"
Dr. Yen got up and walked into the kitchen.
Jed ignored Dr. Young's question.
"Nice to see you, finally, moving around Doctor." He called out to Dr. Yen.
"For a moment there, I thought I lost you."
Dr. Yen called back, from the kitchen. "For a moment, there, Jed, you did.
As I was listening to Dr. Young, I was thinking very seriously about what he was asking you and to the significance of your response."
He filled the jug with tap water and put it back into the fridge.
Then, he returned, with Caly, to the middle of the living room.
He remained standing.

Caly slumped down beside Clem.

"You see, Jed, the six of us in this room, including Caly, have all been, at one time, for one reason or another, induced with the calyx."

Jed looked at Nurse Rogers.

She returned his look.

She nodded.

Jed looked down at Clem.

"You too, Clem?"

Clem smiled.

"My teeth ain't dis white just because I be from dem islands, man. After you tell I what time it be, man, go and check out dem teeth in dem bathroom mirror. You gonna need dose shades dat you be wearin' on dem catwalk, man." He looked at Nurse Rogers.

Jed laughed.

"I should have known. No wonder everybody here looks like a Hollywood movie star. It whitens your teeth? Is that what it does Doc?"

"Yes, indeed, Mister Jed; among other things.

It is not, as you questioned, the result of exchanging favors with dentists."

Jed smiled.

"Oh you did hear me when I asked that, back there, on the catwalk?"

Dr. Yen nodded.

"I hear everything, Mister Jed.

Everything!"

He took a sip of his water.

"It's all starting to make sense." Jed walked around to the other side of the half wall.

"Oh, by the way, in case anybody is still interested, it is now exactly 11:30 a.m."

Dr. Young walked into the kitchen. "Does anybody need more water?"

No response.

Instead, Dr. Yen raised his half full glass of water and held it out towards Jed.

"There are certain things that you will need to remember after you leave us."

He paused.

"You must drink a lot of this."

He took a sip.

"Those of us, who have been blessed with the calyx, are more susceptible to dehydration."

Jed nodded.

"I figured so.

What other things, as you so eloquently stated, doctor, will I need to remember?"

Dr. Yen raised his index finger towards the ceiling.

"I will respond to that question, Mister Jed." He took another sip.

"I will be right back."

He went into the kitchen. He crossed paths with Dr. Young, who was returning to the living room.

Dr. Yen went to the fridge and filled his glass.

Everybody, in the room, studied his moves.

Dr. Yen returned.

"The liquid that is inside this glass is very clear, very precious and very important."

He paused.

He looked closely at the water, inside the glass.

"It represents 70 percent of the earth's surface. You know that, of course."

He sounded scholarly.

"If you think of this glass as the land and the water inside as that which surrounds and engulfs the land, then you will have a clearer picture of how the calyx works."

Clem rubbed behind Caly's ear.

He pulled at one of his dreadlocks and told Dr. Yen, "You be usin' good metaphors, man."

"Thank you, Clem, but I must make a point of clarification. Those were similes, Clem. Metaphors do not include the words like or as."

Clem shrugged.

Jed smiled.

Nurse Rogers stood up.

"Always the teacher, Dr. Yen—and a good one at that."

Jed sat down, in Nurse Rogers' spot, on the couch.

"It's like we're playing musical chairs, here."

Clem laughed and hummed a couple of bars from Bob Marley's 'Redemption Song'.

Jed sipped his water.

"I understand your simile, Dr. Yen, but I am sorry, I do not understand how it addresses my question regarding what other surprises are in store for me."

Jed looked at Dr. Young.

"Dr. Young, you were correct when you stated, earlier, that I now possess certain strengths that I did not possess when I was first brought in here.

I know, now, that my memory is much sharper than it used to be."

He paused and sipped again.

Dr. Young nodded.

Jed continued.

"I also know that I do not need to wear a watch to know what time it is."

Jed looked at Dr. Yen.

"Dr. Yen, I understand the importance of water.

Unlike its clarity, I am still unclear as to what else I should know before I leave this place." He looked around the room.

Dr. Yen called for Caly. She came immediately.

"I will show you something, Mister Jed, with Caly here to assist. She will, once again, serve to put your mind at ease."

Dr. Young, Nurse Rogers and Clem all moved in closer to where Dr. Yen and Caly were standing.

Jed smiled and said:

"This is good."

Dr. Yen placed his hand on Caly's head. The minute he did, she sat down, by his side. She looked like a sentinel guarding a fortress.

Jed looked at Caly.

Caly looked at Jed.

They exchanged a trusting glance.

Dr. Yen continued.

"As you know, Mister Jed, you and Caly share some common ground."

Jed smiled.

Clem said "Ya man" and Nurse Rogers rolled her eyes, for the third time.

This time, Jed was not certain if the eye roll was affectionate or not.

"Have you any idea what common ground you two share, Mister Jed?"

This time it was Dr. Yen, Jed thought, who looked and sounded like a preacher.

His question was not threatening, though.

Even though his tone was serious, Jed was not uncomfortable.

He was not one to let fear control wit.

"Dr. Yen!" Jed stood up, " I know that Caly and I have a lot in common."

Caly yawned.

She was getting bored.

It was as though she had been through all of this before.

"Mister Jed!"

Dr. Yen raised a pleading arm. This time, he looked more like a schoolboy than a preacher.

"Just as she is endangered, so are you, Mister Jed. You are endangered, like Caly."

"We're all in danger, Doc!"

Jed finished the last drop of his water.

"You, me, Caly."

He looked at the others.

"We're all in danger!"

Clem nodded.

"Irae man, Irae!"

"Mister Jed!"

Dr. Yen held up his glass.

"I said endangered, not in danger."

Jed frowned. "What's the difference, Doc?"

Dr. Yen ignored his question.

He continued.

"Seven tenths of the earth's surface are made up of this."

He raised his glass higher.

"On a good day, most people use only ten per cent of their brain to solve problems and deal with every day life."

"I don't mean to sound sarcastic, Doc, but tell me something, I don't already know."

Dr. Yen smiled and Caly licked her chops.

"How is she going to help, Doc?"

Jed pointed at Caly.

"Mister Jed!" Dr. Yen took a sip.

"I will be frank."

He paused

"Just as she," he knelt down beside Caly, the same way he knelt in the catwalk, examining the grass.

"Is here to help you – and others like you."

He touched Caly's head and then, stood up.

"You, Mister Jed, are here to help her—and others like her."

Jed frowned.

"There are others like her?"

"Well?" Dr. Yen tilted his head.

"Yes and no!"

Jed frowned. "Yes and no? I'm confused."

Dr. Young stared at Caly. Jed thought that he looked like a zombie.

Nurse Rogers was smiling and giving Jed her usual, reassuring look.

Clem had one hand on his hip and the other was held, in a 'thumb up' position by his side. Like Nurse Rogers, he, too, was smiling.

Caly lay in the middle of the floor. She looked relaxed.

Dr. Yen remained beside Jed, on the couch. He placed his hand on Jed's arm.

"Let me rephrase. I know that my words might be confusing, to you, but Jed, you are bright—brighter than you have ever been and you possess dynamic, extra sensory power."

Jed nodded. "I know. I know. But Dr. Yen, you're still leaving me with some unanswered questions."

Dr. Yen stood up. He shook his head. "No, Mister Jed, it is you who is leaving me."

He paused.

He pointed at the others.

"It is you who is leaving them."

Dr. Yen walked into the kitchen. He took the jug, from the fridge and returned, with it, to the living room. He filled Jed's glass and then gave the jug, to Clem.

"Tanks, man."

Clem topped up his water and did the same for Nurse Rogers and Dr. Young.

Dr. Yen sat down in the chair opposite Jed.

"You have three choices, Mister Jed."

Dr. Young corrected.

"Excuse me, Dr. Yen, but I think you mean four."

He held up four fingers.

Jed was happy to hear Dr. Young talk, again.

Dr. Yen ignored Dr. Young's interruption and his four, outstretched, fingers.

"One:" he said.

He pointed at Jed.

"Like Caly, you can stay here, with us, at The Center, to help others heal from their injuries, as you have. I can set you up, here, and, in time, you will learn more about our wonderful profession and of course, the calyx."

"Now Doc," Jed interrupted.

"You're not going to lay the guilt trip on me now, just because I am leaving and don't want to practice medicine." Jed corrected himself. "I should say, practice 'unique medicine'."

Dr. Young looked startled. He looked at Dr. Yen, for his reaction. Clem sat down, in his usual cross-legged position, on the floor, beside Caly.

Nurse Rogers took a seat beside Jed and Dr. Yen stood up.

He told Dr. Young to sit in his chair. Dr. Young complied.

Dr. Yen continued:

"Two!"

He made a peace sign.

"You can leave."

He shook his head.

"No guilt trip. No hard feelings. No offense."

He laughed. "Yes, our techniques are quite unique, aren't they, Mister Jed?"

He sipped his water.

He placed his glass, on the table.

He continued.

"But if and when you do leave, Mister Jed, I want you to imagine what it would be like if Caly were to leave this place." He squinted. He moved to get closer, to Jed.

"Just imagine that, for one minute, Mister Jed, if you can." He tapped Jed's arm.

"Can you?"

He looked more serious, now. Jed thought that his expression was bordering on the unfriendly.

"Returning to the wild, for her, would be extremely dangerous." He pointed at Caly.

Clem nodded.

Nurse Rogers touched Jed's hand.

Dr. Young was back to his staring, again.

Now, Jed figured that Dr. Young had issues.

"And returning for you, Mister Jed, is going to be dangerous!"

Jed frowned.

Dr. Yen raised his eyebrows.

He took another sip of his water.

Jed did the same.

They did not take their eyes off each other.

Dr. Yen put down his glass.

"And three!"

He sounded enthusiastic.

He looked friendlier, again.

"You can disappear, Mister Jed."

He put his hands on his hips. Then he snapped a finger.

"Just like that, Mister Jed. You can disappear."

He stopped talking.

He went into the kitchen. This time he did not go to the fridge. Instead, he went to the table and picked up his briefcase.

He returned.

Nobody moved.

Nobody said a word.

Dr. Young kept staring.

Clem remained cross-legged.

Nurse Rogers kept her hand on Jed's.

Caly was now, passed out.

Jed smiled. He found the whole ordeal rather entertaining.

He figured that Dr. Yen intended it that way.

Finally, he spoke.

"Disappear?" He was surprised.

"Just like that?" He laughed. "How?"

Dr. Yen moved his glass to make room for his briefcase. He placed it on the coffee table.

Jed lifted his glass. Dr. Yen smiled. "Thank you, Mister Jed."

He opened his case, slowly and dramatically.

He pulled out a piece of newspaper, slowly and dramatically.

From Jed's vantage point, he could see that the newspaper clipping included a picture and an article.

Dr. Yen held it up.

Then he held it out on display, for all to see.

"Can all of you see?"

Everyone nodded.

He took a sip of his water.

He cleared his throat.

He spoke:

"This is a very famous picture."

He paused.

He looked at Jed.

He held the picture right in front of Jed's face.

"It is from a turning point, in history."

Jed nodded.

"The man in this picture," he pointed to the man, "Who is holding his side, had just been shot, by this man."

He pointed to another man whose back was to the camera. He was wearing a hat. He looked like a large man.

Dr. Yen continued:

"The man who is holding his side," he pointed to the

man, "Is apparently, as history has recorded, the assassin, of John F. Kennedy."

He took another sip of his water.

Jed sipped, too.

Nobody else moved.

Dr. Yen slammed the clipping down on the coffee table.

"He disappeared, Jed."

He snapped his finger.

"And—as you put it—just like that."

He snapped his finger, again.

Jed looked at the picture.

He looked up, at Dr. Yen.

He nodded.

"Yes, but he had some pretty darn good reasons for disappearing, Doc."

"And do you know any of those reasons, Mister Jed?"

"Well when you put it that way, Doc, no, I don't." Jed swallowed.

"Not exactly. But I can hazard a guess."

Dr. Young sighed. Jed thought that he still looked like a zombie.

"What?" Jed frowned. He looked around at everyone.

"What?" he repeated.

Dr. Young spoke. "Do we have to tell you again, Jed? Think!

Don't guess."

Jed looked down at Nurse Rogers' hand. It looked like a kind hand.

Caly got up and stretched—then she slumped down, again.

Clem stood up. He made an announcement: "Ossie soon come, man."

Dr. Yen nodded.

"Yes. Ossie is coming! Thank you, Clem."

"Ossie's coming?" Jed was surprised.

"When?"

Nurse Rogers answered. "Soon."

She removed her hand, from Jed's.

She stood up.

She straightened her dress and then ran her fingers through her hair.

"More water, anyone?"

"No thanks."

She went into the kitchen.

Jed stood up.

"Dr. Yen?

Why would I ever want to disappear?"

"You might have your reasons."

Jed nodded.

"Okay, I might, but at the present time, I don't."

Dr. Yen shrugged. "Fine."

Jed pointed at the man, in the picture. "Did you know his reasons, Dr. Yen?"

"Some of them, Mister Jed."

Dr. Yen walked over and knelt down, beside Caly. He rubbed her back.

She purred.

Jed looked around the room.

Clem nodded. "We all be on dem same link, Mista Jed.

Stay cool, my man. Ya'all be cool."

Jed said that he was cool.

"Clem?"

"Yes, man?"

"You said a few minutes ago that Ossie was coming?"

"Ya man! Ossie be here. Him take you where you wanna go, man."

"But I'm not supposed to leave until tomorrow."

Dr. Yen interrupted. "You can leave today, Mister Jed. If you choose to." He shrugged.

"You are healthy. You are good to go."

"Where is Ossie, now?" Jed was concerned.

"Are you ready to leave, Mister Jed?" Dr. Yen was direct.

Jed looked at Caly. She yawned.

"Ossie is waiting for you in the lab, Mister Jed. He knows that you are ready to leave. You understand, don't you Mister Jed?" Dr. Yen sounded impatient.

"I guess so."

Dr. Young sighed, again. He stood up. He shook his head.

Caly stood up. She arched her back.

"Dr. Young?"

"Yes, Jed?"

"May I ask you a question?"

"Absolutely!"

"What was my fourth choice?"

Dr. Yen put up his hand signaling for Dr. Young not to respond. "I will answer that for you, Doctor."

"It was, Jed, to leave—but to leave, here, with no memory."

"You mean with amnesia?" Jed laughed.

"As if!" He was curious. "What do you mean by that?"

"Think, Jed. You should know what I mean by that." He pointed at the newspaper.

"Perhaps it might be better described as having *selective amnesia*."

Jed nodded. "I understand. I choose to remember what I should remember. It's not like you're going to inject me with anything, is it Doc?"

Clem was the first to make a move.

"No problem, Mista Jed, man. No problem!" He turned to Nurse Rogers and Dr. Young.

"C'mon you two—let's leave dem three cats alone.

I tell Ossie, man, dat Jed soon come, man." He shook Jed's hand. He turned. He walked towards the door. Nurse

Rogers hugged Jed and said that it was not goodbye. "It's just so long, for now."

Dr. Young was the last to leave.

Jed thanked him for coming. He responded that it was his pleasure.

Jed closed the door, behind Dr. Young. He walked back into the living room. He looked at Caly and Dr. Yen. He sat down.

For at least a minute, the three of them just sat. Nobody moved. Nobody spoke.

Dr. Yen was on the couch.

Caly was on the floor.

Jed was in Dr. Young's chair.

Jed, finally, spoke.

"You know that I have mixed emotions, Doctor. You know that, eh?"

"So does she." Dr. Yen pointed at Caly.

"Am I going to be able to deal with all this?"

"Yes."

Jed looked around the room.

"Dr. Yen?"

"Yes, Mister Jed."

"Is Dr. Young okay?"

Dr. Yen rubbed his forehead.

Jed noticed, for the first time, that he didn't have any wrinkles—no forehead lines—no crow's feet – nothing—just a perfect complexion—like a wax figure.

"Dr. Young is a wise man, Jed." Dr. Yen stood up. He walked to the middle of the room.

"But he is a scared man." He looked at Caly. She got up and stood by his side.

Dr. Yen continued:

"And you know that there is danger where there is fear. It is not healthy to be in a state of fear."

"What is he afraid of?" Jed scratched the back of his head.

Dr. Yen looked up.

"What we do and say here, Mister Jed, stays here. You understand?"

"I understand."

"What you know about Kennedy's *supposed* assassin stays here, too.

You understand that, don't you?"

"I understand."

"Well, he doesn't."

"Who?"

"Dr. Young."

"Why not?"

"Fear."

"Of what?"

Caly got up. She walked into the kitchen and went to her water dish.

She slurped, loudly.

Jed laughed.

"Wow! She's thirsty!"

"Yes." Dr. Yen nodded.

"And frustrated too.

She would love to answer your question, Mister Jed." He pointed, in the direction, of the kitchen. "She knows about fear. But right now she is choosing water over talk. I will answer for her."

He returned to the couch.

"Dr. Young is afraid of the wild."

"Afraid of the wild?" Jed frowned. "C'mon, Doctor?" He was confused.

"Yes!" Dr. Yen was serious.

"What wild?"

Dr. Yen looked at the patio doors. He pointed at the catwalk.

"That place, out there, beyond the walls of this place."

He looked back at Jed.

"Dr. Young is always here, Mister Jed. Not out there."
Jed nodded.
"I understand."
He paused.
"And Nurse Rogers and Clem?"
Dr. Yen nodded.
"And Caly, too. They are all here and always will be. It is safe, here, Mister Jed.

That is why one of your choices was to stay here, with them—with me—with her."

He was referring to Caly.

Jed stood up. He picked up the newspaper article.

"You healed this guy?"

Dr. Yen nodded.

"I healed the man who was accused of being an assassin. But I did not heal the real assassin." He paused. "Or assassins!"

"Assassins?" Jed was shocked.

"Yes, Mister Jed. There was more than one."

Jed shook his head.

Dr. Yen pointed at the paper.

"You've been to his home, in Juventud?"

Jed nodded.

"I have."

"You've read Caroline's book?"

"I have."

Dr. Yen got up. He gathered his brief case and carefully tucked the newspaper clipping, back inside.

"I have, too." He looked at Jed.

"Now it is time for me to leave." He paused.

"And, now, it is time for you to leave, too, Mister Jed.

It is the right decision. But, I had to give you other options." He smiled.

"You understand?"

Jed nodded.

"Ossie is waiting for you, Mister Jed. You must be anxious to see him.

I will tell him that you will be by, shortly."

He looked back at the kitchen.

Jed looked, too.

Caly was lying by her empty dish.

"You need a few minutes."

"Thanks Doc. Tell Ossie, I won't be long."

Dr. Yen held out his hand.

"I will see you again, Mister Jed." He smiled.

"Nice teeth." Jed smiled.

"You too!" Dr. Yen shook Jed's hand and told him to be careful.

Jed assured him. "Of that, you can be sure!"

Jed looked into Dr. Yen's caring eyes.

"Thank you, Doctor Yen."

Dr. Yen shook his head. "No. No. Thank you, Mister Jed."

He turned.
He walked away.
Just like that.
He was gone.

Jed went into his bedroom to gather up his gear.

Then, he went into the kitchen.

Caly looked up.

"So what do you think, of all this?"

She purred.

Jed smiled.

"Heh look! Either, I stay or I go."

For a second, Jed thought that Caly rolled her eyes, just like Nurse Rogers.

"Caly! Ossie is waiting for me, out there. I either stay or go."

She purred, again.
"Okay!"
Jed got down, on a knee, beside her.
He touched her paw.

Then, he got up and flung his backpack, over his shoulder.

Then, like Dr. Yen, he turned.
He walked away.
And...
Just like that.

He was gone.

PART SIX

FULL CIRCLE

- CHAPTER ONE -

VERY SUPERSTITIOUS

Ossie looked like he had put on some weight.

"Edmonton restaurants must be feeding you well." Jed and he shook hands.

Ossie laughed. He rubbed his stomach like he was proud of his belly.

"Although, the beer, in this neck of the woods, Jed, is more expensive than in Juventud, its taste is hard to resist."

Jed laughed. He agreed. "I know what you mean. I'm looking forward to havin' a cold one, myself."

"It's good to see you, Jed. It's been a while. How ya' doin'?"

"I'm okay, Os. All things considered."

Ossie opened the passenger door. "There ya' go, amigo."

"Valet service to boot! Impressive." Jed smiled.

He chucked his backpack, into the back seat. "Nice Jeep." He settled in. "Yep, it's good to see you, too, Os."

He shut the door.

As he waited for Ossie to make his way around to the driver's side, Jed opened his window. He inhaled a breath of fresh air.

Ossie buckled in. "So how's it goin', anyway?"

Jed shook his head. "Well, to tell you the truth, Os, it feels more like four months than four weeks. Thanks for being here."

Ossie turned the key to the ignition. "You're welcome."

"So how do you like driving Lana's Jeep?"

"It's good," Ossie appeared to be quite at home, in the driver's seat. "I'd like to take it back, with me, to Juventud."

Jed agreed. "It would be a great vehicle, for 'de island', man."

Ossie gave him a look.

They moved along, at a moderate speed, down the Whitemud and along Jasper. They made small talk. They spoke about the weather, the roads and the oil patch.

At Jed's mention of the rig, Ossie changed his tone.

"Jed, there is something that I've been wanting to tell you, for a few weeks, now."

He looked focused. Jed thought that he also looked concerned.

"A few weeks?" Jed smirked. "Slow but sure, Os. Slow but sure."

Ossie licked his lips. Jed lowered the volume, of the radio.

He left it so that both he and Ossie could hear some background noise. Jed figured it would be more comfortable, with a little music, accompanying them, on their drive.

Ossie cleared his throat.

Jed was interested. "So, Os, what's on your mind?"

Ossie gripped the steering wheel, like he was gripping the helms, of the COPS tug.

"I want to rule out any earlier suspicion of foul play, Jed." He swallowed.

" I don't think it was human malice."

"No?" Jed wasn't convinced.

"You've been to the rig?" Jed was already pretty certain that he had, but he needed to be sure.

He studied Ossie's hand, as it moved the gearshift.

In the distant quiet depths, of the dashboard, the sounds of a familiar song caught Jed's attention.

He leaned forward.

He turned up the volume.

Ossie shifted gears.

Jed said that the Jeep was sort of moving to the beat of the kick and the piano.

Ossie shrugged. "I guess." He had other things, on his mind.

"I might have jumped the gun a little bit, Jed, when I said the things I did, way back when you first came out of your coma." He looked at Jed.

"Your rig just had a blow–out, Jed. I mean, you know as well as I, that those things can happen."

Jed agreed. "Yep. Those things can happen." He scrutinized Ossie's profile.

His jaw looked tight.

Jed looked ahead, at the road.

He tapped his foot.

Ossie remained focused.

Jed took a breath.

He said that he was glad to hear that Ossie didn't think that it was malicious intent.

Then, he changed the subject.

"I haven't heard this song, in a while." He turned up the volume.

"What's this song called again?" He looked at Ossie. "Very Superstitious? Is that it?"

Ossie nodded. "Yep. I think that's it."

"One of Stevie's best." Jed added.

Ossie raised his voice a little. He wanted to be heard, over the singing but not, intentionally, to drown out the song. He still had more to say.

"I remember telling you guys, years ago," he emphasized years ago, "That those fuckin' diamond bits can sometimes do more harm than good."

He down shifted. The streetlight turned yellow.

"Rig 2 hit some gas, Jed."

He down shifted.

"That bit hit some gas and sent that derrick into orbit—plain and simple."

He repeated: "Plain and simple." He sounded definite. Jed thought he sounded a bit like Dr. Yen.

Jed chose not to respond.

Instead, he reclined his seat.

He loosened his seat belt.

The Jeep approached the off ramp and made its way towards The Calgary Trail. The song came to an end.

Jed lowered the volume, again.

He asked Ossie how Lana was doing.

Ossie said that she was just getting over the flu.

"Has she missed work?" Jed knew how much she hated missing work.

"Only a couple of days, I think."

Ossie touched the dashboard.

"She hasn't needed the Jeep. I've been using it to get caught up on some rig stuff and errand running." He paused. "Shit like that. You know."

For a moment, Jed thought that Ossie sounded apologetic – almost guilty.

He decided, once again, to change the subject.

"Have you seen Slim Jim, Al or Stewie?"

"Yep, they're doing fine." Ossie looked relieved that Jed changed the subject.

"Everybody's doing fine." He turned on the indicator light.

He looked at Jed. "So, Jed, will you be going back to Cold Lake or will you be staying at Lana's?"

Jed paused, before responding. He looked out the window at a passing *Brinks* truck.

"I'm going to stay at Lana's tonight, Os, and then I'll probably head back, to the rig, tomorrow."

"You know the rig can wait, Jed. I mean—you just got out of the hospital. Take a few days off. Relax."

Jed shook his head. "I've had more than a few days off, Os. I want to get back.

I need to get back." He looked at Ossie.

"You must know what I mean?"

"Yes and no." Ossie was evasive.

"Yes and no? What's that?" Jed thought about Dr. Yen. He raised his seat.

"You've got to understand that I've got to get back, Os."

"Yes and no." Ossie repeated—this time with more ambiguity.

"That's a crazy response, Os." Jed shook his head. " I don't like yes and no responses, Os. I've heard enough of them, lately."

Jed shook his head.

"Either way, you're right. Either way, you're wrong. It's like sitting on the fence.

Very safe! Very guarded, Os." Jed looked out his window.

"No risk."

"What?" Ossie pulled the Jeep up the hill, in front of Lana's apartment.

"Nothin'." Jed didn't want to talk about it, anymore.

He studied the landscape. He looked at Lana's apartment.

"Before you turn off the engine, Os, let's just sit here, for a minute. I want to hear what the next song is."

"Okay!" Ossie left the engine running. He guided the gearshift into neutral.

"I just need a minute, Os."

Jed looked at the dashboard.

"I want to make sure that I'm not missing a good song before we head out. You know what I mean?" He was fidgety. He buttoned and unbuttoned his shirt collar.

Ossie frowned. "You okay?"

Jed shrugged. "I'm okay. It's been a while. That's all."

Ossie consoled. "I understand. You were sounding a little uptight, there, Jed, for a minute." He undid his seat belt. "You're one of a kind, Jed Sands."

As the disc jockey introduced the next song, Jed said that it was okay to turn off the engine.

Ossie looked at him and asked if he were sure.

Jed confirmed. "I'm sure."

Ossie put his hand on Jed's shoulder. "I've never known you to be anything but cool, Jed."

He pointed at Lana's building.

"Let's go up there and see Lana. She's waiting for you."

"You're right! Let's go."

Before Jed opened his door, he reached into the back seat and grabbed his backpack. Then, he looked at Ossie.

"What? No valet service?" He smiled.

As they walked towards the entrance, Jed stopped.

"You say I'm one of a kind, Os?"

Ossie stopped. He turned and looked at Jed.

"One of a kind? Did I say that?" He paused.

"Well?" He tilted his head. "Now that you mention it, Jed, maybe there are others like you. But only a few." He smiled.

Jed knew what he meant. He flung his bag over his shoulder. He said that he needed to get back into shape.

"I've got to start working out, again. Even this pack feels heavy."

"Once you're back drilling, you'll be fit in no time."

"I hope so. I feel so out of shape."

They walked up the steps of Lana's building.

- CHAPTER TWO -

THE PRODIGAL

Lana looked good. Although she had been laid up for the past few days, she appeared, in the doorway, bright eyed and smiling.

She teased. "Yes, may I help you gentlemen?"

Jed laughed "So formal?"

Ossie responded. "You bet! Look who I found! The prodigal!" He pointed at Jed.

"Do you have it in your heart, to take us in so that this drifter can rest his bones?"

Jed gave Ossie a look. "Drifter? I wish!"

"Entrez mes amis." Lana opened the door. She curtseyed. Jed laughed, again.

"Oh, you speak French now?" Ossie pretended to be impressed.

"Si Senor!" She turned up her nose.

"And Spanish, too!" Jed raised his eyebrows.

They went into the living room. Lana told Jed that she thought that he was looking well.

"Thanks. I'm okay, now. I think?" He pinched his arm. "I was just thinking the same about you. Ossie told me that you're just getting over the flu."

"Yuch! Don't even mention it. It was awful!"

They sat down, all in separate chairs.

Ossie leaned back and adjusted the footrest of the *Lazy Boy* chair.

Lana sorted some magazines that were on the coffee table. Jed thought that they didn't really need sorting.

He looked at her.

She looked at him.

She continued to sort.

She picked up a 'Time' magazine and thumbed through the first few pages.

Jed broke the silence. "So, you must be looking forward to your spring break?"

Lana was relieved that somebody said something.

"Yep! Am I ever! But it's late this year. I think it's the third week in April or somewhere around then."

She put down the magazine.

Jed smiled at her. Then, he looked at Ossie.

"It's great to see you guys. It's been a while."

Ossie nodded. "You too." He put his hands behind his head. He looked comfortable.

Lana stood up. She went into the kitchen. She looked at the calendar. She called out. "Yes, our spring break is the third week in April."

Jed said that it was going to be a long stretch until then. "Oh well, that'll make May and June go by quickly."

Lana agreed. She returned to the living room and to the couch. "Everybody is going to need a break from each other, by that time." She crossed her legs. She looked more relaxed now than she did when she was sorting. "Hopefully the students won't be too rangy."

"And that goes for the teachers, too, I bet!" Ossie pushed himself out of the *Lazy Boy*. Lana agreed. "Especially the teachers!"

"I'm gonna head out for a while—give you guys some space. I want to pick up a few items, at the corner store." Ossie looked at Lana. " I'll be heading back to Miami, tomorrow, and then off to Cuba, the next day. I want to bring back some smokes, for Lee." He looked at Jed. "Need anything?"

301

Jed shrugged. "I don't think so. Thanks anyway."

Lana smiled. She looked like she was up to something. "Hey, Ossie. Pick up some beer." She looked at Jed. "Beer! Bet it's been a while."

Jed nodded. Then, he turned to Ossie. "You don't have to leave, on our account."

Ossie headed for the door. He looked back at Jed and then at Lana. "I'll be back in an hour."

He paused.

He looked over, at the television.

"Do you want me to pick up a movie?"

"Great idea!" Jed hadn't seen one in a while.

Lana hadn't either. "That'll be fun. Pick out whatever catches your eye."

"A western, for Lana!" Jed teased.

She rolled her eyes. "Anything—but a western."

Ossie gave her a thumb up. "Got ya."

Jed asked if he needed any money.

"He shook his head. My treat!" Then, he closed the door.

Jed joined Lana, on the couch.

She touched his lips. She moved her index finger, back and forth.

"I've missed you."

Jed nodded. "I've missed you, too."

"Dr. Yen told me that you weren't allowed visitors."

She paused.

"What kind of a place was that, anyway?"

Jed ran his tongue along his upper lip. He kissed her finger.

"It was a special place, Lana. Very special."

He paused. He shook his head. "A place like no other." He continued to shake his head.

"Like no other. I can't even begin to describe it, Lana."

Lana rubbed the back of his head and then tilted hers towards his.

"Tell me about it." She sat up.

Jed sighed.

He didn't say anything.

He looked at the floor and then at the ceiling.

He stood up.

He walked towards the kitchen.

"Another time," he said.

Lana heard the fridge open – then, the sliding, of the bottom drawer.

"Hey! You've got some beers, in here. Do you want one?"

"I'll try one. I haven't had a drop of alcohol since I got sick."

Lana laughed. "Just the thought of it would have made me barf."

Jed pulled out a couple of Buds. "And you asked Ossie to get some more?"

He called out. "You can tell a lot about a person just by looking in their fridge."

"Oh ya?" Lana appeared in the kitchen doorway.

She walked over and stood by Jed.

"Look here, you party animal." He pointed to some items, on the top shelf.

Lana slid her hand down between the back of his belt and his lower back.

"Ooh," she sounded playful. "Skin! Feels good."

Jed looked at her. He smirked. "As I was saying: This assortment of juices, milk, two oranges and…" He squinted.

"What are those?"

He pointed to a plastic bag that was full of what looked like dried up potato chips or fudge.

Lana giggled.

"Those are dried bananas. And they're good! Try one."

"No, no. That's okay. I'll continue with my analysis."

"Please do." She smiled.

"Now, on this shelf," he pointed to the middle shelf, "On this shelf, I see a variety of different sizes and shapes of Tupperware containers." He paused. He scratched his chin.

"Very interesting and most revealing!" He raised his eyebrows.

"Not only do you not want to waste any food, you are very neat, very organized and very creative." He addressed how Lana had everything strategically placed by size and accessibility.

"See?" He sounded like an instructor.

Lana nodded.

She was smiling.

She was entertained by Jed's serious and focused tone.

She poked his side.

"What kind of drugs are you on, anyway?"

Jed turned and looked at her.

"And," she was laughing, now. "Whatever they are, I want some."

"Drugs?" Jed pretended to be lost.

He opened a side compartment that, as a rule, would house cheese, butter or margarine.

He changed the subject. "Now, this is different." He pulled out a well-used tube of skin cream and a tiny bottle of ointment.

He read the label: "For cold sores." He nodded. "I agree."

He looked at Lana. "After all, it is recommended that we keep medication in a cooler place."

"Oh ya?" Lana was interested. "And how do you know that?"

Jed took a breath. "Remember? I've just come out of the hospital."

He paused. He looked at the counter.

"What?" Lana frowned.

He reached over and took one the unopened beers and cracked its lid. He gave it to Lana.

Then, he opened the other.

The sound of the cracking lids was loud – louder than usual.

He looked up at the ceiling.

"High ceiling." He nodded.

"Good acoustics!"

He took a sip of his beer.

"Aah, that tastes good!"

He raised the can.

"Cheers!"

She did the same, with hers.

"I've been in a hospital, for a few weeks." Jed shook his head.

Lana frowned. "I know." She shrugged her shoulder. "So?" She kissed his cheek. "And now you're out!"

Jed took another sip. He held up his can.

"They don't let you quench your thirst, with one of these."

He studied the can. "King of beers!"

Lana took a sip, of her beer. "Ooh, that tastes good! Feels great on the throat."

"Is your throat still sore?" Jed closed the fridge.

"Nope. I'm better, now."

"That's good." He rubbed his stomach. "I feel like some pizza."

Lana's eyes lit up.

"That sounds great! I haven't had a pizza for a long time!"

"Mushroom, pepperoni and green pepper?"

Lana nodded. "Yep! My favorite."

305

"Mine too."

" I'll call *Louie's*. It's still the best in town."

She walked towards the phone table.

"I forget the number. I'll have to look it up."

"484-7186." Jed chirped the number off, like it was his own.

Lana turned and looked at him. She placed her hands on her hips. "Now how on earth did you remember that?" She was surprised.

Jed shrugged.

He smiled.

"Good drugs, I guess."

He laughed.

Lana curled her lip and gave him a look.

Then, she picked up the phone.

- CHAPTER THREE -

THE DRAGON

After a couple of beers and catching up on the events of the past few weeks, Lana shared with Jed how frightened she was on the day she got the call from Marty.

She said that she couldn't even remember driving to the hospital.

"I got there, somehow, I guess." She shrugged.

She picked up her third beer can. "These are going down well."

She held up the can.

She studied the ingredients.

"This stuff is made with rice?"

Jed read his can. "I guess so."

"Have you heard from Lee lately?"

Jed frowned.

"Lee? Why would I have heard from him?" He looked at Lana. He was puzzled.

"You mean Ossie's dad? Right? That Lee?"

Lana nodded.

She told Jed that on the day after the explosion, she got a call from Lee but never actually spoke with him.

"I just got the message, from Laura, that a guy named Lee, from Cuba, called."

Then she told Jed that she had also received a call from Ossie, on the same day.

"He called from Miami."

Jed nodded. "Yep! He told me that he had been down

there, doing some business, when he got the call, from Lee."

"A lot of people care about you, Jed." She touched his arm. "And you frightened us."

Jed looked apologetic. "Sorry." He shrugged. "I didn't mean to scare anybody." He paused. "But, I sure did. I even scared myself."

There was a knock at the door.

"That must be the pizza guy." Lana leaned forward. "Don't get up. I'll get it."

Jed went to the door.

When he opened it, he was surprised to see Ossie. He was holding a pizza box.

"Large pepperoni, mushroom and green pepper, sir?" He was smiling. He handed the box to Jed.

"I ran into the delivery guy downstairs and asked him where he was going."

Jed brought the box up close to his nose. "It smells great!"

"I picked up a movie too."

"Oh ya? Which one?"

"It's called '*The Dragon*'. It's the Bruce Lee story."

"Great! Sounds good."

Ossie also had purchased a carton of Players' cigarettes and a 12-pack of beer.

He threw the cigarettes on the coffee table and brought the beer to the fridge.

"Anybody want a cold one?" He cracked open a Bud.

Lana said that she could go for another and Jed said that he was okay, for now.

"I'm still working on number three."

Ossie brought Lana a beer. He noticed that she was looking at the cigarettes.

"Those are for Lee."

"And these are for us." He held up two beers.

"What movie did you get?" Lana was curious.

"It's called *The Dragon*. Have you heard of it?"
"Oh ya! I hear it's great. Good choice!"

Jed sat down beside Lana.
Ossie returned to his spot on the *Lazy Boy*.
Lana snuggled in, close to Jed.

Ossie enjoyed his beer.
Lana didn't appear to be having any trouble with hers.
Jed said that he was going to switch to water.

"A six-pack is too much for you, now, Jed?" Ossie teased.
Jed said that he wanted to keep a clear head and not miss any of the exciting fight scenes.
Lana smirked. "The more clouding in the head—the better. That flu bug bit me badly, guys. These are working, though." She raised her beer. "Cheers!"
"Good alliteration, Lana." Jed smiled. "Bug bit, badly."
Lana stuck out her tongue.
Ossie frowned.

They devoured the pizza. Everybody was starving.
They polished off the beer. Lana and Ossie drank most of it.
They viewed the film—well, Jed viewed the film – the entire film.
He enjoyed it.
Ossie fell asleep before it ended.
Lana hung in there – until the closing credits.
There were moments when she struggled with the 'heavy eye lids'. It was a battle. The lids fell. Lana dozed off, in Jed's arms. She put up a good fight, though.

After helping her to her bed, Jed returned to the living room. He covered Ossie with a blanket. He looked out the window, at Alberta's majestic sky. He tried to locate the Big Dipper. He saw a shooting star. It dropped in seconds.

He went back to Lana's room. He lay down beside her. She kind of woke up. She apologized for passing out.

Jed told her that was okay. "Don't worry. I'm glad that you were able to unwind. You've needed it."

She fell asleep. Jed watched and listened to her breathing. It reminded him of Caly's purring.

He couldn't sleep.

He wasn't tired.

He got up.

He figured that he had slept enough, during the past few weeks. He didn't want to miss the opportunity of seizing every waking moment.

He sat down in the chair that was in the middle of the alcove.

Again, he looked up at the sky. He panned the Edmonton skyline. From the alcove window, he could see the northern and most of the eastern sections, of the city.

He caught a glimpse of the quarter moon. It was putting up a good fight with the already well-lit, star-filled sky. The stars were winning the 'illumination' battle.

From the multitudinous chimney stacks, Jed followed the rising smoke. For almost an hour, he followed it dance and slither, from its sleeping giants, to the enlivened heavens.

At times, it looked like snakes. At other times, it reminded him of belly dancers, he had seen, years ago, at the *Que Pasa,* in Havana.

Even the lights, emanating from the ghostly offices, moved in epicurean rhythm.

Sparkling crystals enhanced the mood. They provided

Canada's 'gateway to the north', with a dreamy, magical aura.

Jed enjoyed the solitude.

He respected the peace.

He was familiar with the quiet. He had become accustomed to it.

He mused upon the scene for another hour.

The night moved slowly and faded into day.

Sunrise crept onto the dancing lights like a wild cat encroaching its prey.

Jed stood up.
He walked to Lana's telephone table.
He opened its top drawer.
He took out a pen and two pieces of paper.
He looked for an envelope.
He couldn't find one.
He returned to the window.
He began writing:

Dear Lee,
He paused for a moment. He looked out the window. Then he put pen to paper.
I am sending you this letter, via registered mail.

I want you to receive it quickly and to respond to it, as soon as possible.

You can call me at the rig (I will be heading back) or you can write me there.

I hope that it is not lost or intercepted, en route.

I know that you know what happened to me. Lana told me that you called the day after the blow–out. You, likely, got a call from Slim Jim's mother, notifying you about his condition – and mine, of course. Then, after that, you probably called Ossie, in Miami, to inform him. I'm not 100% sure of the details, however.

People were told. They demonstrated their concern. I appreciate that, Lee.

Thank you.

I have a couple of questions, though.

Don't get me wrong, Lee, I am glad that you and others care, but, at the same time, I'm surprised.

I question—why the extreme care? I also question—why me?

If it's about Dr. Yen and the calyx – I, sort of, understand. That might make sense. If it were because another person was going to be and is now induced with the drug—that person, of course, being yours truly – well, that does make sense. But, Lee, I don't know for sure.

Enlighten me, please – if you can.

I understand that your rigs were threatened.

Is that true?

Coincidence or what??

Do you know or have any idea who would threaten them?

Do you think the two incidents are related?

Anyway, apparently, I got hit in the head with a drill pipe.

And ... At the time, I wasn't wearing my hard hat.

Another coincidence—Imagine that!—Me not wearing my hard hat.

According to the rig cook, just prior to the explosion, something (or someone) caused me to leave the driller station. Supposedly, I approached the edge of the tower stairs and took off my hard hat. (I took off my hard hat? Ya right.) Something smells fishy, Lee.

The only time I would remove my hard hat would be at

the end of a shift or to give it to the sticker guy. The sticker guy would often visit the site with the latest and greatest in Mustang stickers. You remember how I used to love collecting those COPS stickers to put on my hard hat?

Well, I still like collecting stickers! But I don't remember the sticker guy being at the rig, the night of the blowout. Anyway, who knows? It's all behind me now and it's still a bit of a blur and probably will remain that way for a long time ... possibly forever.

The funny thing is—when I'm working, I always keep my hat on. Always. You know that!

But for some strange reason, seconds before the blowout, I removed my hat.

Now tell me this, Lee—was that bad timing or what? (Ha ha—and I'm now supposed to be the expert in punctuality and timing. They call that irony, or something, don't they?)

Anyway, I'm okay now.

Dr. Yen has worked his wonder, once again.

I am not certain if he has spoken to you. But when I was in rehabilitation, he and I shared some very enlightening things. In hindsight, now, they make perfect sense.

I guess you know what I mean.

My life has taken on a whole new meaning.

My perspectives have changed.

I guess you know what that means, too.

I am told that I am going to be thirsty for the next three or four months.

Along with that, my memory is as photographic as that picture taken of you, in that garage, in Dallas.

Pretty wild!

I suppose that from now on, I'll never look at the world in the same way, ever again.

Dr. Yen told me that my need for water will subside but as for the other 'side effects', well, the calyx is going to leave its mark. It has provided you with some unique experiences, I bet!

I'm going to go back to the rig, Lee.

Ossie insists that the blow-out was an accident and that my injury was not a result of foul play. To be honest with you, I'm not that convinced.
I'm not saying that somebody was intentionally trying to hurt or even kill me, but I am saying that I believe that our rig was intentionally tampered with. That's all I'm saying.
Nevertheless, I am going back! I have to."

Jed paused.
He heard the sound of a toilet flushing.
He looked over his shoulder, at the couch.
Ossie was still asleep.
He told himself that it must be Lana.
He put the pen down.
He got up.
He headed for the bathroom.
"Are you okay?"
"I'm fine." Between the sounds of the toilet flushing and the tap running, Jed could hear her.
"I'll be right out."
"Can I get you anything?"
The toilet flushed again.
"No! I'm fine. I'll be right out," Jed thought that she sounded upset.
"Look Lana!" Jed spoke, to her, from the other side of the bathroom door.
"It's okay, you know. You've had the flu. You had a few drinks. Big deal!
I mean, your system is still on the mend."
He knew that he was grasping at straws.

He wanted to help but figured that Lana, most likely, wanted to be left alone.

The door finally opened.

"Don't look at me."

Lana looked pale.

Her hair was wet.

She was holding her forehead.

"I feel horrible. My head hurts. I just took a Tylenol."

Jed gave her a hug.

"You need some rest, that's all. Can I get you anything?"

"No. I'll be all right."

She looked at him. She frowned.

"Why are you still up?"

"I was writing a letter."

"A letter?" She squinted.

"To whom?"

Jed scratched his head.

Before he was able to respond, Lana moved from the bathroom doorway and dragged herself towards the alcove.

She noticed Ossie on the couch.

"How's he doing?"

"He's okay. He fell asleep before the movie ended. Remember?"

Lana shrugged her shoulders. "We shouldn't talk too loudly."

She slumped in the chair that Jed had been sitting in.

He sat on the ledge, of the alcove window.

He asked her if she wanted something to eat.

Lana looked at Jed with a look that didn't need words.

"Okay. Okay. I thought I'd ask. Are you feeling any better?"

Lana shook her head.

Jed told her that she would feel better soon.

Lana noticed the letter, on the ledge, beside Jed. "So! You're writing a letter? To whom?"

Jed looked at her.

"I am writing Lee, Lana, Ossie's dad."

"I know who he is." Lana shook her head. She frowned.

"Why are you writing him?"

"I don't know. I felt like it, I guess."

She frowned, again.

"You felt like it? You guess?"

Jed nodded.

"I have a few unanswered questions, that's all."

This time he shrugged his shoulders.

"I thought maybe he could answer some of them for me."

"May I read it?"

Jed looked at Lana.

"What?" He asked.

"I mean, pardon?" He smiled.

"May I read the letter?" Lana extended an opened palm.

Jed paused.

He glanced out the window and then looked down at the letter.

For a second, Jed thought that it looked like a secret document.

He sighed.

Then he picked it up.

He, reluctantly, handed it to Lana. He told her that he wasn't finished, yet.

"Here's what I have written, so far."

"Thank you," she smiled.

"You're so suspicious, Jed. Really."

Jed returned her smile. "You think so? Why? Whatever gave you that idea?"

Lana dropped an elbow on the arm of the chair and rested her head inside the palm of her hand.

"Ooh. I hope this Tylenol kicks in soon."

After she finished reading, she handed the letter back to Jed.

"You write a good letter," she complimented.

"Thank you, Lana, but what do you think?"

"I told you, already. You write well."

"I don't mean my style, Lana. I'm asking about the content; about what I wrote, not how I wrote."

Lana looked at Jed and then looked over at Ossie sleeping on the couch.

"We should move from here. Let's go into the kitchen. Our talking is going to wake him up."

They tiptoed into the kitchen. Lana asked how much more he had to write.

"Not too much more." Jed replied that he wanted to ask Lee a couple of more questions.

He wanted to make some inquiries about Caroline Bouvier.

"Caroline Bouvier?" Lana squinted. "Why her? What on earth would you want to know about her? And what would Lee know about Caroline Bouvier?"

Jed ignored her question.

He needed to reflect, for a moment.

He wasn't certain how much Lana knew about Lee, Caroline or Rachel.

He didn't know how much Ossie had shared or how much he had told Lana before or since his accident. He looked down at the floor.

He decided to change the subject.

"Well, anyway, I'll talk to you about Caroline later." He walked towards the sink.

"Are you thirsty? Do you want something to drink?"

"No, I'm alright. I was going to make some coffee though. Do you want some?"

Lana stood up and joined him at the sink.

Jed touched her hair. "You're not going back to bed?"

"Well, ya, I was, but I don't think you are. You've got a letter to finish." She smiled and gave Jed a friendly hip check, moving him away, from the sink.

"Get out of the way, fat boy. You're crowding me."

Jed laughed.

Lana laughed. She took the coffee pot from the maker and filled it with some water.

"So do you want a coffee or not?"

Jed shook his head. "No, I'm okay. I'll have some of that water though."

He pointed to the pot. Lana placed it on the coffee maker. Then she rinsed a glass. She filled it.

"There ya go."

Jed thanked her. He asked again about his letter.

Lana was blunt. "If I were to tell you what I was thinking, you wouldn't like it."

"No, no, really Lana. You can tell me. I can handle it. I need to know what you think. I'd love to know."

Jed took a sip of his water.

Lana poured the water, from the pot, into the back of the coffee maker.

She turned to face Jed.

He was now sitting in one of the kitchen chairs.

"Your letter is well written, Jed."

"You've already told me that." Jed interrupted.

Lana put up her hand signaling for him to stop.

"Let me finish." She sounded frustrated.

She turned to the counter and pressed the start button.

"Is there any coffee in there?" Jed pointed to the coffee maker.

"Did you put the coffee in, Lana?"

Lana smiled and rolled her eyes as though she were bored with Jed's questions.

She opened the door that housed the filter and the coffee granules.

She moved away from the counter and gestured with her arm as if she were presenting somebody on stage.

"Ta da!" She smirked. "I'm way ahead of ya, Jed. Way ahead of ya."

"That's incredible! I didn't even see you fill it.

When did you put the coffee in?"

Lana smiled again.

"Yesterday morning. I filled it but I never turned it on. Ossie didn't want any and I had juice instead. There's fresh water in there now, though."

"I know. I just saw you fill it. But it was the coffee that I had missed." Jed shook his head.

"Oh well."

Lana pressed the switch to start the coffee maker.

"Let's go back to the window." She walked, quietly, into the living room.

Jed followed – glass in hand.

Lana looked over at Ossie and then sat down in her chair, in front of the alcove.

She put her finger up to her lips, gesturing for Jed to keep quiet. "Shh."

He placed his water on the ledge.

He sat down on the floor, beside her.

He brought his knees up close to his chest. He looked up.

"Nice view, eh?"

"Yep," Lana agreed. "And a nice spot for letter writing."

He got up.

He sat on the ledge.

He looked down, at the street below. A few cars were making their way, slowly up the hill, towards The Whitemud. He turned to Lana.

"Tell me what you think of my letter. It is important to me."

He leaned over. He touched her knee. He smiled.

"I don't know if I'm being too nosey, too paranoid or too reflective."

Lana looked at Jed as he struggled to say the right words.

She loved it when he tried to justify.

She touched his cheek.

"Relax. Your letter is fine."

Her hand felt nice. "You're handsome," she spoke with warmth.

"I will tell you but you're not going to like what I'm about to say."

"I can deal with it." Jed was honest. "I need to know the truth."

She let her hand drop slowly, from his cheek.

He did the same with his, from her knee.

She stood up.

She looked out the window.

She sighed.

She whispered in his ear.

"I loathe the fact that you're going back to the rig."

She ran her fingers through her hair.

"You almost get killed, Jed. You suspect foul play. And you're going back? What is that?"

She waited.

Jed did not reply.

"Can't you look for something else; something in town; something safer?"

She raised her voice a little.

"Sometimes, Jed, I just can't figure you out."

In was obvious that she was frustrated. She moved away from Jed and looked in the direction of the kitchen.

Then she turned to him, again.

"Why do you have to go back, Jed?"

Jed looked over at Ossie. He was stirring, a little. Then he looked up at Lana.

"We better not speak too loudly."

He noticed that her eyes were watering.

"Can't you stay?"

Jed took a sip of his water.

As he swallowed, his mind scrambled. He searched for words that he thought she might like to hear.

He placed his glass on the sill.

He looked out the window, hoping to find the answer in the friendly, morning sky.

He turned to her.

He shrugged his shoulders.

He shook his head.

"I just have to Lana. I just have to go back. That's all."

He swallowed. His throat felt dry. "I just have to. My work, at the rig, is incomplete."

Lana placed one hand on her hip and pointed at him, with the other.

"You frustrate me so much, Jed. Sometimes, I think you just like being away and free to do whatever you feel like."

She paused.

"You want to be free from responsibility? Is that it?"

Jed shook his head.

"Free from mortgage payments?

Free like a little kid to go and play in the mud patch?"

She paused. She looked directly into his eyes.

"Is that what it's all about?"

Ossie stirred.

Lana wasn't whispering, now.

Jed felt badly that she was so upset.

"I didn't know you felt that way."

"Yes you did, Jed. You must have known. All those

nights when you left me after long change or short change or whatever the heck you call it."

Lana turned away.

She rubbed her eyes.

She sniffed.

She pressed her hand against her chest and then she held her forehead.

"And sometimes, Jed, I think you just want to be away from me."

She began to sob.

Jed got up to hold her.

She pushed him away.

"I think you just like being a free spirit, Jed. Free from everything and everyone."

She walked away.

Jed followed her towards her bedroom.

She shut the door.

Jed could hear her press the lock.

"Open up, Lana. Please open the door. I want to talk. I want to explain.

I can't end a conversation this way."

No response.

"Lana, please open the door."

No response.

Jed stood there for a couple of minutes.

He leaned against the door.

He rested his head on his forearm.

After a few minutes, he walked away.

He went into the kitchen.

The light from the coffee maker caught his eye. He switched it to the off position.

The pot was full.

The coffee smelled good.

He debated about having a cup.

He chose not to.

He returned to the alcove.

He sat down in the writing chair and picked up the unfinished letter.

He reread it.

Then he folded it and placed it beside the pen on the window ledge.

He leaned back.

He looked out the window, at the brightening sky.

His eyes felt heavy.

He closed them.

- CHAPTER FOUR -

BEEP BEEP

The first thing that Jed noticed, when he opened his eyes, was that he was covered with the blanket that he had given to Ossie.

He was tired.

His mouth was dry.

He turned to look back at the couch.

Ossie wasn't there.

He rubbed his eyes.

He got up and leaned on the ledge of the alcove.

He panned a dull and overcast sky. The weather had changed.

He figured that it was about 10:30; 11:00—latest.

He folded the blanket and placed it neatly, over top the back cushions, of the couch.

He rummaged through his backpack to find his shaving kit.

He headed for the bathroom, to grab a quick shower. En route, he noticed that Lana's bedroom door was still closed.

After his shower, Jed made his way into the kitchen. He was hungry. He was also, very, thirsty.

He saw that the coffee pot was still in the maker but that some of the coffee was gone.

The pot was three quarters full. He poured himself a cup and lightened it with milk.

He sat down in one of the kitchen chairs.

He looked around. Something caught his eye.

On the counter, tucked under a mug, was a piece of paper.

Jed got up. He looked at the paper. It was a note, from Ossie.

He read:

Dear Lana and Jed,

I'm off to the port (taxi).

I didn't want to wake either of you to say goodbye (late night, I'm sure).

Lana! Thanks for everything.

Our driller has returned.

My flight is at 10:00.

I'll be in Miami by 4:00 and then off to Havana.

Glad you're back, Jed.

See ya in Juventud.

Oh, by the way, I'll drop the movie off at the Mini Mart.

Jed, your truck is parked out back.

Love you guys... I'll call.

The Oz.

Jed placed the note back on the counter. He covered part of it with the same mug.

For a second, his mind drifted. He stared at the mug.

Then, he pressed the 'off button' of the coffee maker.

He walked down the hall.

He reached for the handle, on Lana's bedroom door.

He tried to turn it.

To his pleasant surprise, the door was unlocked.

Jed pushed the door open.

The room was dark.

The curtains were drawn.

The numbers on Lana's digital clock read: 10:48.

Jed looked at the comforter. He wasn't certain whether

or not Lana was beneath it. The folds looked like someone was in the bed but Jed had to get closer, to be sure.

He recognized a hand that was poking out, from beneath one of the pillows. It was a familiar hand.

It was Lana's.

As he approached the bed, Jed caught sight of the back of Lana's head.

He sat down. He touched the lone hand. It was warm.

She moved. She turned her head. Squinting with one eye, she said hello.

"Your voice sounds raspy. How ya doin'?" Jed touched her hair. He moved a strand from her forehead.

"I don't know." She cleared her throat.

Jed smiled. "You look good."

Lana smirked. "Ya right; in this light—maybe. It's a good thing it's still dark. I know I must look awful."

She reached out and touched his chin. She ran her fingers along his freshly shaven face.

"That feels nice." She smiled. "Smooth."

Jed kissed her arm. "Never mind." He smiled. "Your hand feels nice."

He got up. He opened the curtains—slowly. "The light of day!" He pointed outside. Lana squinted. "Ooh, that's bright."

He returned to her bed. "It's actually kind of dull, today." He touched her hand. "Can I get you anything—a coffee or something? There's still some in the pot. Ossie had a cup before he left."

"Ossie left?"

"Yep. Early this morning – I guess – and he left a note."

"Did he say goodbye?"

"He did in the note." Jed stood up. "He left while I was asleep." Jed yawned. "I passed out on the chair, in front of the alcove."

"You slept?"

"Yep! Believe it or not, Lana, I did."

"So you didn't finish your letter?" She leaned forward and pulled her knees and pillow up against her chest.

"No, I didn't. I'm not sure if I ever will."

"What?" She frowned. "Why not?"

Jed tilted his head. "I'll tell ya later." He smiled.

He walked towards the door. "I'll go zap ya a cup of coffee."

Upon returning to the kitchen, he opened the cupboard, above the microwave.

He looked for Lana's favorite mug.

Finally, he found it. It was easy to see, tucked in behind a couple of school cups.

It was a bright red mug with a picture of the Canadian flag.

He poured some coffee. He placed the mug into the microwave and set the timer for thirty seconds.

As he listened to the seconds tick down, he thought about the letter that he had written to Lee. He went into the living room to reread it. He sat on the ledge, of the alcove.

He picked up the letter.

Beeps from the microwave beckoned his return.

Okay, okay, I'm coming!

He returned to the kitchen, with letter, in hand.

Lana called out, from the bathroom, saying that she was going to have a quick shower.

"Wait a second. Your coffee is ready."

"I'll have it when I get out. I won't be long."

Jed heard the sound of the shower.

He placed the letter on the kitchen table.

He removed the cup from the microwave and placed it on the counter.

He looked at the letter. He thought that it still appeared to be secretive.

He picked it up. He reread it—in its entirety.

He looked at the ink.

He ran his fingers across the words like a blind man reading Braille.

I press down pretty hard, he told himself.

He thought about the blind and how their four senses, especially their sense of touch, must be so acute.

He closed his eyes and ran his middle and index fingers across the page. He tried to decipher some words.

Then, he stopped. He opened his eyes.

He looked down at the paper.

His fingers were resting upon the word: ***calyx***.

He smiled.

Jed looked at the word for a few seconds and then folded the letter. He placed it in the upper pocket, of his vest.

He took a sip of Lana's coffee.

He decided that he would drink hers and pour her a fresh cup, after she got out of the shower.

Despite the fact that it had been sitting in the pot all night, it tasted pretty good.

Mmm, that's good! It warmed his throat.

I must remember to tell Lana that she has great taste in coffee.

He sat down.

As the caffeine worked its way through his system, Jed's thoughts returned to the letter. He thought about the power of the written word.

He realized how much he enjoyed writing, now—and reading, too.

He told himself that he should do more of it.

Maybe it's the calyx. I've never had that urge before but I feel like recording things, on paper and referring to them for direction. Sort of like a diary.

I've got to do something more than finish unfinished letters.

He pondered.

With what I know now, and after what I've experienced, I should write a book!

He finished his coffee.

He looked down at his hands and outstretched fingers.

"Now, I know what Dr. Yen was getting at."

He stood up.

He opened the fridge.

He looked inside.

He panned the assortment of foods and beverages. He thought, again, about how one's personality is reflected in what's in their fridge and how it is all arranged.

He reached into the fruit bin and pulled out, what looked like, a juicy apple.

He leaned against the counter.

As he bit into the apple, he thought about Caly.

He wondered how and what she was doing. This was their first 'full day' apart. He hoped that she was all right.

He took another bite.

What a gift she has. What a gift she shares!

Juices splashed within Jed's mouth. His teeth and tongue came alive.

His taste buds, like his mind, became energized by its cool, refreshing taste.

He heard Lana turning off the shower.

She was humming.

Her voice sounded nice.

Jed called out to her.

"Lana! Do you want some toast and peanut butter?"

"And jam!" She sounded awake, now. "Ooh! Is it ever steamy, in here!"

Jed smiled. He found a jar of peanut butter, on the middle shelf, in the pantry. He placed it on the counter. He took out a loaf of bread from the bread bin.

He looked into the fridge for some jam.

He was pleasantly surprised to find his favorite: raspberry.

"Way to go Lana," he whispered. "You're the best!"

He popped two pieces, of bread, into the toaster.

He finished the apple.

He listened to the sound of Lana turning on and off taps.

"How's it going, in there, anyway?"

"The shower felt great!" Not only did she sound awake, she sounded happy, too.

"I'll be right out."

Jed stood by the toaster.

He caught a glimpse of his reflection in the metal surface. *Well, I, certainly, look better now, than I did a week ago, that's for sure.* He studied his reflection.

Thanks Dr. Yen. Thanks Clem. Thanks Nurse Rogers.

"Holy crow!" Jed noticed how well his scar was healing.

"Thanks to you too, Caly!" He spoke out loud.

Lana entered the kitchen. "Who are you talking to?"

Jed laughed. "The toaster."

The toast popped. "Breakfast of champions, Lana. Coming right up!"

Jed covered one piece with peanut butter and the other with jam.

He cut, both pieces, into four triangles.

He invited Lana to 'dig in'.

She was sporting a blue towel around her head and a red one around her body.

She sat down.

Jed commented on the blue towel.

"You look like a Smurf, Lana." He laughed. "It 'kinda' suits you."

He asked if she wanted a coffee.

She gave Jed a look and then, nodded. "Please."

She bit into one of the triangular pieces.

Jed poured the coffee. "Ah! Your favorite mug!" He held it up.

"I drank out of it, this morning." He set the timer, on the microwave. He asked how she liked the toast.

"It's delicious!" She approved. "I'm hungry." She chewed.

Jed reached over and stole a piece.

The microwave beeped. He liberated the mug, from its beeping imprisonment.

"Ooh, that smells good. Good choice in coffee, by the way, Lana."

Jed tested its temperature. He asked if she wanted some milk.

"Please." She continued chewing.

As he poured the milk, Jed caught sight of Ossie's note.

He handed it to Lana.

"Here, read this. It's the note, from Ossie."

"Oh, Ossie's note." Lana swallowed. "You mentioned that he had written."

"Thanks." She read.

Jed returned the milk to its shelf, in the fridge.

When Lana finished reading, she placed Ossie's note, face up, in the middle of the table.

"Nice note."

"Yep. He says a lot in few words." Jed sat down, beside her.

"He's probably at 35,000 feet, right now."

"En route to Miami?" Lana took a sip of her coffee and then, double-checked the note.

"Ooh, that is good coffee, Jed! Thanks."

Jed agreed. "Yep it's delicious. I enjoyed mine, this morning."

Lana took another sip.

"It's nice and hot!"

Jed put his arm around her shoulder.

"How ya doin', anyway?"

She paused.

She looked at Ossie's note.

"He was good company, you know, Jed." She pointed at the note.

"When you're away, it gets so quiet around here." She looked around.

"It was nice having another person to talk to and to have meals with."

She looked into Jed's eyes. "He's a good man." She paused. "He's a good friend." She emphasized friend. "Do you know what I mean?"

Jed nodded. "I do." He looked at Lana. "I understand."

He leaned over and kissed her forehead.

"Jed?" Lana touched his arm.

"Yes?"

"If I go get the blow dryer, will you dry my hair?"

"I'd love to."

"I'll meet you at the alcove. I'll take in the skyline, while you dry this mop."

She removed the towel from her head. Her hair was still wet and hard packed.

She stood up.

She gave her head a shake and then loosened some of the hair, from its depressed state.

She ran her fingers through it and freed some of the tangles.

"I'll go and get the dryer—and my comb."

She walked towards the bathroom.

"I think the dryer is in there and my comb should be on my dresser. I'll be right back."

Jed picked up her coffee and headed for the alcove.

He looked out the window.

He thought, again, about the significance of the written word.

"I've got to remember to write things about the Alberta sky."

"Pardon?" Lana entered the living room.

Jed turned towards her.

"Oh nothing, I was just thinking out loud."

"Oh ya? Having a conversation, with the window like you did with the toaster?"

She smiled and sat down in front of the alcove.

She was still wearing the red towel.

She was holding on to a hair dryer and a comb.

"I was just telling myself some stuff that I have to remember to do."

Lana looked up. She pointed the hair dryer like a gunslinger pointing a pistol.

"And what might that be, cowboy?" She raised an eyebrow and puckered a lip.

Jed asked if he could plug in the dryer. Lana took her time handing it over, to him. He plugged it, into the outlet.

He told her that he was not intending to finish or mail the letter that he had written to Lee.

Lana frowned. "Why not?"

Jed looked into her eyes and shared with her something that he had learned, as a result of his treatment, in the hospital and at the Center.

"The calyx works its magic in more ways than one, Lana.

It doesn't just coagulate blood and stop internal bleeding."

Lana tugged at her hair.

"Go on." She settled into the chair.

"Lana," Jed swallowed. He took a deep breath.

"I know that to a certain extent, we all have E.S.P."

"What?" Lana tilted her head. Her hair was still wet.

It looked darker and heavier than usual. She ran the comb through some of the tangles.

"Instead of writing this letter." Jed removed the letter from his upper pocket.

"I have decided to write a book."

Lana looked up.

"Oh ya?"

He returned the letter to his pocket.

"Yep! I think the idea came to me in my sleep."

"Really?" Lana was interested.

Jed nodded.

"Yep! Extra Sensory Perception!" He smiled.

Lana made a face. "As if!"

"Seriously, Lana. Shortly after I woke up, in that very same chair that you're sitting in, I went to the kitchen and read Ossie's letter."

Jed looked serious.

"After that, my mind went *kind* of blank." He shook his head. "No, No! I should say that I thought my mind went *kind* of blank."

He shook his head again. "But it didn't!"

Lana frowned.

"I went on a journey down the *path of realization,* back to my sleeping moments, in that chair, in front of this very window."

He pointed to the chair and window.

It was now his turn to hold the hair dryer like a gunslinger.

Lana sat up.

"And what did you discover on that 'path of realization'?"

Jed smiled.

"Thanks for asking."

He shrugged.

"I guess," he thought for a second. "I guess, I discovered that I have a story to tell."

Lana frowned.

Jed corrected himself.

"No, no Lana. I should say that I have a story that I must tell."

He paused.

He looked at Lana.

She looked at him.

In trust and understanding, their eyes met.

Jed turned on the dryer.

- CHAPTER FIVE -

HOT AIR

Jed moved his fingers through Lana's hair like he was sifting sand, on a beach, in Juventud.

He massaged her scalp.

"I'm glad you have strong fingers." She tilted her head, forward.

"Strong but gentle." She closed her eyes.

"The way I like it." She touched his arm.

The air, from the dryer, warmed Lana's head and neck.

"That feels good—on my upper back, too." She lowered the towel. She lifted her hair.

The tangles, slowly, began to magically, disappear.

Her hair evolved into a shiny flow, like the mane, on the back of a thoroughbred.

She opened her eyes.

She looked up at Jed.

She smiled.

"This is nice."

Lana enjoyed having Jed, back again, by her side.

She was happiest when he was in Edmonton.

Once again, she closed her eyes.

She thought about Jed's comment regarding 'E.S.P.' and what he said about writing a book.

The sound of the dryer was mesmerizing.

The heat was stimulating.

With one hand, Jed massaged her neck.

With the other, he moved the dryer, slowly, up and down.

Like a surfer's wave, her hair climbed and curled.

Like the changing tide, it ebbed and flowed.

Lana loosened the towel.

She let out a sigh. "Ooh, that feels better."

Jed looked at her shoulders.

They looked attractive.

There was a sprinkling of freckles on her upper back and a tiny purple birthmark, in the middle. It looked like it had been strategically placed.

Jed thought that it was becoming—even sexy.

He continued to move the dryer, up and down.

He aimed the heat towards her hips.

He continued massaging.

Her skin felt smooth. Jed thought that it looked like the color of an Okanogan peach.

Lana opened her eyes. "This feels great!"

She turned to look at him.

"You make me feel special."

Jed smiled. "That's good, 'cause you are."

He continued drying.

His wrist moved with wave-like rhythm.

He warmed Lana's head, her arms, her back and her hips.

He warmed her everywhere.

She raised her arms. She crossed them, behind her head.

She made a moaning sound. She told him not to stop.

"I want the heat all over me."

Like a cat, she arched her back.

The towel fell to the floor.

She turned to face him.

Jed thought that she looked beautiful.

"Dry me here." She pointed to her neck.

"And here." She reached out and guided his hand towards her chest.

She remained in the chair and elevated herself to a kneeling position.

She looked into Jed's eyes.

"Hi." She licked her lips.

She directed his hand to the middle, of her belly.

Jed continued to spread the heat.

He moved the dryer back and forth and up and down.

He moved it like a painter, painting a masterpiece.

He moved it like a gardener, spraying a garden.

He moved it with art, with precision, with tenderness.

He wanted it to be perfect.

She moaned.

He dried.

"You have a nice tummy."

"Blow here." She pointed to her navel.

"Dry me all over."

She freed his hand to raise her arms. Once again, she crossed them, behind her head.

Jed asked her if it were too hot.

Lana smiled. "I like it hot!" She laughed.

Jed smiled. "Ooh la la!" He laughed.

She tilted her head back. She ran her tongue sensuously along her upper lip. "Don't stop."

She pulled Jed's arm close to her mouth and like a cat, she licked it—slowly –affectionately—passionately.

"You taste good."

She slithered from the chair.

She stood up.

She moved to him.

She looked directly into his eyes.

Then, she lifted her leg and rested it against his knee. "Dry me here."

Jed raised his eyebrows.

He moved the dryer up and down her thigh.
She turned and leaned against the chair.
She arched her back, again, for the second time.
Jed swallowed.
He let out a breath. "Whew!"
Lana closed her eyes.
"Do my back."
Like a waterfall, the warm air cascaded upon her back.
"Lower."
She reached behind and pulled him into her.
"I want to feel you, as you dry me."
He reached around and held her.
He ran his hand up and down her stomach and between her breasts.
She reached out and held the hand that was holding the dryer.
"Turn it off, baby." She turned to him.
She licked her lips.
Jed looked into her eyes. They looked playful – frisky and playful.
The noise subsided.
The room was quiet – sensuously quiet.
She took the dryer from his hand and carefully placed it on the ledge of the alcove. It was still hot.
She put her arms around his shoulders.
She pressed her body against his.
She curled her leg around the back of his knees.
Jed smiled.
She kissed his lips.
With her tongue, she encircled his.
She slid her hand down between his pants and his shirt. She tugged. "Let's get rid of these."
Jed nodded.
He swallowed.
Against the walls of his chest, he could feel the ac-

celeration and pounding, of his heart. He tried to think of something good to say, but, before he could, Lana kissed his mouth—again – and again—and again.

She released. "Let's go to my room."

Again, all Jed could muster was a nod.

They walked, slowly, in the direction of Lana's room. As she slipped off his vest and unbuttoned his shirt, Lana ran her fingers erotically up and down Jed's waist and chest.

He finally spoke. "That feels good. Your hand is warm."

His shirt fell to the floor.

Now, it was his turn to close his eyes.

"I am warm in other places, too." Lana ran her tongue along his back and up and down his neck. She nibbled his ear.

Then, she inserted her tongue inside his ear and dragged it across his jaw bone and down, towards his mouth.

Jed took a breath.

His heart continued to accelerate. "Wow! That's quite a feeling."

Lana smiled.

She touched his mouth with her index finger and then brought it back to hers. She licked it. Then, in a slow circular motion, she caressed Jed's lips with it.

He opened his eyes.

"Whew!" He managed a word.

She continued to lead him, towards her room.

With each step, she paused to kiss his mouth, his neck and his chest

She teased.

She tugged his belt.

"Let's get rid of this." She loosened it and unzipped his pants' zipper.

She kissed his chest and then, with outstretched fingers, slid her hand slowly and sensuously down his back.

She asked him to tell her about the book he was thinking of writing.

She sat on the edge of her bed. She pulled him closer. She kissed his stomach.

Jed could hardly think.

He tried to speak.

Her request about the 'book writing', took him by surprise.

He remained standing.

He held her head.

Lana continued to kiss his stomach.

He took a breath.

"Well," he paused. He collected some disoriented thoughts.

"It will be about Caly and Lee and you, of course." He swallowed. He was grasping at straws.

Lana dragged her tongue slowly up and down, Jed's chest.

She nibbled at his belly button. "I like yours, too."

"Pardon?" Jed was almost peaked.

"Yours tastes good."

"Oh!" He took another breath.

He tried to concentrate.

Lana looked up.

Her hair was covering her face.

For a moment, Jed thought that she looked wild—untamed.

"Tell me more."

Lana lowered his jeans. She nibbled at his shorts' strings.

"Black Boxers." She rubbed his inner thigh. "I like black."

She pulled the string.

"What are you going to call it?"

Jed took a breath.

It was getting harder to think – harder to speak – harder to stand.

Everything was hard.

Everything!

Jed told himself to stay focused.

His knees, however, responded to another force.

Like a stallion, he locked his legs.

Like a mare, Lana loosened hers.

Jed swayed.

Lana pulled.

Jed relinquished.

"I'll call it something Canadian." He unlocked a knee. Lana lifted his leg and rested it, by her side, on the edge of the bed.

She slipped off his sock.

For her, his skin felt warm.

For him, the sheet felt smooth.

She put her hands around the back of his shorts.

She squeezed.

"I was thinking about calling it *The Canadian Links*."

"After Caly?" she caressed his leg.

Then, she blew a long, warm breath along his thigh and down his shin.

Jed lowered his leg stepping out of his jeans. "That feels better."

Lana ran her hands up and down both his legs.

Jed took a breath.

She repeated her question.

"The lynx? After Caly?" She pulled him closer. She kissed his stomach and then rubbed her jaw against his flesh.

"No, no. Not after Caly—After us. We're the links." He placed his palm against her cheek.

He spelled out the letters: L—I -N—K—S.

"Oh that kind of links!" She ran her tongue along his inner thigh.

He almost fell forward.

She held his wrists. " I'll hold you." She looked up at him. "Your arms are warm."

Jed laughed. "I wonder why!"

He ran his fingers through her hair. "Your hair looks great."

"Thanks for drying it."

She moved her hands up and down his arms. "I like your limbs." She smiled.

"I like yours, too." He touched her elbow.

"The links! The links to what?" She wrapped her legs around him.

"Pardon?" Jed held her head.

He ran his fingers through her hair and then lifted her chin.

He looked into her eyes.

"The links to what?" She kissed his hand.

With her feet, she rubbed the back of his legs.

"Ooh." Jed sighed. "It's getting difficult to think." He paused. "And talk."

He hung in, there—barely.

"The links to a lot of things."

Lana leaned back. She was still holding on to his arms. She pulled him closer.

"Why don't you call it *The Calyx*?"

"After the drug?" He could feel heat emanating from her thighs.

"Yes, partly." She rubbed his side with the inside of her calves.

With her tongue, she wet his chest.

He looked up at the ceiling.

He closed his eyes.

"But not exclusively." She lifted herself and then nestled into him.

"*The Calyx* could mean many things." She pulled the back of his neck.

Their faces met.

"It means Caly. The lynx! And us! The Canadian Links."

She made a sound of pleasure.

Jed smiled. "You're smart!"

Their lips met.

He kissed her.

ISBN 1-41204772-2